Westlake Village

Tengo Amor

A Novel

Written by
James Welch

Copyright © 2020 James Welch
All rights reserved
First Edition

NEWMAN SPRINGS PUBLISHING
320 Broad Street
Red Bank, NJ 07701

First originally published by Newman Springs Publishing 2020

ISBN 978-1-64801-817-6 (Paperback)
ISBN 978-1-64801-818-3 (Digital)

Printed in the United States of America

Dedicated to:
My three favorite Indians

Tom Nardini
Selina Jayne
Geeta Bunsraj

Special Thanks to:

Stacey Johnson-Whaley

I

Jack stepped outside into the bright morning sunlight. It was a beautiful warm California day. A tiny storm had moved through the area the night before, and the slight scent of rain was still in the air.

Jack glanced at the clear blue sky, then the rolling green hills that surrounded his domicile, and smiled. A little rain, then a lovely warm sunny day. That was the beauty of living in southern Cal, Jack thought, as he took a deep breath.

He closed the door behind him and jiggled the handle to make sure the door was securely locked.

Jack was wearing shorts, a sweatshirt, baseball cap, and military style sun glasses. The previous night he'd dyed his hair dark brown, and his scalp still stung from the endeavor.

He felt a warm gentle breeze as he stepped away from his room and immediately encountered one of the motel maids, Maria.

"Buenos dias, Maria. ¿Como esta?"

"Bien, bien. ¿Usted?"

"Estoy muy bien, gracias. Un otro dia en paraiso."

"¿Si?"

"Si," Jack said with conviction. He was in love, and it seemed like nothing could dampen his spirits that day.

As he walked briskly along the side of the motel toward Agoura Road, the exquisite weather made him think once again, how lucky he was to be living in this wonderful little corner of the world.

His room was located at he rear of the well kept Cape Cod style motel complex that sat on the northwest edge of the City of Calabasas. It was just off the Ventura Freeway, and about a quarter of a mile from Malibu Canyon Road.

Surrounded by beautiful rolling hills the area offered somewhat of a country contrast to the city of Los Angeles only thirty miles away. Jack liked being close to L.A., without actually being in L.A.

As he walked along the grounds of the motel, he cheerfully greeted two more Mexican maids in Spanish. In each case, he paused for a few moments to exchange pleasantries with the pretty young girls, addressing them both by name.

Once he reached Agoura Road, it took him only a matter of minutes to walk to the nearby McDonald's located at the corner of Agoura and Malibu Canyon Road. Being in love, coupled with the perfect California day, was the best feeling on earth, Jack thought, as he entered the familiar fast food joint.

The place was not particularly crowded. That was always subject to change since the establishment was located on one of the busiest routes over the Santa Monica Mountains to Malibu Beach.

It was late in the morning and Jack realized he'd missed the cut off time for ordering breakfast, but it also seemed a bit early to bite into a Big Mac. Undecided about what he wanted to eat, he stepped into a short line and only had to wait a few moments before approaching the counter to order.

During the months he'd been living at the motel, Jack had made quite a few friends around the immediate area.

From behind the counter, his friend Blanca, an attractive young Latina, greeted him in Spanish with a smile.

"Buenos dias," Blanca said. "¿Como esta?"
"Bien, bien," he answered. "¿Como esta mi amiga, Blanca?"
"Muy bien, gracias," she replied. "¿Quieres?"
"Ah,...no se."

They continued their small talk as jack tried to make up his mind. He finally settled on a chicken sandwich and a cup of joe.

In the meantime, a casually dressed middle aged white couple had stepped into line behind Jack. The couple quickly became unreasonably impatient while listening to Blanca and her customer converse in Spanish.

Unaware of the couple, Jack continued to chit chat in Spanish and in the process the term Gringo was used.

Apparently unable to contain his xenophobia, the Caucasian man mouthed off in a loud contemptuous voice that was seething with hatred.

"Why don't you filthy people learn to speak English?" He growled. "Or better yet, why don't you go back to where the fuck you came from!"

Startled, and caught off guard by the sudden and unexpected tirade, Jack turned abruptly to confront the verbal assailant. He immediately noticed that the burly white man reeked with the smell of booze.

A little early in the day to tie one on, jack thought, as he quickly switched languages and addressed the nasty hombre in perfect American English, making it suddenly clear that he too was an Anglo.

Speaking Spanish, along with his newly acquired dark hair, and his light blue eyes hidden behind sun glasses, Marine Corps veteran Jack Hardin had been mistaken for a Hispanic.

Jack set the record straight in short order, reverting to a stern voice style that recalled his days as a platoon sergeant in the Corps.

"Go back to where the fuck I came from? I guess in my case, that'd be Culver City, Pal!"

This wasn't the first time Jack had encountered anti Latino sentiments, and Jack hated racism. More in Blanca's defense than his own, Jack continued. Hard working Latinos often had to put up with this crap, he didn't.

"Ever hear of the First Amendment? I think I'm entitled to say anything I want, in any language that I want! Now if you've got a problem with that, you can kiss my ass!"

Blanca tried to follow Jack's angry retort, but some of the words confused her. She noticed the burly antagonist was taken aback by Jack's sudden revelation, and his aggressive reply.

It had only been a few days since the last incident where Jack was forced to hold his temper. In that case, the women he loved, a Mexicana, had begged him not to retaliate. He had acquiesced to her wishes, but the sting of the incident was still fresh in his mind.

"Oh, you're an American,…I thought you were a,…"

"You know, I don't really give a shit what you thought."

"Hey, I heard you call me a Gringo!" The surly man spat back.

"Look, I wasn't taking to you, or about you!" Jack replied, as his anger began to build. "I was talking to my friend, mi amiga, Blanca!"

Outside, a Sheriff's black and white patrol car pulled into the restaurant's parking lot. The Malibu Sheriff's Station was just over a mile away, and their presence in the area verged on being ubiquitous. Blanca noticed the cops, Jack did not.

Two uniformed L.A. County Deputies slipped out of their car in no particular hurry. It was time for their lunch break.

Jack turned slightly and again addressed Blanca, but he continued to speak English.

"You know I wish some of these dump ass Gringos would learn to speak Spanish. I think there'd sure as hell be a lot more understanding."

Outside, the cops were almost at the point of entering the establishment. Blanca tried to say something to Jack, but he cut her off as he switched back to Spanish for the sole benefit of antagonizing his adversary.

For a moment he thought about the women he loved, and briefly wondered if he should hold back a little, then he noticed the pure hate in the man's blood shot eyes.

"No me gusta la actitud mala de algunos Gringos," Jack said, looking the man straight in the eye. "yo odio racismo, Gringo!"

"Okay, that's it! I've had it. Looks like I'm goin' have to kick your butt suckin' beaner lovin' ass!" The burly man growled.

"Kinda looks that way, doesn't it, punk," Jack replied, in a manner that indicated he was more than ready to defend himself.

Just as the large man started to pull back his fist to throw a punch, Jack instinctively moved forward and grabbed the man's offending hand and twisted it into a half nelson arm lock, then drove his opponent's fist up his back until it almost touched his hairy neck. Jack effectively employed a move he hadn't used since his days as a Marine Corps M.P.

The cop in the lead opened one of the restaurant's double glass doors the second the man's wife screamed at the top of her lungs.

Jacks slammed the aggravating Gringo's face into a nearby soda dispensing machine just as the two cops charged into the place.

Soon the joint was surrounded by squad cars, fire trucks, and paramedics. Jacks perfect southern California day had come to a sudden end.

II

For Jack Hardin, the quintessential Gringo, the whole Spanish speaking thing had started with a girl. Una Mexicana.

It coincided with his starting a new job. A job he didn't really want, but desperately needed. Jack was in his early forties, broke, and facing eviction. His problem was both a result of hard economic times, and his seeming inability to make intelligent adult decisions when it came to career choices. Jack also had a problem with women. He liked 'em.

It was an unseasonally rainy day when jack pulled the black Lincoln Towncar he had just received from the dealership into the driveway of the upscale home in tony Westlake Village.

It stopped raining just as Jack stepped out of the car clutching a black umbrella. Within seconds the front door of the house swung open and a cadre of wild children disgorged screaming in unintelligible unison. Several started using the sloping wet lawn as a water slide. By Jack's count there seemed to be six or seven including an older girl who appeared to be in her early teens. Her name was Terri, and she was trying desperately to wrangle the rampaging children. A beautiful Mexican girl soon emerged from the house to lend some assistance.

When Carmelita spoke it was with authority and in Spanish. She snapped off commands, and the children instantly responded by retreating to the house, whinning all the way, but offering no real resistance.

Jack marveled at her beauty, and her command presence. She looked like she was in her middle twenties, Jack thought. She also had a killer body, long black hair, and seemed slightly over dressed for the occasion. Tight jeans, white tennies, and a light pink sweater. She flashed Jack a look with her intense black eyes just as the youngest kid in the brood slipped past her from inside the house, and took another turn at the slide.

The tiny blond three year old girl was wearing pig tails and a muddy yellow party dress.

Carmelita screamed in Spanish as the tyke in pig tails slid down the well manicured lawn headed straight for the busy street below. Jack immediately responded and blocked her way before she reached the sidewalk. She probably wouldn't have gone into the roadway, but Jack was glad he was able to at least give the appearance of coming to her aid.

Jack thought about taking the little girl in his arms and returning her to the pretty Latina, but the kid was filthy, and he didn't want to risk ruining his light grey suit.

Instead of grabbing the little girl's hand and leading her onto the sidewalk then up the driveway, Jack stood by as the pig tailed one crawled back up the slippery wet lawn, eventually reaching Carmelita's position at the bottom of the house steps. She was now totally covered with mud.

"What's your name?" Jack asked in a clear voice.

"Betty," the little girl screamed with glee.

"No, your name?" Jack shouted at the at the beautiful Mexican girl, who was now reaching out to grab little Betty.

Jack actually thought he knew her name was Carmelita. Amid the cacophony earlier he'd heard the kids call her by name, but he wanted to open a line of conversation and he couldn't think of anything else to say.

Just as Carmelita reached out to grab Betty's hand, the tiny girl turned and hit the slide again, causing Carmelita to lean forward slightly and lose her balance.

Jack watched in horror as the light pink sweater hit the muddy grass and Carmelita slid helplessly to the bottom of the slick lawn just behind baby Betty.

A litany of rapid fire Spanish swear words filled the air, and poor Jack suddenly felt he was probably off to a bad start with the sexy Señorita.

He dashed to the bottom of the hill and snatched Betty with determined dispatch, soiling his hands and suit in the process.

Carmelita had some trouble getting back on her feet due to the slippery grass, and Jack wanted to help, but baby Betty proved to be a handful. He didn't want to lose her, and the swearing on Carmelita's part continued as she grabbed the little girl from Jack and headed back up the driveway toward the house.

"I'm sorry," Jack said, as he watched her quickly disappear through the front door with Betty laughing, as the other children surrounded them and cheered with loud laughter at Carmelita's misfortune. It seemed she had lost charge of her charges.

The residential street in front of the house was alive with morning traffic. SUVs and other luxury vehicles whizzed past the house with most of the hurried drivers yakking on their cell phones and paying little attention to their surroundings. The irresponsibility of it all caught Jack's attention for a moment. These spoiled self indulgent yuppie types were already starting to get on Jack's nerves, and this was only his second day on the job.

The day before, his first day, he had arrived in the early afternoon. The house was quiet then, only Jack's new boss and his beautiful wife were at home.

After all the confusion with the kids and Carmelita, Jack suddenly found himself alone in front of the house. Soon Tammy, the attractive wife of his boss appeared in the doorway at the top of the porch.

Tammy was blond, sexy, and seemed completely unfazed by all the turmoil Jack could hear behind her. Jack still wasn't quite sure just how many kids there were, but it seemed like there were at least two or three too many to make things manageable.

"Good morning, Jack. Would you like a cup of coffee?" Tammy said in a cheerful voice as she stepped outside onto the porch.

"Ah, no thank you. I'm fine."

"You sure?"

"Yeah, but thank you."

"Dan will be out in a minute," Tammy stated, then she struck a sexy little pose.

"I'm really sorry about what happened to,…what's her name?"

"Carmelita. Don't worry about it," Tammy said.

Tammy was a real looker, and she made Jack a little nervous. She too seemed a bit over dressed for this early in the morning, and Jack knew she didn't have a job.

I wonder what her plans are for the day, Jack wondered as Dan stepped through the doorway.

"What happened to Carmelita?" Dan asked. "Jack shoved her into the mud," Tammy teased.

"Good," Dan replied, as the couple chuckled at Carmelita's expense.

"You want a cup of coffee before we go," Dan added, but also looked like he was in a hurry to leave.

"No thanks, I'm fine."

Dan quickly turned and gave Tammy a kiss. She did something kind of cute and slightly theatrical with her foot during the brief smooch.

"Bye honey. I won't be home before midnight," Dan said, as he quickly bounded down the steps. Tammy just rolled her pretty blue eyes.

"Okay, have a good day. Bye Jack," Tammy said, with a sigh.

"Bye," Jack answered, as he and Dan climbed into the Lincoln.

Jack carefully backed the big car out of the driveway, then wheeled the shiny sedan off down the street, as Tammy watched them go from her position on the porch.

That day Jack learned that Tammy was thirty two years old, and had been married three times.

Another little boy named Anthony, and baby Betty were from her marriage to Dan. Terri, the older girl, and a boy of ten named Roger, were from her last two marriages. Then there was John, the eldest, who was from one of Dan's previous unions. The other two children who were in attendance belonged to one of Tammy's sisters.

Westlake Village, located some thirty nine miles northwest of Los Angeles, was the absolute height of yuppie heaven. A place where getting married was more like an adult version of going steady.

Jack thought, in this sphere romance was something more akin to a metaphoric square dance. Fall in love, get married, have a couple of kids, then change partners.

Suddenly a Hummer, a Caddie pick up, and a huge SUV, all full of kids, passed the Lincoln on the right. In each vehicle, the female driver was chattering on her cell phone.

Well, at least it probably kept the local law firms busy, and the Little League and soccer fields full, Jack mused.

During that first week, Jack picked up Dan at 5 am, well before anyone else in the house was out of bed. Dan had a series of meetings in far flung places like San Diego, Santa Cruz, and on one occasion over the border into Mexico.

Also, within that first week on the new job, Jack was evicted, and moved into the motel. By landing this job, Jack had escaped homelessness by a matter of days.

Most nights during the week of long day trips, they usually didn't return until close to midnight.

Jack learned from the guy who got him the job, that Dan had a law degree, but that he didn't actually practice law. The guy told Jack that Dan was some kind of consultant.

Dan was pretty quiet, and aside from imparting the information about Tammy and the various kids, he usually had very little to say. He didn't go into details, but for some reason he needed a driver for a year. The new Lincoln was leased for this purpose.

Dan only touched on the subject briefly, saying that he had lost his license. Jack figured it was probably a DUI thing, and he was grateful, if it worked out, to have a steady job for a year.

For some reason, Jack's military background had played a major role in his getting hired. He wondered why? Was Dan just a fan of former marines, or was there something else?

Dan appeared to be in his mid to late forties, and seemed fascinated by the military, but lacked any personal experience.

In many ways, it was a pretty good job, but early on, Jack started to wonder about a lot of things.

Accept for the long hours, on the surface everything seemed to be okay, but he soon started to wonder if there was going to be some kind of catch. There was something mysterious about Dan, but Jack couldn't quite put his finger on it.

III

Tammy entered the room quickly, and immediately caught Jack's attention. It was a pleasantly warm California afternoon, and Jack was waiting for Dan. He was relaxing in a comfortable chair reading the L.A. Times, and having a cup of coffee.

The spacious living room with its high ceiling accentuated by large wooden beams was tastefully filled with antiques and techno crap that somehow oddly blended together well.

Tammy was wearing a cute little tight fitting tennis outfit. The skimpy attire seemed expensive, and aptly showed off her well toned body. Tammy also really knew how to milk the machinery. Jack promptly put his newspaper aside.

"Sure is quiet when most of the kids are at school," Tammy said.

"What time do they get out?" Jack inquired.

"Different times," Tammy replied. "Depends on the kid. The first one's out at 2:20, the last one's out at three, and they're all pretty much back here by 3:30. Circus time. Where's Dan?"

"Upstairs in his office, I think."

"What time's his flight?" Tammy asked.

"Five-fifteen."

"Boy, you're really gonna hit traffic."

"Yeah, I know. Both ways," Jack said, with resignation.

"How does Dan pay you? By the day, or by the hour?"

"I'm on an hourly."

"So do you get paid while Dan's gone?"

"No, I don't think so."

"You know, I could probably use you while he's away. I'll ask him. Do you want some extra work, Jack?"

Before Jack could answer, Carmelita entered the room with some freshly cut flowers in a vase. She passed Jack without saying a word as she went about selecting a suitable place to set the flowers.

"I could really use some help shuttlin' the kids around after school, Jack," Tammy purred. "Carmelita can't drive. I could probably use you for some other stuff, too."

"Oh, yeah?" Jack replied. "Well, ask Dan."

"I will," Tammy said, then she looked at her dainty diamond studded wristwatch. "Oh, I gotta go. Time to play," she added, as she noticed Jack watching Carmelita.

Tammy swung her arm like she was wielding a racket, then she bounced out of the room.

Jack digested the various implications of the foregoing conversation for a moment, then Carmelita caught his attention again as she quietly passed him on her way out of the room, the flowers having found a home on a nearby table.

"Hola," Jack said.

"Hola," Carmelita responded in a soft voice. "Do you speak any English?"

"No quiero hablo ingles," Carmelita answered.

Jack had no idea what that meant, but she wasn't being very friendly, so he assumed the worse.

God, she was beautiful, Jack thought, as he watched her exit through the arched passageway into the next room. Carmelita had intense dark eyes, beautiful skin, and long straight black hair. She also had a quiet air of dignity that impressed Jack.

Dan was late coming down with his luggage, and the trip to LAX was a total nightmare. Twenty-one miles east on the 101 Ventura Freeway in heavy traffic, then another twenty some miles south on the 405 San Diego Freeway in bumper to bumper traffic.

Dan almost missed his flight, and his mood was foul. They were often almost late, regardless of the nature of the appointment. Dan virtually never allowed a sufficient amount of time for them to get where they were going, thus making Jack's job that much harder.

Dan always rode in the front seat, and shuffled through large stacks of business papers. He also listened to sports radio, and talked almost constantly on his cell phone.

With the cell phone chatter and the moronic sports talk, Jack tried to tune it out as much as possible by thinking about something else.

His move to the motel had been a good one. Jack decided during the trip to the airport that he had to learn to speak Spanish. Almost all the people who worked at the motel were from Mexico or Central America. What a great place to learn. There were also some really cute Señoritas working at the motel as maids. Jack thought, what a splendid opportunity to get to know some Latina cuties.

Jack was determined to turn his situation into a positive one. Also, if he learned a little espanol, he could communicate with Carmelita.

At the last moment, just before Dan jumped out of the car at the busy airport, he mumbled something about it being okay to work for Tammy while he was away. She had phoned him on his cell during the trip and interrupted a business call, much to Dan's annoyance. Jack was beginning to realize that there was more than a little tension between Dan and his pretty spouse. Whenever Tammy called, the conversation was always somewhat terse.

Tammy had called a second time, and this call really irritated Dan. No degree in family counseling was necessary to conclude that their marriage wasn't going very well.

Jack didn't know the exact nature of the call, but if looks could kill, Tammy would have been dead. It sounded like it had something to do with money. Dan was always real touchy about money.

As he got out of the car Dan told Jack he'd probably be in Washington for about a week, and that he would phone him once he had information about his return flight. He also tipped Jack twenty dollars and told him to take good care of Tammy and the kids, before he disappeared into the airport crowd. Dan was a hard man to read, Jack thought.

Tammy was alone in the bedroom on the phone. Her mood was quite serious.

"I haven't totally made up my mind yet, but I think I'm going to have him killed. And I know exactly how to do it. There's a new character I want to bring into the mix, and I think we can set him up to take the fall."

IV

Jack maneuvered the large Lincoln through light traffic along Thousand Oaks Boulevard headed for one of the kid's favorite haunts. The cacophony of a car load of screaming children just about drove Jack crazy in the first ten minutes. They were on their way to Chuck E Cheese, and from time to time Carmelita's voice would rise above the din in colorful Spanish.

There were three little ones in the back seat with Carmelita. Terri, the older girl, was riding up front with Jack. Terri would occasionally chime in with some command in an effort to assist Carmelita. Being a teenager she liked assuming the role of an adult.

Tammy had taken John, who was a year older than Terri, to his soccer practice. Terri confided to Jack, that without John, whom she considered her arch enemy, it was actually a pretty easy day.

For a moment, Jack's mind drifted back to his eight years of comparative peace and quiet in the Marine Corps. M.P. duty, or even running a rifle platoon, seemed to pale next to wrangling a car load of rowdy kids, Jack thought.

Later, after using the john, Jack emerged alone from Chuck E Cheese. As the big door closed behind him, the loud sound of screaming children mercifully subsided.

He walked over to the Lincoln, retrieved a pack of smokes from the car, and lit a cigarette. Although it was still early in the day, Jack felt very very tired.

Carmelita barely acknowledged him. Her use of English didn't seem to extend beyond the words yes and no. The less she said, the more Jack became intrigued. Her ability to control the gang of unruly children, even with her limited English, completely fascinated him. Her acute sense of intuition surfaced constantly in spite of the communication problem. Even with the language chasm, Jack sensed that Carmelita was highly intelligent.

The more he watched her, the more he was enchanted by the dark strong Aztec features of her classically beautiful face. Her long black hair glistened in the sunlight, and her eyes sparkled with intense expression whenever she spoke. When she smiled, which was seldom, two rows of perfect white teeth made her lovely face absolutely glow.

Jack wondered about her past, her family, and her plans for the future. He also thought about what it would be like to make love to her.

For the next hour or so, Jack smoked a series of cigarettes, and continued to think about Carmelita. His concentration was interrupted when she suddenly exited the kiddie establishment with baby Betty in her arms.

Carmelita was followed closely by the rest of the brood, with little Anthony proudly announcing that Betty had an accident that cut short their sojourn in the play room restaurant.

"I never poop in my pants anymore," Anthony shouted to the world in general as they all piled back into the Lincoln.

When they returned to the house, Jack backed the big Lincoln into the driveway so its hood was facing the street. He was busy cleaning kid related debris out of the car when Tammy suddenly appeared.

"How'd it go?" She inquired, noting that poor Jack looked very tired and frustrated.

"Okay, fine," Jack responded.

"Here, maybe this will help," Tammy added, as she handed Jack a can of air freshner.

"Thanks."

"Carmelita said, the kids were really terrible. Muy <u>terrible</u>," Tammy said, using the Spanish pronounciation.

"You speak Spanish?" Jack asked, as he applied the air spray to the interior of the car.

"Not really. I know a couple of words. I took it in high school," Tammy answered.

"So how do you communicate with Carmelita?"

"I don't know. She always seems to understand most of what I say. She just doesn't speak English very well."

"How long has she been here?" Jack asked.

"With us? Or here in the States?"

"Both," Jack replied.

"She's been with us a little over two years. I think she's been here from Mexico for four of five years." Tammy responded, while striking a sexy little pose. Tammy was always striking sexy little poses. She was very theatrical, and her use of body language verged on being seductive. "Why?" Tammy added.

"Oh, just curious."

"You like her, don't you?" Tammy offered this question in a tone that caught Jack a little off guard.

"Ah, yeah. I think she's cute. And she's really great with the kids."

"Yeah, she is," Tammy agreed, as she leaned forward letting Jack get a glimpse of her well rounded breasts beneath her low cut blouse. "And the kids listen to her."

"I thought maybe the kids spoke Spanish," Jack said, as he handed the can of deodorizer back to Tammy.

"No, but they seem to understand what she means when she tells them to do something. It's weird."

"But she doesn't seem to think much of me," Jack lamented.

"Really?" Tammy replied, stroking the can of deodorizer just a tad with her bejewled well manicured hand.

"Maybe she just doesn't like Gringos," Jack speculated.

"No. I think it's you," Tammy said, still lightly stroking the can in her hand.

Tammy was a little closer than necessary, which made Jack just a little nervous. What was on her mind, he wondered, when her pager suddenly went off sounding a melodious tone. She instantly checked the tiny device's display screen.

"Oops, I gotta make a call," she said, as she started to walk quickly back toward the house. Just as she reached the porch, she turned back and looked at Jack.

"By the way, you have to take Carmelita home today," Tammy informed Jack.

"Home? I thought she lived here?"

"She gets three days off every three weeks. She has family here, some brothers and a sister, I think. Anyway, they have a house over in the Valley, an' she stays there on her days off. She'll be ready in about twenty minutes. It'll take you about an hour, then you're done."

"Okay," Jack replied.

"Funny, as busy as this place is,... I'm going to be home alone all weekend," Tammy said, flashing a sly smile.

"What about the kids?" Jack asked, surprised by her comment, and wondering where the tribe of children were going?

"On Carmelita's days off, the little ones stay with their Grandma. The two that aren't Dan's stay with my ex's, and the oldest one has a Boy Scout camp thing this weekend, so I'm free."

"Oh, yeah," Jack said, as he tried to assess what was on her mind.

Tammy did something kind of cute, then she jogged up the steps and turned back and said, "Any big plans for the weekend, Jack?"

"Ah, no. Why?" Jack replied.

"Oh, just curious. Maybe I'll give you a call," she said, as she waved good bye and popped back into the house.

Oh, dear, Jack thought. If Tammy's on the make, how will he handle that? If he turns her down, she'll probably get him fired by telling Dan he hit on her. The other way, if he gets caught, he could get fired, or worse. Something in his instincts told him that Dan was a dangerous man. He wasn't sure just what Dan did for a living, but he sure met with a lot of shady looking characters. Jack couldn't afford to lose his job. He'd be on the street in a matter of days. Why was nothing in his life, ever simple?

V

Some time had passed, and Jack was still standing next to the car waiting for Carmelita. He checked his watch. It had been close to an hour since Tammy told him Carmelita would be ready to leave in twenty minutes.

He waited a few more minutes, then decided to walk down to the street and have a cigarette. He fished a Camel non-filter out of his dwindling pack. Next, he tapped both ends of the short cigarette on the surface of his watch, then lit up using a blue throw away lighter. He took a deep drag on the strong tightly packed cigarette, and thought about Carmelita, then Tammy. He'd smoked Camels since his service days, and other milder brands just didn't cut it with Jack.

Neither Dan nor Tammy smoked, so he always tried to distance himself from the house when he had the urge. He couldn't really smell it, he'd smoked too long, but he knew his mighty little Camels packed a pervasive aroma. He was going to try and quit again, but somehow this just didn't seem to be the right time.

What was it with Carmelita? Why didn't she like him, Jack thought? It wasn't his fault she slipped and ruined her pretty sweater when they first met.

Maybe on the half hour drive to the Valley, alone in the car with Carmelita, I might have a chance to redeem myself, Jack thought.

"Damn, I should have learned some more phrases in Spanish," he muttered to himself.

He figured she'd probably pull the, 'No comprendo,' thing again. Jack was sure, no comprendo, actually meant selective comprehension in Carmelita's case. This little girl was sharp as a tack, and getting through to her was truly going to be a big challenge.

Unseen by Jack, who was facing the street, Carmelita came out from the side of the house carrying a couple of medium size bags and a nice new compact stereo.

Still unnoticed by Jack, she set the bags and the stereo on the ground behind the Lincoln. Then she quickly dashed back the same way she came to get some more of her stuff.

Jack finished his smoke and crushed out what was left of the cigarette in the street with his foot. He then turned and walked back toward the Lincoln. As he walked, something caught his attention.

As he approached the car, Jack noticed a soccer ball wedged underneath the front of the Lincoln. He bent down and tried to reach under the car and retrieve the black and white ball.

"Damn," he said to himself, when he realized he couldn't quite reach the ball.

Next, he pulled his keys out of his pocket, and jumped into the car. He started the engine and immediately dropped the gear shift into reverse. As the long Lincoln started to roll backward the quiet of the sunny afternoon was suddenly shattered by a loud scream.

"Stop!" Carmelita cried out in an anguished voice that could clearly be heard a block away.

Carmelita had just rounded the house carrying another travel bag. The Lincoln's rear wheel was about to back over her new stereo.

Jack jammed on the brakes stopping the wheel less than an inch away from crushing Carmelita's prized little boom box.

Carmelita quickly grabbed her stereo and other bags as Jack killed the engine and jumped out of the car.

"What happened?" Jack asked, responding to the panic in her voice.

Carmelita lit into a litany of colorful phrases in Spanish. In a literal sense Jack didn't understand a word, however, on a visceral level her dissatisfaction with him was very very clear.

"I'm sorry!" Jack said.

"¿Que?" Carmelita responded.

Oh, boy. Here we go with the no comprendo crap, again, Jack thought, as he tried to make his face look as conciliatory as possible. Then her incredible beauty in the natural afternoon sunlight aroused his attention again.

"You're so beautiful," he said, cracking a slight smile.

"¿Como?" She replied.

"Bellissima."

Jack used an Italian word for beautiful, and immediately felt stupid. The word had no effect on Carmelita who was now throwing her things into the Lincoln.

Jack recomposed himself and took solace in the fact that he hadn't almost backed over a kid. That was his first thought when he heard Carmelita scream.

"Wow. You scared me. I thought I almost backed over a kid," Jack said.

The idea of backing over a child held a particular horror for Jack. It triggered a terrible memory time couldn't erase.

She finished loading the car, and jumped into the front seat. A look of, let's go, crossed her pretty face as she impatiently folded her arms.

Jack noticed that Carmelita had changed her clothes. She was now wearing short tight shorts, sandals, and a snug fitting mid drift tee shirt. As Jack pulled out into the street, a loud pop emanated from beneath the moving car. They drove away leaving a black and white soccer ball dead in the driveway.

The seat belt ran between Carmelita's breasts in a way that made their firm outline very obvious. With the air conditioner running full bore, the shape of her large dark nipples showed through the thin tee shirt, and made Jack jittery as he tried not to look with little success.

Carmelita didn't say a word all the way to her brother and sister's house except to give Jack directions using hand signals and a smattering of terse staccato phrases in broken English and Spanish.

It took them a little over a half an hour to reach the house which was located in the Pacoima area of the north San Fernando Valley. Just before they reached the well kept little house, they passed through a large commercial section where almost all the stores sported signs in Spanish.

In a way, this part of the Valley was very much like being in another country, Jack thought. The area was alive with shoppers, busy retail establishments, and a myriad of vocal street vendors. Blaring from a series of large unseen stereo speakers, lively Latin music filled the afternoon air and created a very festive atmosphere.

When Jack dropped Carmelita off at her relative's house, she declined his offer to help her with her stuff, and scampered inside without saying another word. To Jack, the chances of ever getting anywhere with this gal seemed hopelessly slim.

What was it about these Latinas, that Jack suddenly found so overwhelmingly attractive? He had also noticed a number of hot little cuties shopping in the commercial district on the way to Carmelita's house, and then the bevy of beautiful Señoritas who worked at Jack's new abode crossed his mind.

Before returning to the motel in Calabasas, Jack stopped at a big book store and hit the foreign language section.

It took him over forty minutes to find exactly what he wanted. He bought some easy to read instructional books that pertained to learning Spanish. He also picked up a couple of cassette tapes on conversational Spanish, and found a flyer that advertised some local Spanish classes for beginners. Probably armed with enough material to teach an army, Jack left the book store ready to face the great challenge ahead.

VI

Once Jack returned to his room, he dug into his new Spanish studies with gusto and determination. He realized that learning another language was going to be difficult, but not impossible. Years before, he'd peripherally tackled another language while serving in the Marine Corps. He never achieved fluency, but he learned enough to make himself understood.

Lots of people mastered new languages, he told himself. Look at all the folks that come to this country and learn English. If they could do it, he could, Jack concluded.

That night, while he was busy studying one of his new Spanish books and listening to an audio tape, the telephone rang.

Jack wasn't expecting any calls. Almost no one he knew had knowledge of his new residence. He decided not to answer the phone, thinking it just might be Tammy. He didn't want to blow his deal with Dan, and he thought the boss' wife had that look in her eye. He also knew that she was going to be home alone all weekend.

Tammy and Dan had been married almost seven years, and for Tammy that was a new indoor record. After the phone rang four times, it stopped and the red message light began to flash.

Jack promptly picked up the receiver and checked the motel's voice mail, and realized the caller had hung up without leaving a message. He quickly returned to his studies.

About an hour later the phone rang again. Once more, he let

it ring four times, then checked the voice mail as soon as the red light started flashing. Again, the caller left no message.

Jack continued to study his books and listen to his tapes late into the night. By the time he finally went to bed it was almost three in the morning. He slept well, and didn't get up until a little past ten the next day.

When he got up he made himself a cup of instant coffee using hot water from the tap. He made several cups this way and smoked a half a dozen cigarettes before he finally felt ready to resume his studies. He started by listening to another audio tape on beginning Spanish.

After an hour or so, he showered, dressed in shorts and a tee shirt, then donned his favorite baseball cap and ventured out into the world to test his newly acquired knowledge.

The first person Jack encountered was Maria, one of the cute young Mexican maids that worked at the motel.

"Buenos dias," Jack said, as he greeted her with a smile.

"Buenos dias, Señor," she replied, also flashing a big smile.

When Maria returned the phrase and the smile, Jack's spirits were instantly buoyed by the cheerful response he'd received.

Soon he passed another housekeeping Latina named Rita. All the housekeeping staff wore little name tags, so he was able to address them each by name.

"Buenos dias, Rita."

"Buenos dias, Señor."

"¿Como esta?" Jack inquired.

"Muy bien, gracias. ¿Usted?"

"Muy bien, gracias," Jack answered, very pleased that he had actually engaged in a short conversation. He broke into a broad smile as he continued down the walkway.

The sun was shinning and the sky was blue. Another beautiful day in Southern California. Un dia bonito, indeed, Jack thought.

Jack spent the rest of the weekend practicing his Spanish, and getting to know some of the pretty girls who worked around the motel.

One in particular caught his eye early on. She was the first one with whom he had exchanged a few words in espanol. Her name was Maria, una Mexicana, and she was absolutely beautiful.

Maria didn't look as traditionally Mexican as the others who worked at the motel. She had high cheek bones, beautiful hazel eyes, and soft brown hair with slight blond highlights. During work the girls were required to wear their hair straight back in a bun, or a ponytail. Maria's ponytail hung to the middle of her back and swayed in a most interesting way when she walked. With her hair pulled straight back nothing obstructed her classically beautiful face. She had thick wonderful lips, lovely white teeth, and a winning smile that would light up a dark room or a man's heart in a second. She also spoke absolutely no English.

Jack found much to his amazement that most of the women there spoke little to no English. Some were married with children, and others were single. Most had family in the area, and Jack also presumed that many were working in the country illegally.

He also quickly developed a friendship with a young man named Raul who worked as a maintenance man at the well kept motel. Raul proved to be very helpful in Jack's quest to learn Spanish. His new friend spoke very good English, and Jack could ask him very specific questions and get answers in both languages. Raul also gave him a rundown on some of the girls.

That weekend was one of great discovery on many levels, and Jack was happy he had landed in this interesting little oasis in Calabasas.

Jack also received a number of calls over that weekend, where no one left a message. Then once, responding to a call in the middle of the night, he grabbed the receiver, but only a dial greeted him. Who was calling? Jack could only speculate.

The following Tuesday Dan came back, and he and Jack returned to their regular routine, more or less. The days all started early and ended late. Carmelita's sister apparently drove her back to Dan and Tammy's, and Jack was disappointed he wasn't asked to pick her up for the return trip. He only encountered her once that week, and she remained as distant as before, or maybe more so. Jack was now anxious to try out a little of his newly acquired espanol on her, but the opportunity just didn't present itself.

Tammy was totally nude and walking around her spacious sky blue bedroom having a heated conversation on her cell phone.
"No. I've made up my mind. I've given this a lot of thought, and I detinitely want him killed!" Tammy said passionately, lowering her voice slightly as she uttered the last two words.
Outside the bedroom, Carmelita had just approached the closed bedroom door. She was holding a handful of Tammy's neatly ironed blouses. Several hours of work had gone into the ten tops she was carefully carrying on hangers. Tammy would blow through the blouses in less than two days.
Carmelita hesitated at the door as if she had just overheard Tammy's final comment on the phone. She waited for a moment, and pondered whether or not she should knock on the door.

VII

After work one day Jack encountered Raul working close to his room. Jack, still dressed in his suit, listened as Raul patiently taught him a new phrase in Spanish. Jack repeated the phrase perfectly several times.

"Muy bien, Jack," Raul complimented.

"Ah,…muchas gracias, Raul."

"Oh, that's okay. Any time you have a question, Jack," Raul replied in precise English.

"Una pregunta. A question," Jack said, making the statement sound almost like a question.

"Si," Raul replied. "If you want to say, I have a question, it's,… tengo una pregunta."

"Tengo una pregunta," Jack repeated.

"Hey, that was great. You're learning fast. I think you'll be speaking Spanish in no time," Raul responded.

"Gracias, Raul. You're a good teacher. Yo tengo un maestro excelente. ¿Es correcto?"

"Si. Absolutely correct," Raul replied.

"You really speak good English, Raul."

"Thank you, I try."

"Did you take it in school?"

"Yes, in Mexico. Four years in school, then I've been here for almost five years. I like to help you with your Spanish, to teach you words, phrases. I have to practice my English so I can explain things to you. Is good for me."

"Well, you're very helpful."

"Oh, it is my pleasure. Es mi gusto. I help you, it help me," Raul said, with a big smile.

Just then Raul noticed the motel manager approaching.

"I have to go back to work. Necesito regreso trabajo. Hasta luego, Jack."

"Yeah, see ya later," Jack said, repeating Raul's last phrase in English.

In just a matter of days, studying Spanish had started to open up a whole new world to Jack. Attacking the challenge on many fronts, he also enrolled in a night school Spanish class.

Jack had never cared much for school, and he had acquired most of his knowledge empirically. The class was held at a local high school and met two nights a week.

The class was attended by fifteen students. Twelve were Anglo, the other three were Asian. The class was taught by a very stern looking middle aged man named Raphael.

"Me gusta el color anaranjado," Señor Raphael said, employing an air of arrogance that made the short fat instructor resemble a South American dictator.

"Me gusta el color anaranjado," the class repeated, a little out of unison.

"No! No! No! Me gusta el color anaranjado." Señor Raphael repeated sternly.

Next, he singled out an Asian woman who was having a very pronounced problem with the tongue twisting phrase.

"Señorita Lee. Repita por favor," Raphael commanded.

"Si, Señor. Me gusta el color anaranjado," Ms. Lee said, hesitantly.

"No! No! No! Me gusta el color anaranjado," the instructor repeated, just short of shouting at the shy woman.

Ms. Lee repeated the phrase once again. There was no hiding Señor Raphael's disapproval of her pronunciation. In disgust, he mercifully let Ms. Lee off the hook and pointed a pudgy finger at Jack.

"Señor."

Jack eloquently executed the sentence to Señor Raphael's satisfaction. However, from that night on, Jack never cared much for the color orange.

A couple of days later Jack got off work early and returned to the motel in the middle of the afternoon. It wasn't long before he was having an animated conversation in Spanish with an attractive young maid named Nancy. Nancy was a pretty Mexicana whom Jack had secretly nicknamed the Aztec Princess.

Nancy was a tall girl who was blessed with natural beauty, soft bronze skin, intense dark eyes, and long straight jet black hair. She wore her hair in una coleta, a ponytail, like all of the girls at the motel, except Nancy's coleta hung clear to the small of her back.

She also possessed a regal presence due to her height and near perfect posture. Jack thought the Princess sobriquet fit her to a tee. Nancy had long slender fingers and a wonderful figure that sported a couple of breasts that Jack found totally irresistible. He practically got a hard on just looking at her.

When Jack encountered her near his room, Nancy was still on duty and standing next to her housekeeping cart. She was in between stops, and asked Jack if he would share a cigarette with her.

Jack was the perfect cover. Nancy would look around, then take a puff off Jack's cigarette, then hand it back to him, so she wouldn't get caught smoking on the job. They were near the back of the motel, so their little game of subterfuge was fairly safe.

"Nancy, tengo una pregunta. ¿Tu casada?" Jack asked, as he pointed at his ring finger.

"No," Nancy replied.

Jack had just asked her if she was married, and her reply pleased him.

Jack had run into Nancy a few times, and on those occasions there had always been a slight state of flirtation between them. Jack had heard from someone that she had two kids, and he assumed that she was married. The news that she was not, now tipped the Nancy scale in another direction.

She then asked Jack if he was married. She too, pointed at her ring finger while posing the question first in broken English then in Spanish.

"No. Soy divorciado," he replied.

"Si. You no married?" Nancy confirmed.

"No, ahora."

Nancy then went on to explain using a mixture of Spanish and halting English, that she had two young children at home, but she was no longer married because her husband was dead.

"Oh, I'm sorry. Lo siento," Jack said, sympathetically.

"My husband, he was killed in a robbery."

"Oh, my God. That's awful!" Jack replied.

"Si," she said. "The cops shot him coming out of the store with the money."

This little slice of reality hit Jack like a sledge hammer.

Nancy quickly handed the cigarette back to Jack just a second before Yolanda, the watch commander of the housekeeping staff, rounded the corner of the building. As Yolanda approached the chatting couple Nancy turned her head away and slowly blew the smoke out of her mouth. Jack knew this was his cue to leave.

"I gotta go. Yo voy. Muchas gracias por mi leccion," Jack said.
"De nada, Jack."
"Adios. Hasta luego, Nancy."
"Si. Hasta luego."

Jack walked away as Nancy resumed pushing her cart.

VIII

Dan worked out of a rather nice office complex in the center of trendy Westlake Village. The low slung California Spanish architecture of off white two story red tile roofed office buildings appealed to Jack's esthetic side. Wooden balconies with potted plants accentuated the old California Spanish look. The well tended compound included a duck pond and grounds that abounded with greenery.

The complex blended well with the surrounding hills that were dotted with huge ancient oak trees. Situated in the heart of the Conejo Valley, Westlake Village is approximately forty miles northwest of Los Angeles, and is part of the City of Thousand Oaks. The Spanish translation for the word conejo is rabbit or bunny. Somehow, Bunny Valley, sounded much better in Spanish, Jack thought.

Jack's imagination often drifted to thoughts of what this area was like almost two hundred years ago when California was part of Mexico, and before that when it was still the property of Spain. New Spain, they called it, much like the northeastern portion of the United States came to be known as New England during the British Colonial era.

Jack slipped out of the office and crossed the parking lot to have a smoke.

Jack would bide his time while waiting for Dan at the office, either by sitting at an empty desk in the big outer office, or he would retreat to the parking lot to smoke, and chat with the other smokers.

At the desk Jack would usually read the paper, or study one of his Spanish books.

Outside, he often ran into the Latino gardener Juan, whom he had come to know through his extended visits to the parking lot.

Juan was one of two Latinos who worked at the office complex. His duties included gardening and general maintenance.

Early on, Jack found that the phrase, buenos dias, opened the door to a number of new friendships.

Within a very short period of time, Jack had learned quite a bit of Spanish from Juan. Any Hispanic within Jack's sphere, was fair game to turn into a teacher. Jack also helped Juan with his English. The student/teacher thing was usually a two way street, Jack learned soon after he began his linguistic journey.

Jack liked Juan. He was bright, funny, somewhat shy, and had soldiered in jungle combat for five years in the Salvadorian Army. This fact also made them brothers in the veteran sense.

Juan seldom spoke about his war experience in El Salvador, but Jack surmised his friend had seen a lot of shit. Men who saw the most generally said the least.

They had a brief but lively chat, that was suddenly cut short, when Juan noticed his boss drive into the complex at the far end of the parking lot. Juan indicated that he had to go return to work and promptly excused himself, leaving Jack standing alone next to the Lincoln.

Jack lit another cigarette and thought about his latest encounter with Tammy earlier in the day.

Tammy had really looked hot again that morning when he picked Dan up at nine. Jack wondered what her story was? And that morning there was also no sign of Carmelita. He hadn't seen her in a couple of weeks.

He wasn't even sure if she still worked there. He also didn't want to ask. Dan had acted a little funny when Jack asked him a question about her once before, and he didn't want to take a chance, just in case there was something going on between Dan and Carmelita. God, he hoped there wasn't, even though he figured his chances with the mysterious Señorita were somewhere between slim and none.

Suddenly, Jack felt someone's presence close by and he turned around to discover Dan standing next to him.

"Oh, you startled me!" Jack said. "If you were the enemy, I'd be dead."

Dan laughed, and said, "You got another one of those?"

"A cigarette?"

"Yeah."

"I didn't know you smoked?"

"I do sometimes," Dan replied.

Jack gave Dan a cigarette and lit it for him.

"Thanks."

"Sure."

Dan took a puff off the strong non filtered Camel, and got a little tobacco on his lip and in his mouth. He subtly tried to spit the bitter taste off his tongue. Also, Dan's eyes started to water slightly.

He should have warned him, these little Camels pack quite a whollop, Jack thought. He also figured Dan was probably using the cigarette thing as some sort of ice breaker, and Jack's instincts proved right.

"You know Tammy can be a real pain in the ass sometimes. We're pretty much on the verge of getting a divorce. Has Tammy said anything to you?"

"No," Jack replied. "This is the first time I've heard about it."

"Well, Tammy thinks I'm seeing another woman," Dan said.

"Oh."

"An' she's right. Now, it's the kind of thing, where with you being around all the time, you just might catch on to it, so that's why I'm tellin' you."

"Okay," Jack said.

"You don't have a problem with keeping your mouth shut, do you Jack?"

"No. Of course not."

"Good," Dan said, as he flipped his unfinished cigarette away, "Come on, let's go. I have to be in Century City by 4:30."

As Dan started to jump into the car, he turned his head back as if he'd forgotten something.

"Jack, run in the office and get my briefcase, I forgot it," Dan snapped.

Before Jack could reply, Dan answered the cell phone that seemed perminately affixed to his hand, and slipped into the car.

Jack quickly glanced at his watch as he dashed to the office to retrieve the briefcase. It was almost three forty-five, and they were forty miles from Century City. Here we go again, Jack thought, the 405's gonna be a nightmare at this hour.

Jack promptly returned with the briefcase, popped a mint in his mouth, and the two men sped away headed for the West Side of L.A. They only sped for a block, however, until they hit the 101.

In heavy traffic, first on the Ventura Freeway, then on the 405, it took them almost an hour to reach their destination.

As usual, Dan had little to say as they crept along in traffic, and Jack wondered if he was having an affair with Carmelita?

Dan's meeting in Century City lasted until a little past six. The traffic was awful on the return trip as well. L.A.'s vast freeway system was far too overcrowded, an observation made by thousands of commuters every day.

The terrible traffic, the sports talk radio, which Jack hated, and Dan blared between business calls, coupled with the reasonable likelihood that his boss was having an affair with that incredibly beautiful little niñera, Carmelita, kept Jack's stomach on the verge of nausea the rest of the day.

Dan's curt attitude earlier really pissed Jack off, and he hadn't quite settled on how to deal with it. And why was this gal Carmelita having such an effect on him, Jack wondered? He just couldn't get la Señorita off his mind.

Why can't I stop thinking about her, Jack thought? Why her? There were plenty of pretty girls around, and his chances with Carmelita seemed rather slim at best. She always acted very distant with him, and besides, if his boss was in that saddle it also made Jack's situation very precarious if he hit on her, and maybe even dangerous. Dan didn't seem like the type of man who would take that kind of transgression lightly. Jack also knew he really needed this job. No job, and he'd be on the street.

Yet, even weighing all this, there was something absolutely enchanting about la Señorita, and no matter how hard he tried, he couldn't get Carmelita out of his mind.

They didn't get back to the office until almost eight, then Dan attended to something in his office until just before ten.

When they returned to Dan's house around ten that evening, the kids were all in bed, and Tammy was nowhere in sight. Dan went immediately upstairs to the room he used as an office in the house, and asked Jack to wait, on the off chance that he had might have to go out again.

Soon Jack went into the garage to retrieve some Windex and paper towels. His intention was to kill some time by cleaning the Lincoln's windshield and windows. While in the garage, he noticed that the washer was running. It immediately occurred to him that Carmelita was probably doing the laundry.

He quickly checked the washing machine's timer, and realized the laundry would be finished in five minutes. The opportunity of a chance encounter over the laundry loomed, and the quick formulation of a plan took root.

As Jack passed back through the kitchen leaving the garage, he heard a strange sound upstairs. Kind of a thumping. He also thought he heard something break.

His plan was to quickly clean the Lincoln's windshield, then return to the garage in five minutes and hope to accidently run into Carmelita.

Jack did a perfunctory job on the windshield, and headed back for the garage via the kitchen in exactly five minutes.

The machine, a large nice model, clicked off on the dot, and a pleasant sounding alarm sounded to notify its user that the cycle was finished.

Jack returned the Windex and roll of paper towels to a rack near the laundry area, and waited to see if Carmelita would turn up to transfer the clothes to the dryer.

A few minutes passed, and Jack wondered if Dan had started to look for him. He always expected Jack to wait next to the car, or in the living room. Dan would become immediately agitated if he had to wait even a second for Jack.

Just as Jack decided enough time had passed and he needed to check in by the car, Carmelita entered the garage.

Jack was struck again by the quiet glow of her beauty, then a large bruise just below her eye caught his attention. When she noticed Jack standing near the washer, she smiled sheepishly, and acknowledged him with a nod of her head.

Jack was taken aback slightly. She was actually responding to him in a somewhat friendly manner.

"Hola," Jack said.

"Hola," Carmelita replied.

"¿Que paso tu hojo?" Jack asked, pointing at his eye, and hoping he had used the right words in Spanish.

"Es nada," Carmelita stated. "¿Habla espanol, usted?" She asked, somewhat surprised that Jack had learned some Spanish.

When she spoke, she spoke quietly with her eyes cast down. It occurred to Jack that Dan may have hit her, and if that was the case it certainly presented a problem. How to handle his new and delicate dilemma posed a conundrum. Also, the fact that she was responding to him for the first time in a manner that wasn't cold and indifferent gave Jack a glimmer of hope. He decided to try and communicate with her at another time, concerned that Dan might be outside by the car waiting for him.

Jack quickly scribbled the phone number at the motel and his room number on a scrap of paper and handed it to Carmelita.

"Si, tienes un problema aqui, llama me. ¿Entiende?" Jack said, as he handed her his phone number.

"Si, entiendo," she affirmed, as she furtively slipped the paper with Jack's number into her pocket. "Gracias," she added, then turned to the wet clothes in the washer.

"Hasta luego," Jack said.

"Si. Hasta luego," she replied softly.

Afraid he might incur Dan's wrath if the boss was waiting, Jack slipped out of the garage and returned to the driveway to find no sign of Dan.

He lit a cigarette, and considered what had just transpired in the garage with Carmelita. Was she in danger? If so, what could he do? Also, if he did anything, his job would be on the line, and on the street he'd be no good to anyone.

"Hey, Jack," Dan called out from the porch.

"Yeah," Jack replied.

"You can take off. We're done for the day. Be back at seven in the morning. We have to go to San Diego again tomorrow. And maybe Mexico. Give you a chance to speak a little Spanish," Dan added, sarcastically, before he slammed the front door shut.

Boy, that sounds like fun, Jack thought. With Friday traffic it'll be seven and a half hours each way, with lots of stupid ass sports radio, and Dan. Jack slightly exaggerated the travel time in his mind, but not by much.

When Jack got back to the motel that night, there was a voice mail message waiting for him. Dan had called to change Jack's start time in the morning. Dan now wanted to leave for the trip south at five am.

Jack looked at his clock. It was almost eleven thirty. On the way home he'd gassed up the car and gotten a bite to eat. He cracked a beer and smoked a couple of cigarettes before he went to bed. He quickly fell into a deep sleep, but only for a few minutes. The phone rang and jolted Jack back to consciousness.

"Hello," Jack said, then responded with a tone of surprise when the caller identified herself by greeting him in Spanish.

"Oh, bola," Jack said, as he sat up in bed.

Jack flipped on the light and reached for a cigarette as he tried to gather his thoughts and translate them into Spanish.

"¿Qué pasa, Nancy?" Jack asked.

IX

There were cops everywhere in the Westlake area. Jack would usually observe their ubiquitous activity first thing in the morning on his way to work. The commute from Calabasas up to Dan's house in Westlake Village was just over seven miles. Six miles of which were on the 101 Ventura Freeway. During this six to eight minute trip, Jack would pass through north Calabasas, Agoura Hills, Oak Park, and then into Westlake Village, located at the southern tip of the City of Thousand Oaks just over the L.A. Ventura County line.

This little stretch was patrolled by the L.A. County Sheriff's Department, the Thousand Oaks Police Department, the Ventura County Sheriff's Department, and the California Highway Patrol.

All these communities were predominately lily white, rather conservative, and very well protected. The Captain in charge of the Malibu Lost Hills Sheriff's Station which serviced the area often boasted in the press about their zero tolerance policy.

It all looked like over kill to Jack, who had experienced no problems while driving the Lincoln, but had been stopped twice while driving his own decade old dilapidated sedan.

Just that morning Jack witnessed three traffic stops during his short journey to work. Two of the stops were attended by more than one patrol car. Criminals beware, the police are everywhere, Jack thought, as he pulled off the Freeway exiting at Westlake Boulevard.

A few days had passed since he encountered Carmelita in the garage. He'd picked Dan up very early each morning and dropped him off late at night, and he hadn't run into la Señorita since that night when she was doing the laundry.

This morning Dan had told him to arrive at the house around ten. The kids were in school, and he remembered that Tammy was off to Hawaii for a week with her girlfriend Annie Horwitz. That morning he saw no sign of Carmelita while he was waiting for Dan.

Jack sat in his usual chair in the living room and read the newspaper cover to cover. He helped himself to some coffee from the kitchen, and went outside a couple of times to grab a smoke. It was almost noon when Dan finally came downstairs.

"Carmelita's going to make us some lunch before we go," Dan announced, as he reached the bottom of the stairs.

"Okay," Jack said.

"She makes great tacos," Dan continued, as he headed for the kitchen.

Jack followed his boss and was surprised to see Carmelita busy at work in the kitchen. How long had she been out there? He wondered. There were two back doors to the large house, and a side entrance into the kitchen. Had she purposely avoided him that morning?

Jack and Dan eat hearty portions of tacos, beans, and rice, as Carmelita quietly went about her tasks cleaning up the large kitchen.

"I love Mexican food," Dan said, as he finished the last bite of his forth taco.

"Yeah, me too. I could eat it every day. Esta comida es muy deliciosa, Carmelita," Jack complimented.

"Gracias, Señor," Carmelita said, without turning her head in Jack's direction.

Jack tried to remember, had it been five or six days since he last saw Carmelita?

The way her hair was hanging slightly over her face, it was hard for him to see her bruise. Then he saw it as she turned to pick up a dirty plate.

The bruise under her eye seemed larger, Jack thought, then he realized that this was a new bruise under her other eye. Should he say something and risk angering Dan, or keep his mouth shut like some pussy?

Jack didn't think Dan spoke Spanish, but he wasn't absolutely sure. Jack also realized that his Spanish was still very very simplistic, and someone with even rudimentary knowledge of the language might understand his crude phraseology.

"¿Como esta tu hojo, Carmelita?" Jack asked.

"Bien, bien," she said softly, then returned to the sink with her back to Jack.

Fine, fine, Jack thought. Yeah, I can see it's just fine.

"Bien," Jack said, under his breath. Then he noticed that Dan was glaring at him as he spoke Spanish.

Jack had noticed that a lot of Gringos glared when they saw him speaking espanol.

Carmelita kept her eyes focused on the dishes she was washing.

Jack could sense the tension in the room. Had he stepped over some line? And what would he do if he found out his boss was slapping the pretty little Señorita around every now and then? Kick the guy's ass and end up homeless, I guess, Jack speculated.

"Okay, let's go, Mr. Hardin I have to be in Santa Monica at three," Dan said, in a fairly warm tone. "Thanks, Carmelita."

"You're welcome, sir," Carmelita said, her English somewhat halting.

Dan's change of mood caught Jack off guard. Dan was smiling as he got up and left the table.

"Come on, Jack. We've got to go by the office first, and I want to give us plenty of time for a change. I hate fighting traffic at the last minute, don't you?"

"Yeah, really," Jack said. "Gracias, de nuevo, Carmelita."

"De nada," she said quietly, again without turning her head.

As they exited the kitchen Jack looked back at Carmelita. Her long black hair hanging straight and glistening in the light, along with the tall shadow she strangely cast against the wall, gave her an almost mystical Madonna aura. That's weird, Jack thought, as the image settled in his mind, where it would remain for the rest of the day.

X

Over the next two weeks, Dan arranged his schedule in such a way that Jack never ran into Carmelita. He and Dan would leave very early in the morning, usually before dawn, and return late at night, when none of the lights within the house were burning.

After the Madonna day, Jack slowly tried to push thoughts of Carmelita into the outer recesses of his mind, until she, or somebody else, made another move. Keeping Carmelita on a front burner was far too painful. Since he still thought his chances with Carmelita were slim, and the situation possibly dangerous, Jack let his eye drift toward a couple of other ladies. Even when he tried, it was always hard for Jack to suppress his horny side.

Of the few women Jack had been with recently, he was most fond of fucking a gal named Flora.

Flora worked in a sandwich shop that Jack visited often when he had a lunch break in the vicinity of the office in Westlake Village. Dan had recently started working out of another office close to the L.A. Airport, in addition to the Westlake complex. Now, when they weren't on the road, they split their time between the two office sites.

It had been four or five days since Jack had stopped by the shop for one of their great submarine sandwiches. As he entered the uncrowded shop Jack greeted his friend Flora behind the high counter in Spanish.

Jack always wondered why they built the counter so high? Poor little Flora, who was barely five feet tall, had to stand on her tip toes, or on a box, during her entire shift.

Always cheerful, Flora often said, her job just made her short legs stronger, something Jack could attest to with great fondness. Yes, Flora was one hot little Señorita, Jack thought, as he looked into her deep set sexy eyes while they exchanged small talk.

From El Salvador, Flora had been in the States for almost ten years. Her English was quite fluent, and she had an infectious sense of humor that Jack found very appealing. She was thirty-six years old, and made no bones about the fact that she was trying to find a husband. Flora found Jack attractive, and told him so frequently. Today, she was in strong flirtation mode, and Jack sensed that sex was as much on her mind as it was on his. She took his money, and handed him his sandwich in a basket, in a way that suggested the matter should be explored further as soon as possible.

"Gracias," Jack said.

"De nada, Jack," Flora replied. "Your Spanish is sure getting better."

"Gracias. Yo trato," Jack said, not really sure if he had used the correct phrase for, 'I try.'

"When are you going to call me?" Flora asked, putting an emphasis on the word call that was wrought with double-entendre.

"Ah, soon. I've been really busy. Si, pronto. Yo estoy muy ocupado, ahora." Jack said, saying basically the same thing in English and Spanish.

"¿Muy ocupado? You too busy for sex?" She asked.

"¿Cuando es tu proximo dia de libre?" Jack responded.

"Mañana. Yo estoy libre esta noche," she said, informing him that she was free that night, and off the next day.

"¿Cuando quieres encontramos?"

"Ocho."

"¿Ocho esta noche?" Jack asked.

"Si."

"¿Tu vino quarto de mio?" Jack said, asking her if she was coming to his room.

"Si. I come to your place at eight tonight." Flora answered, with a smile.

"Muy bien. Hasta a las ocho esta noche," Jack replied, also sporting a smile.

"See you at eight," Flora stated, then suddenly looked real embarrassed when she realized that her foregoing conversation with Jack was clearly overheard by one of her nearby coworkers.

Later that afternoon, Jack and Dan returned to the house to retrieve some documents he needed for a meeting later that day at the L.A. Airport office.

Jack went inside to use the restroom and encountered Carmelita and Tammy at the same time. Tammy was the closet to Jack, and she immediately struck one of her dramatic little poses the instant see spotted him.

"Hi, Jack," Tammy greeted.

"Hi, Tammy," Jack replied.

Tammy had been out in the backyard by the pool, and she was wearing the skimpiest bikini possible. A tiny Hawaiian print job probably purchased on her recent trip to the Islands, he thought. It also occurred to Jack that Tammy's tan body was probably one of the most perfect he'd ever seen.

"Beautiful day, isn't it Jack" Tammy offered.

"Yeah, it's great," Jack replied, as he watched Carmelita slip out of view.

Tammy noticed Jack glancing at Carmelita as she left the room, and gave him a look that was hard to read. She turned her taught body slightly as Jack made a move for the bathroom.

"I hear you like to eat tacos, Jack?" Tammy said, in a matter of fact way.

"Very much," Jack replied. "To me, Taco Bell is high cuisine, how about you?"

"I was kinda referring to something else," she said, before she turned abruptly left the room.

Jack made his trip to the john a quick one, and returned to car in the driveway. When he saw that Dan wasn't out there, he fired up a smoke and leaned against the car while he waited.

It wasn't long before he noticed Carmelita standing almost hidden at the corner of the house.

When he saw her, he flipped his unfinished cigarette into the street and quickly approached her.

Before Jack could say, 'buenas tardies' they heard Dan exit the house through the front door.

"Jack!" Dan shouted, when he didn't spot him near the car.

"I call you tonight," Carmelita said.

Did she say she'd call me tonight? Jack thought, as Carmelita turned and ran off toward the back of the house along a narrow pathway out of Dan's view.

"Coming boss," Jack said, as he started to dash toward the car where Dan was waiting with his hands full of stuff.

Jack hit the unlock tab on his key chain, and opened the back door so Dan could deposit his brimming box full of documents.

Dan was on edge all the way to the airport office. He made a couple of terse telephone calls and cranked the sports radio.

Jack continued to ponder the incredible dilemma he was facing. Carmelita said she was going to call, and Flora was showing up at eight. He can't talk to Carmelita with Flora in the room, and what if Carmelita wants to get together? Or, maybe she won't call.

Complicating matters, Jack didn't have Flora's home telephone number, and he couldn't call her at work because he was on the road. Then Jack glanced at the car clock. It was already after four, and Flora's shift ended at four-fifteen. So much for calling her once they reached their destination, Jack thought, just as he passed the Century Boulevard exit.

"Jack! You just passed Century!"

"I know. I'm sorry. I'll get off at Imperial an' go back," Jack said.

Great time for me to miss an exit, Jack thought, as he stepped on the gas and got them to Dan's office using a round about route that seemed to displease Dan enormously.

Later that night, after he dropped Dan off at the house, Jack got back to his motel room just before eight. Flora was sitting in her car waiting for him, and Jack had to do some very quick thinking as he stepped out of the car.

Flora jumped out of her car in a way that offered a view of her legs all the way up to her thighs. Jack noticed that Flora had forgot to wear panties.

She was dressed in a short low cut spaghetti strap dress that revealed she wasn't wearing a bra. Flora was looking hot, Jack thought, her hair hanging long and clean.

They greeted each other with a kiss. Flora liked his rugged good looks, and the fact that Jack was learning Spanish also impressed her. So many Gringos were prejudice and offensive, but Jack was handsome and fun.

The kiss quickly got deeper and hotter, and Jack could feel her nipples getting hard against his chest. Her long wet kiss was so passionate that it damn near put him in a trance, and he had a lot of trouble pulling away. Once the kiss was broken, he had a little problem keeping his balance.

"Flora! I have to go back to work. I couldn't call you, so I drove down here, but I've got to go right back to work, or I'll get fired," Jack lied.

They were standing within a few feet of his room, and suddenly Jack thought he heard the telephone ringing inside his room. He couldn't go inside to answer it, because it would blow his story. He had to leave.

"How 'bout tomorrow night? ¿Mañana noche?" Jack asked.

"Maybe. You sure you have to go back work? Or do you have another girlfriend for tonight?" Flora inquired.

"I don't have a girlfriend. No tengo novia," Jack answered honestly.

"You sure?" She questioned. "¿Seguro?

"Si, seguro. No girlfriend, but I do have to go. Necesito yo voy a la casa de mi jefe, inmediatamente." Jack stated, then glanced at his watch for affect. "I gotta go right now!"

"Okay, tomorrow night. Promise? ¿Promesa? She asked.

"Si, promesa. Misma hora," Jack said, indicating they'd meet here at the same time tomorrow night.

"Okay," Flora replied, looking very sexy, and equally very disappointed. She also didn't look like she believed his story.

"Hasta luego," Jack said, as he gave her a quick kiss, then jumped back into the Lincoln and sped away.

Jack made a wide three mile circle before returning to the motel ten minutes later. Fortunately Flora had left, and Jack quickly entered his room. The red light on his telephone was flashing, but a check of the voice mail produced no messages.

The phone remained silent the rest of the night. No Flora, no Carmelita, no nada, Jack thought, feeling totally had by the circumstances. He finally fell asleep shorty after midnight.

Jack felt like shit the next morning when he picked Dan up at six. They headed straight for the airport office where he and Dan spent the rest of the day. Jack lamented the fact that he didn't have the chance to pop by the sandwich shop to comfirm his date that night with Flora. All day long Jack wondered if she'd even show up.

After dropping Dan off a little before seven, Jack returned to his room, and waited for Flora. The phone was quiet all evening. Flora failed to show, and again Jack fell asleep late.

XI

Later that week, for reasons that were unclear to Jack, Dan abruptly scuttled the office near the airport, and all the real action shifted back to the office in Westlake Village.

This suited Jack just fine. The airport location was in a dreary section of Inglewood that Jack found absolutely depressing. He hated the long drive down the 405 to the airport, the frustrating traffic, and the talk radio. It was nice to be back stationed in pleasant surroundings.

The first chance he had to return to the sandwich shop, found his friend Flora in a very chilly mood. After the cold reception, and a sandwich that seemed to include all the ingredients that Jack didn't like, he returned to the office where he intended to study for his Spanish class that evening.

However, an unscheduled afternoon trip to Arcadia suddenly changed his plans. The traffic sucked as they snaked their way along the 101 across the Valley to the 134. East of Pasadena, close to the Santa Anita Race Track, Jack's boss met with some tough looking gents behind the walls of a very secure mansion.

While Dan commiserated with these characters, Jack was briefly able to study some Spanish. He didn't want to face Señor Raphael unprepared. However, that wasn't Jack's only concern that day, as he sat in the car and studied one of his Spanish books.

His thoughts kept drifting back to Tammy. Sexy little Tammy had left a couple of vague and mysterious messages on his motel voice mail over the last two days. She alluded to the necessity of a meeting, which made Jack a little nervous.

Women. Women had always been Jack's number one problem in life. When he gave the Tammy situation some thought, he had to admit, she actually scared him. Every time he saw her she had managed to look a little sexier. What was Tammy up to, Jack wondered?

If she and Dan got a divorce, who would get the house? The house had to be worth at least a million and a half, but Jack also figured it was probably mortgaged to the hilt. And how did he fit into all of this? These questions preyed heavily on his mind, along with a strong sexual curiosity concerning Tammy, that he found very hard to suppress. God, life is complicated, Jack thought.

Back in Spanish class, Jack was more than pleased to see that Señor Raphael had been replaced by a very attractive Mexican American woman in her mid thirties named Maria Mendez, who taught the class in a cheerful manner.

"La estoy limpiando," the teacher stated.

"La estoy limpiando," the class repeated.

Jack couldn't imagine why they replaced ol' fun loving Señor Raphael, but he was delighted with the change. The new teacher certainly had a winning way.

Señorita Mendez noticed Jack sitting off by himself toward the back of the small classroom. Only seven other students were in attendance that night. Jack smiled at her as she complimented the class.

"Muy bien, clase," Maria said.

"Gracias, Señorita Mendez," the class responded.

Jack raised his hand and immediately caught the teacher's eye.

"¿Señor?" She inquired, flashing a bright smile.
"Si. Tengo una pregunta," Jack said, with confidence.
"¿Si?" Maria replied.

That night produced another phone message from Tammy when Jack returned to his room. This one, like the others, was short, arcane, and slightly dramatic.

Outside his room the night was alive with the sounds of nature. Little crickets were singing their songs of love. Jack was busy studying one of his Spanish books when he heard a timid knock at his door. He wasn't expecting anyone, so he answered the door with a slight degree of caution. Much to his surprise, due to the hour, he was pleased to see Nancy the maid with an armful of clean neatly folded towels.

"Rola, Nancy," Jack said.

"Toallas," Nancy said, referring to the stack of towels in her hands.

"Gracias," Jack said, as he looked back at his empty towel rack near the sink. He also glanced at his watch.

"¿Trabajo tarde esta noche?" Jack said, commenting on the fact that Nancy was working late that night.

"Si," Nancy replied.

"¿Un problema con la secadora de nuevo?" Jack asked, as he wondered if he had used the correct words to inquire about the status of the all too often broken industrial size dryer in the motel's laundry room.

"Si." She affirmed. "¿Con permiso?"

"Si," Jack said, as he stepped back and allowed Nancy to enter his room. They exchanged a look and a smile as he closed the door behind her.

Dan's house was unusually quiet when Jack reported for work the next morning. His boss was supposed to be back from the golf course by eleven a.m. Dan had a plane to catch at two. He was going to Paris on a business trip for three days.

Jack glanced at his watch. It was already 11:10 Dan was supposed to be playing golf was his buddy Al. Al Schwartz was a big boozer, and sometimes he got Dan going. Dan also had a weakness for the sauce, and sometimes this played on Jack's nerves. He wondered if maybe Dan and Al where off on a drunk this morning.

Carmelita was at the park with the two small kids, and Jack wasn't sure if Tammy was home. She always parked her SUV in the garage, and Jack had let himself in through the front door. He'd entered the house quietly at ten-thirty, with hopes of running into Carmelita. His hopes however were quickly dashed when he found a short message written in crude Spanish on the blackboard in the kitchen. Tammy's hand written words commanded Carmelita to take Anthony and Betty to the park, where Tammy would pick them all up later at noon.

Disappointed, Jack returned to the living room with a a cup of coffee to wait for Dan. He decided to glance out the front window before he sat down, but he was interrupted when he heard Tammy's footsteps on the stairs behind him.

Jack turned and saw Tammy gliding down the stairs dressed solely in a blue satin bathrobe. Her blond hair was slightly damp and tasseled like she'd just stepped out of the shower.

"Hi, Jack, you're early," Tammy said, just before she reached the bottom of the staircase.

"Dan said eleven. It's ten past." Jack replied.

"Funny, he told me eleven-forty-five," Tammy stated.

Tammy slid past Jack giving him a whiff of pleasant femine fragrance. As she walked by Jack noticed her pretty feet and tone tan legs extending below the knee length robe.

"He's always late. You know that, Jack," Tammy said, letting her robe slip slightly open. She was clearly wearing nothing underneath.

Jack wondered if she was putting the make on him with a zero to maybe thirty-five minute window of opportunity. Now, that's living dangerously, Jack thought. Her close presence and scent made Jack very nervous. It also really turned him on.

"I've got a little proposition for you, Jack, but there isn't time to discuss it now. You know, I find your background very interesting."

"Oh?" Jack said, wondering which area of his background Tammy meant?

Suddenly they both heard the sound of a car door opening and closing outside.

"See ya later, Jack," Tammy said, then quickly turned and ran back up the stairs and disappeared a second before Dan walked through the front door.

From her upstairs bedroom window, Tammy watched as Jack and Dan drove away. She was having a conversation on her phone as she left the window area and let her robe fall to the floor.

Tammy glanced at the reflection of her beautiful naked body in the long mirror located opposite the huge four poster bed that dominated the bedroom, as she continued her phone conversation.

"Well, honey, they're gone. I guess we could grab a couple of hours."

Tammy listened for a moment as she continued to admire her tan naked body in the mirror.

"No, I didn't. I didn't have enough time to make it happen this morning. It's a shame too, 'cause I was really in the mood. Maybe tonight."

Again, Tammy listened for a couple of moments. "Okay, see ya in an hour. Love ya, bye."

That night, all the lights in Jack's room were off, and a DO NOT DISTURB sign was hanging on the door handle. Noisy crickets were again engaged in their melodious concerto, and the sounds of amor were emanating from inside Jack's room.

"Oh, God,…harder, harder, harder," she cried. "Fuck me like you love me, Jack!"

Oh, boy. Jack knew he was in trouble now. Why had he let her seduce him into having sex?

"Harder, harder, fuck me harder, Jack!" She pleaded, as her incantation continued and Jack worked to please her seemingly insatiable sexual appetite. It wasn't long before they both exchanged the satisfied squeals of more or less mutual orgasms.

"Oh, I love it when you scream when you come, Jack," she said, as she relaxed and pulled his tired body down hard against her tingly nakedness. She groaned and moved her warm wet body in a manner that invited another round, but after two hours of almost non stop sex, Jack was pooped.

Women and sex had always been a problem for Jack, especially when he was horny. And Jack was always horny. Another two bouts followed that night with the aid of a little blue pill.

The next morning, after she left, Jack was forced once again to acknowledge something he'd known for years. At times he was basically just a body attached to the back of his dick.

Jack really felt like shit that morning. He also thought the previous night's sexual activity would probably create some kind of repercussions, as he pulled some blond hairs out of his hair brush.

Also another new wrinkle had recently come into the mix, Maria Mendez, the rather attractive night school Spanish teacher.

After the second class, they'd met for coffee. Jack learned that Maria was a Chicana, a third generation Mexican American. She was in her mid thirties, divorced, and taught high school for a living. Maria grew up speaking both languages, and seemed very impressed with Jack's interest in learning Spanish.

She was well educated, well traveled, and quite pretty in a straight laced sort of way.

She had also called and left a message the night before, while Jack was otherwise engaged in the throws of amor.

XII

More than a week passed before Jack saw Carmelita or Tammy again. Dan had returned from Paris, and things were very tense around the house.

Carmelita was both slightly friendly and distant during their two chance meetings. Women, Jack thought, I just can't figure them out in any language.

Carmelita acted like she had something on her mind, but Jack couldn't quite put his finger on it. and she wouldn't tell him. During their couple of brief encounters, Carmelita repeated her pledge to call him, but she never did. She was being mysterious, and Jack wondered what was going on with her?

He still felt there probably wasn't a chance in hell of them ever getting together, but then again with women, Jack's long experience told him, you never know. Also, there was something about Carmelita that made other women pale by comparison. She was incredibly beautiful, mysterious, and sexy. A very hard combination to beat.

Jack had always liked pretty women. Any color, nationality, or ethnicity. Jack also liked a variety of types, but lately he had really discovered Latinas.

Saturday morning as Jack exited his room he encountered Maria the maid. Jack knew by observation that all the maids worked really hard, but his heart went out to Maria who was working today as the laundry runner. Instead of cleaning rooms, the girl assigned to laundry patrol picked up the dirty towels and sheets from the other maids carts, and replaced them with clean ones from the motel laundry room.

Maria didn't look stereotypically Mexican with her very light brown hair, hazel eyes and light complexion. She was absolutely beautiful, cheerfully charming, and she spoke almost no English. Her eyes sparkled when she smiled, and she almost always had a bright smile on her pretty face.

"Hola, Maria," Jack said.

"Hola Señor Jack," she replied.

"¿Como esta?"

"Bien, bien. ¿Usted?"

"Estoy muy bien, gracias," Jack responded. "Esta dia es muy bonito," Jack added, saying that it was a beautiful day.

"Si," Maria concurred. "No mucho calor."

When Maria mentioned that it wasn't too hot today, Jack again realized how the weather affected the girls who worked at the motel. They all worked real hard, cleaning up to twenty-seven rooms per day. When it was hot their day's work was much more difficult.

Seeing that Maria was struggling with two large bags of dirty laundry, Jack helped her carry the load back to the motel's busy lavanderia.

Rosa-Martina, the pleasant middle aged woman who usually ran the laundry room, was absent today, leaving Nancy in charge of la lavanderia.

When Nancy saw Jack helping Maria, she rapidly spoke to her coworker in spitfire Spanish. Jack didn't understand a thing Nancy said, as words shot off her tongue like a stream of bullets flying from a machinegun.

"Buenos dias, Nancy," Jack offered.

"Buenos dias," Nancy replied, then spat out some more Spanish in Maria's direction. Again, Jack was clueless. He decided to quickly make his visit an official one when he spied some boxes of tissue stacked on a nearby shelf.

"¿Puedo agaggar una caja de Kleen-ex?" He said, then added, "Por favor."

"Si," Maria said, as she turned and grabbed a couple of boxes of tissue and handed them to Jack with a smile.

"Gracias, Maria."

"De nada," Maria replied.

Again, Nancy opened fire in Spanish and Jack decided it was probably time to leave.

"Adios, mis amigas," Jack said, as he excused himself and left the laundry room with two fresh boxes of tissue paper.

The courtyard set up of the motel, the laundry, la lavanderia, as the predominately Mexican staff called it, somewhat reminded Jack of what hacienda life might have been like in these parts, back when Spain then later Mexico ruled this area. A hundred and fifty to two hundred years ago Spanish then Mexican calvarymen patroled the same rolling hills Jack saw daily.

The night air was cool, and again a DO NOT DISTURB sign was hanging from the door handle of Jack's room. The loud strains of passionate amor coming from Jack's dark abode cut into the quite of the night. Inside, things were getting hot, and loud.

Suddenly she screamed something in Spanish and grabbed hold of Jack's hair with both hands. Clutching his hair tight in her fists she moaned loudly with pleasure, then screamed a litte more.

Her climax was anything but quiet, and Jack wondered if there were any guests in the room next to his? If so, he was sure they were being thoroughly entertained.

The night had been long and passionate. Hours of mutual oral sex, and other forms of foreplay that proceeded the actual act of intercourse. When penetration finally commenced, the conjugation lasted for close to forty-five minutes.

Also, while in the throws of passion, Jack learned some new Spanish slang for body parts, amorous positions, and sexual preferences. So far, it had been his best class.

After they finally finished the long first session, they tenderly intertwined their warm bodies and cuddled tightly for awhile.

It wasn't long before her talented wet lips had Jack up and ready for more. They continued to repeat this process for most of the night.

Jack was amused to learn the Spanish slang term for testicles was huevos. By the end of the night, she had certainly fried his eggs.

XIII

Carmelita's younger sister Angela was as pretty as her older sibling. She arrived in the States after a harrowing experience crossing the border from Mexico. She was raped then released by her Border Patrol captor. Angela had managed to put the incident behind her. Carmelita had not.

Angela had worked at one thing or another seven days a week from almost the day she came from Mexico, and she had recently become the owner of a shiny new Saturn sedan. The navy blue car, bought with cash and credit she'd earned, made her beam with a sense of accomplishment. Carmelita had always liked her little sister's spirit, and the two shared a very close releationship.

It was a warm afternoon and the upholstery was hot when the sisters climbed into Angela's new car. As they drove down the street the two Señoritas were noticed by several neighbors who were gathered on porches or in the front yards along the quiet tree lined street of the mostly Latino neighborhood.

Within a couple of minutes the girls were in a commercial area bustling with people shopping and speaking Spanish. All of the merchant's signs were in espanol. The wonderful aroma of foods from Mexico, Central and South America filled the air. The area pulsated with the activity of commerce.

Angela drove her car into the parking lot of a small strip mall. As Carmelita and Angela got out of the car, they both noticed that a black and white LAPD cruiser with its red lights flashing, pulled into the lot behind them.

An older very tough looking LAPD sergeant got out of the cop car. He walked toward the girls with a gait that fell just short of a swagger. The six hash marks on his sleeve coupled with his sergeant's chevrons and a pair of steel blue eyes, reflected his many years on the force. The old cop toyed slightly with his long black nightstick before letting the weapon fall into a chrome ring on his gun belt.

"Buenos dias. Do you speak English?" The old cop asked.

"Yes, of course," Angela quickly replied.

Next, Carmelita watched with fascination as her little sister turned on the charm in an animated conversation with the old white cop. She soon marveled at the young girl's ability to talk her way out of a ticket in English.

Angela's sojourn in the States was just approaching two years. Carmelita was absolutely amazed with her sister's fluency in her newly acquired second language. When did she find time to study?

The cop asked Angela to produce her driver's license, insurance papers, and registration. After examining the documents, the old sergeant admonished the girls for not wearing their seat belts, but he didn't issue a citation.

"Well, okay, young lady, I think you just talked me out of a ticket," he said, then handed the insurance papers, license, and registration back to Angela.

"Thank you, sir," Angela said politely.

"Oh, that's okay. I hate writing tickets. I know how it can ruin somebody's day," the cop said, breaking into a slight smile.

Angela looked relieved. So did Carmelita, who was worried that the policeman might ask about their immigration status.

"But you've got to remember to use your seat belt," the cop instructed. "It's a safety thing."

Angela's relief was compounded by the fact that the cop didn't notice that her driver's license was phony.

"Okay, sir. I will."

"If I ever see you again, and you're not wearing it, I'll have to give you a ticket," the sergeant warned.

"Okay, I'll remember. Thank you."

"You're welcome."

"Have a nice day," Angela added.

"Thanks, you too."

"Bye," Angela cooed.

The cop smiled and returned to his squad car. Just as he slipped into the vehicle a call came over his radio informing him of a 211 in progress. He responded by tearing out of the parking lot with his lights still flashing. An armed robbery call always presented a challenge.

As the girls watched the cop blaze out of the lot Carmelita asked Angela how she learned to speak English so fast?

Angela told her cheerfully that she studied every day. She also stated that she believed that the ability to easily learn another language, was as much a God given talent, as it was a matter of intelligence. She told Carmelita that some of the people in her night school class were never able to get the hang of it, no matter how hard they tried. Angela said she studied hard, but she also felt she had a natural talent for learning languages.

As the sisters walked arm in arm toward their destination, a nearby market named Mercado Mexicano, Angela informed her older sibling that she was starting a new job in a French restaurant, and hoped this would offer her an opportunity to tackle another new language. Angela's thirst for knowledge and achievement had always impressed Carmelita.

As they entered the store Carmelita surprised Angela when she asked her little sister help her with her English. Carmelita understood English fairly well, but in the past, she had showed little interest in learning to speak the language.

Angela responded to her sister's request by answering her in English.

"Why the sudden interest in learning English?" She demanded. "Tengo rezones," Carmelita replied, telling Angela she had her reasons.

"Would it have anything to do with that Gringo who works for your boss? Angela asked, further testing Carmelita's English comprehension.

"Es posible."

"¿Es posible?" Angela questioned.

"Maybe," Carmelita replied.

Angela gave Carmelita a curious look. This was the first time she had ever heard her older sister utter a word in English.

The two girls smiled at each other as they headed toward the bakery section arm and arm.

Carmelita wasn't quite ready to discuss her other reasons for wanting to sharpen her English skills. Had she misunderstood what Tammy said on the phone? Was her pretty boss planning to murder somebody?

Lately, the whole Tammy matter had weighed heavily on poor Carmelita's mind. The damn language thing. Although she understood much more English than she could speak, Carmelita often had a particular problem with English pronouns. She found the words he, him, and her, confusing. This was especially true when she heard someone speak rapidly. Who was Tammy planning to kill?

As Tammy waited for her friend to arrive, she was pondering many things. She gazed at her beautiful body in the big mirror, and wondered how long her youthful appearance would last? Tammy viewed approaching middle age with much trepidation. Would she have to resort to plastic surgery to retain her flawless wrinkle free face? Would her tone body become harder to maintain? Was her sex appeal already beginning to wane?

All these matters worried Tammy to death, but none worried her more than money. Money was important to Tammy. She had her standards. She had a lifestyle to maintain, and acquiring the necessary funds to feed her interests were now causing her more concern than ever.

XIV

Dan was traveling out of town again, and as usual he forgot something and had to go by the office on a retrieval run before heading to the airport.

Dan shared the two story office he used in Westlake Village with a couple of other companies. One was a dot com something or other, and the second was some sort of sales enterprise.

From the beginning this ancillary environment tended to get on Jack's nerves. He didn't much care for the button down yuppie types who shared their office space. A bunch of spoiled white boys who all seemed to possess an unearned sense of entitlement.

Jack tried to avoid them as much as possible. Making money, following sports, and making money, seemed to be their only true interests in life. They all parroted the same clever phrases, undoubtedly gleaned from countless sales seminars, and self help tapes. Devoid of original thought, but quintessentially trendy and cool, by their own admission.

Early on, Jack had a minor run in with one of the hip shirt and tie collage boys, who by his own account, was destined to change the entire method of marketing some kind of new arcane financial plan. This clown was about thirty years old, and Jack suspected he'd probably never done a day's worth of real work in his life. His name was Brad, and his very presence made Jack want to puke.

The problem started when Brad, who'd had a couple of years of Spanish in high school, and a few more in college, left a note.

Jack found the condescending note, written in English, and addressed to the nighttime cleaning staff, when he had arrived at the office early one morning. The computer generated note severely admonished the cleaning team, who were all Latino, for not doing their job properly.

Brad's note was bullshit! They did an exemplary job, and for far less than a living wage. Jack found Brad's classisum, or racism, abhorrent. How many years of academic Spanish, and this jerk couldn't get past buenos dias. Also, this dickhead Brad had bitched about Jack's smoking cigarettes too close to the office's front door, thus banishing Jack to the far side of the parking lot. Jack had held his tongue for the sake of his job, although he was sorely tempted to say to young Brad, 'So what'd you do in boot camp when the Drill Sergeant said, if you got 'em smoke 'em, or are you some dickless piece of yuppie scum who didn't have the balls to serve your country! I have Rights too, punk, Jack thought, and I earned mine.

Although the Draft ended the year Jack finished high school, he chose to join the Marine Corps out of a sense of duty. Jack served a total of eight years in the Corps. He had served in the infantry, then as a military policeman, during his first four year enlistment.

After his first tour he reenlisted and eventually rose to the prestigious role of U.S. Embassy guard abroad. Usually Embassy duty was a three year stint at one station, but after six months in the Danish capital of Copenhagen, he was abruptly transferred to Nairobi, Kenya. After a few months in Kenya, came Lebanon, then finally Rome. This international odyssey eventually made Jack long to return to the United States and civilian life.

Although he achieved the rank of Staff Sergeant, Jack was not inclined to ship over for another four year cruise. He wanted a chance to enjoy some of the freedom he's served to protect. Also, after a few long cold winters in Europe, he yearned to return to sunny California.

In many ways Jack thought the military sucked, but he also maintained a certain contempt for men he felt didn't possess the balls to serve their country. Especially the ones singing the patriotic tunes.

These highfalutin' yuppie types were quick to take advantage of all the capitalistic opportunities this country had to offer, but they were either dickless, or derelict, when it came time to put their asses on the line in terms of military service, or even some kind of safe community involvement. Altruism was truly not on their collective agenda.

Jack was outside grabbing a smoke when Brad from upstairs came out of the office carrying a bag full of soccer balls. He was also decked out in a soccer outfit and looked silly as hell.

As Brad approached his vehicle he yelled something to one of the secretaries who worked in the office next door. She had just pulled into the parking lot in her Saab convertible. Brad began boasting about playing in an adult soccer league in a tone that faintly feigned modesty. The sexy redhead from next door bee lined past Brad acknowledging him as if he had just announced that he was a child molester.

Jack shot Brad a glare then turned his attention to the sexy red head. Her name was Susan and she had a great body. She also always dressed in a way that did it justice.

I just like girls, Jack thought, as he watched her walk from the car to her office. He had never actually met Susan, and he had learned her name from someone else in the complex. She had an alluring quality that reminded Jack of an old film noir femme fatale. He didn't quite dare introduce himself, since he was already juggling more romantic intrigue than he could handle.

Wow, I've just experienced a flash of maturity, Jack thought, as he essentially complimented himself on his restraint. He did, however, continue to watch the cute red head until she slipped through her office door.

Jack took another drag on his cigarette as the Pelé of Oak Park finished loading his soccer balls into his SUV. Brad then gave Jack a dirty look as he drove past leaving the lot. Again, the sight of Brad made Jack want to puke. Brad had one of those silly boyish faces that really looked stupid when he smirked.

Jack noticed the bike rack on the back of Brad's black Chevy Suburban and recalled how clownish Brad also looked when he wore his colorful cross country bicycle riding costume.

Yep, now there's a role model for ya, kids. A true symbol of America today. Fuckin' yuppie asshole, Jack thought. An' all these guy's like Brad, seem to be bursting with this unearned sense of entitlement. Jack's old service injury was hurting him that day, and he found Brad and his kind even more annoying when he was in pain.

Dan suddenly reappeared with a binder bulging with documents. Soon he and Jack were en route to LAX with sports talk blaring from the car's speakers. The banal banter of Jim Rome's call in clones, made Jack long for the sounds of rock 'n roll, or simply silence, as they slowly crept along the crowded 405 Freeway that led to LAX.

As Jack continued to endure the radio and Dan's intermittent phone conversations, he thought about his working class roots.

He wondered what Brad or Dan would do if they had to get real jobs, and actually work for a living? The more Jack thought about it, the more he tended to identify with the hard working Latinos he'd recently come to know.

He also couldn't get Carmelita off his mind. She never called, and the last time he saw her she was still sporting a black eye.

Dan had mentioned something about Carmelita and a bicycle accident. Jack didn't know what to believe, but somehow he just didn't buy the bicycle story.

XV

"No, I won't change my mind. He's got to die!" Tammy reiterated. She was in the garage standing next to her SUV, with her tiny cell phone pressed against her ear.

"Look, I can't talk right now. I gotta go in a minute, and I'm runnin' late. I have to take the damn maid home," Tammy continued, glancing toward the door where she expected Carmelita to appear any second.

"No, I can't see you this weekend. Not with all that's goin' on. An' Carmelita's gonna be gone, so I also have all the kids this weekend. But, that's okay, it actually looks good that way. You know what I mean? It's gonna work out perfect, and Dan's not going to know what's happening until it's too late."

Tammy listened for a moment, then cut the conversation short when she heard Carmelita open the door that led into the garage.

"Love you too, bye." Tammy said, before Carmelita came into earshot carrying her three travel bags and her stereo.

Oblivious to the fact that Carmelita was struggling with her little load of things, Tammy didn't offer to open the car's back door, as she impatiently slid into the driver's seat.

"Come on, Carmelita, I haven't got all day," Tammy said, as she turned the ignition switch.

"Si, Señora," Carmelita quietly replied.

That evening the weather had suddenly gotten cooler, and Jack was a bit chilly wearing only a tee shirt. He was in a small strip mall in the West Valley community of Woodland Hills.

Jack rounded a corner and was walking past a dry cleaners with a big plate glass window, when three very loud gunshots rang out.

Jack's chest exploded with blood as his body jerked violently, then spun backwards and crashed through the plate glass window. Some bystanders screamed in horror as they dove for cover.

Out at the Country Club, Dan and three of his buddies were at the bar downing a few. In the alpha male world, things so far were going well for Dan that day.

Outside Carmelita's house the neighborhood was quiet that night, except for the sound of crickets engaged in their evening serenade.

Inside a back bedroom, Angela had been trying to teach her older sister some English, but Carmelita was having a really big problem with her concentration.

When Angela asked Carmelita what was bothering her, the answer was truly a troubling one. After wrestling with what had been on her mind for days, Carmelita finally confided that she thought the woman she worked for was planning to kill someone.

Angela reacted to this news with a look of alarm and concern, as she reached out and clutched her older sister's hand.

Tammy was trying to work on her computer, but her mind was really elsewhere. The kids were screaming in the background, and being alone with the brood was not to Tammy's liking. The sound of children crashing against the wall in the next room followed by the noise of something breaking, caused Tammy to jump to her feet.

"God! Why do I have to suffer like this? Will you kids hold it down!" Tammy screamed.

Next, she heard something else crash as the loud cacophony of laughing children rose to a deafening crescendo in the next room.

"Christ! I've got to get some help when Carmelita's away," Tammy said, as she left her humming computer and prepared to charge onto the fray.

"You fuckin' kids are gonna make me have a nervous breakdown, damn it!" Tammy screamed, as she stomped her way toward the kid's room.

Nancy was making a late towel delivery to Jack's room, when she noticed the absence of his car in the parking lot. Nancy was disappointed, she'd been planning this late night towel delivery all day.

After a cursory tap on the door, Nancy entered Jack's room using her pass key.

She carefully placed the towels in the towel rack. Then as started to leave the room, she saw a photograph on Jack's small nightstand. She cleaned his room every day, and this was the first time she'd ever seen this picture. It was a photograph of Jack and a cute little two year old boy. Nancy wondered if the boy was Jack's son? She picked up the framed photo.

"Hola," Flora said, as she stepped into the open doorway, catching Nancy by surprise.

"Hola," Nancy replied, rather coldly.

Flora had found herself cruising through the parking lot when she noticed Jack's open door.

"¿Donde es Jack?" Flora inquired.

"No se," Nancy answered. "No aqui."

An ambulance and several black and white police cars were now in evidence at the strip mall. A large crowd of busy folks were milling all over the place. The lights on the cop cars and the ambulance were flashing, and people in blue LAPD uniforms were standing around talking and paying little attention to what was going on inside the dry cleaning establishment. Some of the men in uniform were drinking coffee, eating doughnuts, and smoking cigarettes.

Flora noticed the framed photograph of Jack and the boy that Nancy was holding. The girls exchanged a strained look as Nancy set the picture back on Jack's nightstand.

Dan's party at the Country Club had broken up, and he and his buddy Al were crossing the somewhat dark parking lot headed for Al's brand new 200K Mercedes Benz. Both men were quite drunk, and neither noticed the Sheriff's black and white car waiting in the shadows.

The only advice Angela could think to offer her sister, was to go to the police, or simply never go back to work at Dan's house. Carmelita again brought up the possibility that she had misunderstood everything that Tammy had said.

Tammy had basically finished wrangling the rowdy kids, when her phone rang. Could this be the news she'd been waiting for?

Inside the dry cleaners, Jack was propped up against the wall in a sitting position. The room was heavily ladened with smoke.

A woman was bent over Jack busily dabbing his face with a tiny damp sponge. A man wearing a headset soon spoke up in a strong voice loud enough to be heard above the din of chatter in the cramped quarters. He addressed Jack.

"You're in one more shot, dead, with two cops talking, then you're done. Nice work."

"Thanks," Jack replied.

"You okay?" The assistant director added, almost as an afterthought.

"Yeah, I'm fine. Thanks for asking," Jack said, as the busy A.D. abruptly turned his attention elsewhere.

"Alright, let's get movin', we gotta get the next shot in the can by nine," the officious A.D. shouted at no one in particular, and everyone in general. "Come on, let's go, chop chop!"

Jack always found assistant directors annoying. The movie set was alive with activity as people rushed around in an effort to set up the next shot.

Jack had worked off and on as a stuntman for years, before things kind of dried up not long after he turned forty. During the last couple of years he'd hardly worked at all.

That's why he got into the driving thing. He occasionally also worked as a bodyguard.

Actually, since his Marine Corps days Jack hadn't worked at anything too steady. Then recently, his life had completely fallen apart. After his second wife divorced him, he was forced to file for bankruptcy. Then later things got even worse. He lost his apartment and had to move into the motel. The job with Dan absolutely saved his ass. It was truly a Godsent, because at the time he was just a breath away from becoming homeless.

Dan had been cool about letting him off when Jack got a call out of the blue to do a gag on a little feature film. He also made more money in one day getting killed, then he earned in two weeks working for Dan. And Jack certainly needed the money.

When Jack wrapped about an hour later, he was really sore and tired when he walked to his car. He had dropped the Lincoln off at the dealership to get it serviced, and had used his own car to drive to the stunt gig.

Jack's car was a battered twelve year old Toyota sedan that was on its last leg. Fortunately the job at the strip mall in Woodland Hills was only a couple of miles from his motel in Calabasas. Jack tossed his set bag into the back seat and headed home.

XVI

Tammy and Dan were in the midst of yet another very heated argument. The kitchen was their favorite sparring spot.

"So where'd you get the money this time?" Dan demanded, in an angry voice.

Tammy didn't answer her husband, she just stood there and glared at him.

"Tammy! Was it Allen Horwitz again?" Dan questioned further.

"Yeah, Allen Horwitz." She sheepishly replied. "Yeah, I got the money from Allen. You never seem to have any."

Dan just looked at her. The honeymoon was long over, and they both knew discussing the matter further wouldn't resolve anything.

"I'm sorry," Tammy offered.

Without saying another word, Dan turned and started to leave the kitchen. Before he got out, Tammy grabbed her purse and her car keys.

"I'm going out," she stated, as Dan stormed out of the room.

Tammy went out the other door that led to the garage, slamming it behind her, as she quickly dashed to her waiting SUV.

Angela's first night at the fancy French restaurant was not a very pleasant one.

The customers were jerks, the waiters were arrogant, and the manager was an absolute asshole. Why did people with a litte bit of power have to act so poorly, Angela wondered?

Aside from learning a new English word for the anal part of the anatomy, the only other benefit of the miserable evening was meeting a cute Mexican busboy named Carlos.

Angela met Carlos for a drink after work. They ended their date by shaking hands and exchanging phone numbers. It helped after getting fired at the end of her first shift.

Jack got up early by his old standards, still very sore from the three squib burns on his chest where the bullets had exploded, and from crashing through the candy glass window and hitting the hard cement floor the night before.

He made a couple of cups of instant coffee using hot water out of the tap. He also had another warm bath, before he rubbed Ben Gay into the sore areas of his body to ease his aching bones. He'd soaked in the tub the night before for close to an hour, then he spent the night sleeping on a heating pad. He had never done a stunt job that didn't hurt in some way, and he knew in his heart that he was just getting too old for that line of work.

He took another helping of four Advil tablets in an attempt to knock down the pain in his back and his bruised elbows. Because he was asked by the director to wear only a tee shirt, he wasn't afforded the usual precaution of elbow pads for protection when he landed on the hard concrete floor. Due to the camera angle the young first time director insisted on using, a floor pad was also out of the question.

He had worn pads under his pants on his knees and shins, but as usual he had actually landed on an area of his butt and lower back that was unpadded.

He lit a cigarette and glanced at the clock on his nightstand. It was close to 9 am. He decided to walk up to McDonalds for a bite of breakfast.

At McDonald's Jack ran into his friend Blanca who was working behind the counter. In the short time Jack had resided at the motel, he'd come to know a lot of people in the immediate area. Also, almost any Latino whom he encountered became fair game in his quest to learn Spanish.

After some friendly chit chat with Blanca, Jack sat down with an Egg McMuffin and a cup of real coffee. He'd picked up a copy of the Spanish language newspaper La Opinion on his way to the establishment, and intended to read it cover to cover with the aid of a small English/Spanish dictionary he now constantly kept in his pocket.

Tammy, alone in her bedroom, reached for the phone and quickly punched a number. She waited impatiently as she listened to the phone ring a couple of times. She played with her hair as she waited through four rings, then heard the line she was calling switch to voice mail after the last ring.

Nancy was busy cleaning Jack's room in his absence. Again she noticed the picture of Jack and the small boy. Next time she saw Jack she intended to ask him about the child. Her thoughts were suddenly interrupted by a loud rap on the open door to Jack's room.

When Nancy looked up, she saw Maria Mendez, Jack's Spanish teacher from night school standing in the doorway.

"I'm looking for Jack," Maria Mendez said.

"¿Como?" Nancy replied.

"¿Donde Jack?" Maria asked.

"No se," Nancy answered.

Maria had a package in her hand that was wrapped up like a present. She stepped into the room and put the gift on Jack's freshly made bed.

"Para Jack," Maria informed Nancy.

"Si," Nancy responded.

Maria glanced around the small room, then turned and left without saying another word. Nancy watched her go in silence.

Tammy punched out another number on her phone and this time there was an answer at the other end.

"Hello, Allen? Did I wake you?" Tammy said, then she quietly listened to Allen Horwitz's sleepy reply.

"I'm sorry," Tammy apologized.

Allen Horwitz was completely naked, sitting up in bed, and still pretty much asleep.

He knew he shouldn't have answered the phone, but he'd just had a couple of hang ups in the last few minutes, and he didn't recognize the phone number on his caller ID.

Tammy explained she had recently changed her cell phone number again, and went on to apologize repeatedly for disturbing Allen's sleep.

"That's okay, I'm about half awake,…but I can't talk right now," Allen said in a sleepy voice. "I'll call you later."

"Sure," Tammy replied, unable to mask her disappointment as the phone went dead on the other end.

As Allen replaced the phone on the table next to the bed, an incredibly beautiful African American woman in her late twenties stepped out of the nearby bathroom. She was wearing only a short sexy shear nightie.

As she left the bathroom she flipped off the light switch that also silenced the bathroom's noisy fan. She cracked a big smile and struck a sexy pose for a moment, then quickly crossed the room letting the nightie slide off her curvaceous ebony body as she rejoined Allen in bed.

A long wet passionate kiss soon led the amorous couple into a resumption of the kinky sexual activity that had kept them both awake most of the previous night. The pure sexual pleasure this woman gave Allen was unparalleled in terms of his other preceding sexual experiences. In his thirty two years of life, she unleashed a lust in him that was certainly unmatched, and something that Allen's mother, Lea Horwitz, would never understand.

When Jack returned to his room after breakfast, he was quite surprised to find a gift wrapped package on his bed. He smiled when he saw the card was signed, Maria.

Jack quickly unwrapped the package, and was delighted to find a rather large expensive looking English/Spanish dictionary.

"Wow, this is really nice," Jack said out loud. He was truly pleased with his gift. How thoughtful.

Jack immediately left his room in search of Maria the maid, whom he had seen earlier in passing. In a crass Hollywood sort of way, he felt that Maria was far too beautiful to be working as a maid. She spoke very little English, but she was always more than helpful whenever Jack tried to speak Spanish with her. Jack loved the way Maria's lovely amber eyes lit up whenever she smiled, and he couldn't wait to find her that morning and thank her for the great gift she had left on his bed. He also wondered if this was some kind of one-upmanship with Nancy. He knew the gift wasn't cheap.

Maria knew about Jack's show business connection in the stunt world, and since her childhood days in a small village in Mexico, she had dreamed the almost impossible dream of someday having the opportunity to pursue a career as an actress or a model. However, working as a maid some thirty five miles from Hollywood, so far, was as close as she had come to her dream. It was a lot closer than the village in her homeland, yet still a million light years away.

Maria also genuinely liked Jack. He was not only good looking, he was one of the few Gringos she'd met in her three years in the United States who even attempted to communicate with her in her native tongue. She longed to learn English, but her intense work load coupled with her personal life left little time to study a new language. Also, another element came into play that made any outside pursuit difficult.

Tammy knew her girlfriend Annie Horwitz, Allen's wife, was out of town on business. Getting Allen's attention when Annie was gone was always a challenge.

Maybe, she thought, I should just go by Allen's house in about a half an hour, and say I didn't know Annie was out of town.

"I'll just play dumb. That's easy," she said out loud, as she grabbed her handbag and her car keys.

Allen's rapacious sex partner screamed when she came. Anal sex was her favorite, and Allen really knew how to make her come. After a couple of moments of rest, she was ready to give Allen his due.

Jack finally found Maria on the far side of the motel pushing her heavy cart to the next room on her itinerary. He approached her quietly from behind.

"Muchas muchas gracias, Maria," he said, as he quickly turned her around and kissed her.

The startled Maria instantly stepped back, then slapped Jack, and shouted, "Señor Jack!"

Jack immediately regretted his impulsiveness. Boy, now I've done it, he thought.

"Oh, I'm sorry,…I ah,…Lo siento. Yo solamente quiero a dijo gracias por mi diccionario."

Maria looked completely baffled. She knew nothing about a dictionary. Had Jack lost his mind?

"¿Como? ¿Que diccionario?" Maria asked.

Then it suddenly dawned on Jack that he had kissed the wrong Maria. His mind instantly flashed back to his last conversation with Maria Mendez, his new night school Spanish teacher. He had lightly flirted with her after the last class the previous Friday, when he told her he was going to miss class the following Friday, due to an upcoming movie stunt job. This revelation seemed to impress her. He had also addressed her as Señorita Mendez.

"Oh, please call me Maria," Ms. Mendez had insisted.

Jack could tell that the pretty Latina teacher liked him when she asked where he lived? When he told her, she informed him that she owned a house not far from the motel.

Jack suddenly felt so stupid, standing there staring at Maria the maid, whose two beautiful amber eyes were still burning with anger. He was really embarrassed by his mistake. His face also stung from the swift hard slap, as he grappled for the right words to say in Spanish.

"Lo siento, Maria." Jack said.

"Señor Jack, soy casada," Maria reiterated.

The last time Maria had used that phrase with him, he had apparently misunderstood her. He thought she had told him that she was tired. The feminine word in Spanish for tired is ca<u>n</u>sada, and the two words sounded very similar to Jack. Damn it, now he remembered. Casada was married, and cansada was tired.

During his brief tenure as a Marine Embassy Guard in Rome, he had tackled learning a bit of Italian. Their words for afternoon and tomato were somewhat similar, and he would always get the two words confused. However, telling someone that he would met them tomorrow in the tomato, instead of the afternoon, seemed like a rather harmless faux pas compared to the casada-married thing.

Nearby, Nancy had seen the foregoing encounter. She was very amused. She continued to watch as Jack passionately tried to explain to Maria what had happened in both English and Spanish. He finished with a powerful profusion of apologies.

Maria eventually warmed up to Jack again as she listened to his explanation, and his apologies. She finally smiled, then said, she too, was sorry that she slapped him so hard. They soon ended their conversation with a kind of awkward good bye, and an exchange of smiles that ended in laughter.

Nancy watched as the two parted as friends again. She now seemed somewhat less amused.

Just as Tammy was heading out the kitchen door to the garage, her hard line telephone rang. Since she was on a mission, she decided to monitor the message on the answering machine rather than pick up the phone.

"Hi, honey."

Tammy instantly recognized the melodious female voice of her girlfriend Annie Horwitz, Allen's wife.

"It's Annie. I'm back from New York. I came back a day early to surprise Allen. Call me."

So much for the mission, Tammy thought.

Just then, Carmelita entered the kitchen. She was wearing her hair down loose and slightly over her cheek in an attempt to hide a fresh bruise on her face. The answering machine clicked off a moment after Annie's message ended.

"Ah,…you startled me, Carmelita! Damn, I wish you wouldn't do that. Sometimes you're so quiet."

Carmelita said nothing.

"Are the little ones still sleeping?" Tammy asked.

Carmelita nodded her head. Tammy however was unsatisfied with anything less than a verbal answer.

"Sleeping?" Tammy demanded.

Another couple of moments passed as Carmelita's dark intense eyes almost defiantly glared at her expensively dressed boss.

"Si, Señora." Carmelita replied.

"¿Donde Dan?" Tammy asked, impatiently switching to her high school Spanish.

"No, se." Carmelita said, stating that she didn't know where Dan had gone.

"¿Con Jack?" Tammy inquired.

"No. Con Al." Carmelita answered.

"Oh, great, the drinking duo."

"¿Como?"

"Nothing, Carmelita. I put an outfit in the hamper this morning that I need by noon," Tammy said. "¿Comprendo?" Tammy questioned, using the wrong form of the word.

"Si, Señora."

Tammy quickly walked out of the kitchen and into the main part of the house. Carmelita didn't budge for a moment. Her eyes reflected a very pensive mood, as she contemplated her next move.

XVII

Jack emerged from his room and climbed into a shiny brand new bright red Mustang convertible driven by Maria Mendez. Jack had found her number listed in the phone book and called her minutes after the other Maria debacle. Señorita Mendez lived literally five minutes from the motel.

As the flashy Mustang wheeled down the driveway they first passed Nancy pushing her cart one way, then they passed the other Maria pushing her cart in the opposite direction. Jack waved, as both maids watched the Mustang roll by.

Carmelita had just given Tammy her freshly pressed outfit, meeting the noon deadline right on the dot. Tammy, now dressed in a black bra and a pair of thong style panties, thanked her, then picked up the phone the second Carmelita left the bedroom.

Tammy punched out a number by memory and waited until she heard the beep activating the voice mail on the other end of the line.

"Hello, Jack. It's Tammy. I need to talk to you. Ah, maybe you're out by the pool? Ah, let me give you my new cell number, and my pager number, an' maybe I'll come by and check if you're out by the pool,…"

Twenty minutes later Tammy pulled her SUV into the driveway of the motel. She parked between Jack's old sedan and the black Lincoln.

First, Tammy banged loudly on Jack's door, then when there was no reply, she launched a systematic search of the grounds of the motel, starting at the pool.

Inquiring at the front desk, and dissatisified with the clerk's circumspect indifference, she returned to Jack's room and banged on the door a few more times with her fist.

"Jack? Jack? Jack? Are you there?"

Frustrated, she noticed Nancy watching her from near the door way of the next room.

"Hey, do you know where Jack is?"

"No entendo," Nancy replied.

"¿Donde Jack?" Tammy said, exasperated today by the help's seeming inability to speak or understand English.

"No se," Nancy answered, as she returned to her work removing some cleaning utensils from her cart.

Tammy's patience was spent. She possessed little tolerance for people when things weren't going exactly the way she wanted them to go. How could the world be so inconsiderate to her needs?

The restaurant Jack and Maria Mendez chose for lunch, was an upscale fish place called Fins in the heart of Westlake Village. They were seated at a nice table on the terrace, where they were in the middle of enjoying a delicious meal. They had ordered a tasty halibut special, and a bottle of fine white wine. The vino had very much loosened their conversation by the third glass.

"Muchas gracias, de nuevo por mi diccionario," Jack said, once again thanking the right Maria for his new dictionary.

"De nada," Maria replied. "You know I didn't mean to cause you a problem."

"I know. Too many Marias," Jack replied.

"Yeah, I guess."

"I love the name Maria," Jack said. "It's one of my favorite female names."

"Oh, really?" Maria responded, with a smile.

"Si, verdad," Jack added, saying, yes that's true. "Where are you from?"

"Here, I grew up in Encino. I'm a Valley girl."

"That's right, I think you mentioned that in class. And you're a third generation Mexican American. Una Chicana."

"Si. How about you? Where'd you grow up?"

"Same as you, here in L.A. Culver City. Real middle class. My dad worked in a machine shop, and my mother was a housewife. What do your folks do?"

"My dad's a doctor, and my mom's a teacher."

"Your family did fairly well."

"Yes, they did. Especially when you consider that my grandparents were farm laborers on both sides. They came here from Mexico in the Forties with no money, and no skills except for the calluses on their hands. They worked incredibly hard, and they were damned determined to see that all their children got a decent education."

"Bravo," Jack said.

"When I was in your room, I saw a photograph of you with a cute little boy. Is he your son?" Maria asked.

"Yeah," Jack replied, somewhat sadly. It was a subject he still found difficult to broach.

"Where is he?" Maria inquired.

"Heaven," Jack replied.

Maria saw the sadness in Jack's eyes brought on by the mention of his son.

"Sometimes I have trouble looking at the picture, so I keep it in a drawer. Other times I stare at it for days. He died when he was four years old. His name was Timothy James Hardin, but we all called him T.J."

"Oh, I'm terribly sorry," Maria said, as she reached out and touched Jack's hand.

They were both silent for a few moments.

"How did he die?" Maria finally asked, almost hesitantly. She didn't know if it was appropriate to inquire further. She could see that the subject of his son deeply affected Jack, but somehow she sensed he wanted to say more. "How long ago?"

Jack still found the incident very hard to retell, even after so many years.

"A little over twenty years. He died in a car accident. My first wife, Julie," Jack went on, "T.J.'s mom, accidently backed over him in the driveway."

"Oh, my God! How horrible."

"Yeah, horrible. He was on his little tricycle. Then, three weeks later, my wife Julie committed suicide."

"Oh, my God. What a double tragedy," Maria said, as her heart went out to Jack as he continued his sad story.

"T.J. would be almost twenty-five now, so it's been a long time," Jack said, as he took a sip of wine. "I still miss them both, but you know, life goes on."

"How did you get through it?"

"Well, I was still in the service at the time, so I shipped over for another four year tour," Jack said, as he took another sip of wine.

"I was in the Marine Corps, and I guess I had kind of a death wish. So you know where they sent me?"

"No, where? Vietnam?"

"No. Denmark."

Jack's remark about Denmark lightened things slightly. He then went on to tell her about his subsequent assignments overseas which eventually landed him in Italy. Next, he noticed that her glass was almost empty, and he refilled it with the last of the wine in their bottle.

"Thanks," Maria said.

"De nada."

Maria found herself very attracted to Jack's rugged good looks along with his sensitive side. She was also attracted to the stuntman angle, and the ex-Marine macho thing. Most of the men in her academic circle were not only pretty boring, by comparison, they were also a bunch of whimps.

"So why Spanish?" Maria asked, feeling it was probably time to change the subject.

Jack chuckled. He too, was ready to move on to another less troubling area of conversation.

"Tengo rezones," Jack replied, stating that he had his reasons.

XVIII

Jack pulled the Lincoln into Dan's driveway promptly at 7:30 am. Dressed in his grey suit, he got out of the car and quickly went into the house through the open garage door.

When he entered the kitchen he found Carmelita busy picking up breakfast debris from the kitchen table.

"Buenos dias, Carmelita," Jack said, with a smile. Again, simply being in her presence made him nervous in a boyish sort of way.

Carmelita was dressed in white satin shorts, tennies, and a tight fitting halter top. Even from across the room, this woman generated enough body heat to sizzle a steak without even touching it, Jack thought.

"Buenos dias, Jack," Carmelita answered, in a soft voice as she turned to face him.

Jack immediately noticed another nasty bruise on her cheek. Taken aback, he couldn't remember the Spanish word for face, so he just blurted out his question in English.

"What happened to your face?"

"Mismo," she replied, rather sheepishly.

Jack knew mismo meant, the same, indicating that she wanted him to believe that she had another accident on her bicycle. "¿Mismo? ¿Otro accidente con tu bicicleta?" Jack asked, in an incredulous tone.

"Si," she said, as she dropped her head slightly.

"I don't believe it. Yo no creo. What really happened to you?" Jack said, then he suddenly remembered that the word for face in Spanish was cara. "¿Que paso tu cara?"

Before she had a chance to respond further, Dan came into the kitchen carrying his briefcase. He did not look like he was in a very good mood.

"Come on Jack, we gotta go," Dan said, abruptly.

Jack started to say something to Dan, but his boss quickly disappeared out the open door to the garage. Jack turned back to Carmelita.

"Llama me, por favor. I'm worried about you. Call me, please," Jack said. "Llama me."

"Si. We must talk," she said. "Cuidado, Jack," she added.

"¿Como?" Jack questioned, not immediately able to translate the word, cuidado.

"Be careful, Jack." Carmelita warned.

Jack was surprised by the comment, and also by the amount of English she used today.

"Jack! Come on! We gotta go!"

Jack heard Dan yell in a very irritated voice.

"I'm gonna be late!" Dan continued, impatiently shouting from the garage.

"Call me," Jack said.

"Yes," Carmelita replied.

Jack rushed out to join Dan. He didn't know if his boss was hitting Carmelita, but if he found out that he was, Jack decided he was going to kick some ass.

The night before, Dan had told Jack to pull the Lincoln into the garage when he arrived in the morning.

Jack had parked close to the garage, but not in it, as he was instructed. He forgot.

"I told you to pull into the garage, that's why I left the door open! Come on, we've got to load the car up with a lot of shit!"

"Sorry, I forgot," Jack said, as he got into the Lincoln and pulled it forward into the garage.

Next, they filled the car's cavernous trunk with a bunch of boxes brimming with documents.

Soon, Jack carefully backed the car out of the driveway very slowly.

"Hurry up, Jack," Dan said, impatiently.

"Yes, sir," Jack replied, once they reached the street.

Since they were running late, Jack glided the Lincoln swiftly through traffic maneuvering the large vehicle skillfully from lane to lane exceeding the speed limit by twenty miles per hour.

"There's a couple hundred in it for you if you get me there in fifteen minutes," Dan offered.

Must be an awfully important meeting if his tightwad asshole boss is willing to pony up two bills just to get to Tarzana in less than twenty minutes, Jack thought.

"An' you'll pay for the ticket?" Jack asked.

"Yeah, I'll pay for the ticket."

Oh, what the hell, this could be fun, Jack thought. It'll give me a chance to scare the shit out of him.

"Okay. Fifteen minutes," Jack said, as he stabbed the pedal to the floor and they really started to move.

Jack accelerated to over eighty passing everything in sight.

He cut a path to the freeway in a matter of seconds keeping one eye on the rear view mirror. With no cops in sight, he hit the 101 heading east and cranked the Lincoln up to almost one hundred and ten miles per hour. He zinged from lane to lane, passing cars on the left and right. Jack also couldn't help but notice Dan's complexion grow appreciably lighter as his boss watched the speedometer needle pass the century plus ten mark.

Jack got Dan to his destination in fourteen minutes flat, and was promptly rewarded with two crushed C-notes Dan was clutching during the ride.

As Jack was sticking the crumpled money into his pocket, four tough looking men appeared and unloaded the material from the car trunk.

Jack looked at the big house and opulent surroundings, and he wondered what kind of business they were doing.

"Nice job, and with a minute to spare," Dan said.

"Thanks."

"You're welcome. Now, I've got an errand for you to run," Dan said. "I bought Carmelita a new bicycle, and I want you to go to the bike shop and pick it up while I'm in this meeting."

"Okay," Jack said. "You want me to drop it off at your place before she leaves?"

"No. No, I want you to leave it at her family's house before she gets there."

"Who's taking her home?" Jack asked.

"I don't know. I think she's taking the bus. Do you remember where their house is?"

"Yeah, I remember." Jack replied, disappointed that he had missed a chance to drive her home. Also, he lamented her having to take the bus, knowing that had be a long ride.

"Here's the address of the bike shop," Dan said, as he handed Jack the address scribbled on a yellow slip of paper from a stick on pad. "I already paid for it over the phone with a credit card."

"Okay," Jack said, as he looked at the address.

"Oh, another thing, I don't want Tammy to know about the bike, comprende?"

"Yeah, I understand," Jack answered, noting a hint of sarcasm in Dan's use of a Spanish word. He also used the correct form, Jack noticed, wondering if this clown speaks Spanish?

Dan's business meeting concluded a little quicker than he had anticipated. After the meeting he sat around drinking with a few of the men on the terrace of the huge Tarzana house. Dan slowly lifted his glass to his lips, took a long sip, then said, "Well gentlemen, I think we know what has to be done now."

The men in attendance nodded in agreement. A telling look of total satisfaction crossed Dan's face, as he realized one of his most serious problems was about to be solved.

Jack pulled the car into the driveway of Carmelita's family's well kept house in Pacoima. The single story wood frame place looked like it had recently been painted. It was a light shade of blue that was pleasantly contrasted with snow white trim. The front yard and side areas were generously planted with a wide selection of colorful flowers and lush greenery.

Jack got out and quickly unloaded a brand new, but very cheep looking bicycle from the trunk of the Lincoln. As he wheeled the shiny red bike up to the front door, he noticed that he was being watched by someone who was peeking out the window.

Back at the motel, Nancy was pushing her cleaning cart near Jack's room when she spotted Flora, Jack's friend from the sandwich shop, approaching his room.

Nancy drew closer as Flora reached Jack's door. Nancy spoke out in Spanish, and asked Flora what she was doing?

Flora, annoyed by the inquiry, answered curtly that she was looking for Jack, and that it was none of Nancy's business.

Ignoring the admonition, Nancy informed Flora that Jack was usually at work at this hour.

Flora was aware of Jack's schedule. She actually had written a note she wanted to leave on Jack's door, but now she was afraid Nancy would snatch it, or read the damn thing.

Flora was very frustrated. Jack hadn't come by the sandwich shop in a couple of weeks. The two girls exchanged a look that was not particularly friendly, and Flora soon retreated to her nearby car with the carefully written note still in her hand. She quickly departed the premises as Nancy watched her drive away.

Jack pointed at the bicycle as he talked to a middle aged Mexican man named Ricardo on the porch of Carmelita's house. He repeatedly attempted to explain his intentions in Spanish, but to no avail. He tried rephrasing his sentences a couple of times, but Ricardo seemed very unreceptive to both the gift, and Jack's Spanish.

Sometimes his Spanish didn't seem to work at all, Jack thought, as he continued trying to explain why he was leaving the bicycle.

XIX

Dan didn't say anything to Jack during the short drive to the office. Once they arrived, Jack helped Dan carrying some more cardboard cases into the office. Carting boxes full of documents was becoming a regular part of their routine. What was all this shit, Jack wondered? These guys generate enough paper work to destroy a rainforest a week. Once the task was completed, Dan closed the door to his office without further comment, and Jack stepped outside to have a cigarette.

As Jack walked over to the parkway to have his smoke, he passed that upstairs yuppie who always made him want to puke. This pussy whose name was Brad something or other, like the rest of his breed drove a behemoth SUV, or his wife's flashy Mercedes Benz. Today it was the Benz.

Deeply engaged in a heated business conversation on his cell phone, this bozo was using a hand computer and had a headset in his ear. Brad acknowledged Jack with a nod as he headed for the office door. Jack didn't return the nod, as he subjugated his feelings about this pussy son-of-a-bitch who had instigated his smoking banishment to the parkway.

It was early evening when Jack finally pulled the Lincoln into the motel parking lot and parked close to his room. He felt very tired and frustrated as he climbed out of the car and quickly approached the door to his abode. He let himself in using his key card. He didn't sense that he was being watched.

Jack failed to notice the very mean looking man watching him from the cab of an old pick up truck parked in the dark shadows nearby. The ominous looking man staking out Jack's room, truly had malice on his mind.

Jack had moved so quickly from the car to his room, that the man did not have time to react before Jack was safely inside. The man would have to wait for another opportunity.

Jack took off his jacket as he glanced at the telephone on the nightstand next to his bed. No blinking red light. Alas, no messages.

He'd hoped Carmelita would call. Since Dan was home, she knew it only took Jack less than ten minutes to get back to his place.

Jack popped the door on his tiny refrigerator and removed a cold bottle of beer. Outside, the man on a mission continued to wait.

Over the next hour, Jack went through three more beers, and idly flipped through the myriad channels on the motel television. Suddenly the telephone rang, and Jack grabbed the receiver before the end of the first ring.

"Hello," Jack said, then he listened for a few long moments.

It wasn't the call he'd anticipated. The only woman he hoped would call, was Carmelita. This call caused him great stress.

"No, I don't want to have sex with you again," Jack stated, emphatically. "It's just not right. I'm sorry, but the other night was a big mistake."

Initiating rejection was never easy for Jack. The phone went dead as she hung up on him. Jack dropped the receiver back into its cradle as he reflected on the lust that had so often led him into having sex with the wrong women.

Now that he thought that he was in love with Carmelita, the idea of recreational sex offered little appeal, especially with someone where he knew it was likely to cause trouble. He wanted to kick himself in the butt for his actions the other night. How could he be so stupid? He knew there would be repercussions.

He cracked another beer, leaned back in the chair, and fired up a cigarette. Then he thought about what it would be like to make love to Carmelita.

The small room where Carmelita slept at Dan's house was on the second floor. The tiny room had a bed and a small TV. There was no phone and the room basically lacked amenities. A crucifix hung over her cot like bed, and with the exception of a framless mirror, nothing else adorned the walls.

As Carmelita prepared to leave she slipped into her coat, then ran a brush through her thick mane of long black hair. Once her hair was brushed Carmelita quickly tied it into a ponytail, una coleta. Next, she cautiously peeked out the door to see if anyone was in the hallway, and saw that all was quiet.

After she left the house Carmelita quickly walked a couple of blocks to a bus stop. The buses in this part of town only ran once an hour at this time of night. She knew the next one should be due in about ten minutes.

She sat down on the bench and contemplated what she was about to do. How had her seemingly simple little life become so very complicated? As she wondered about this she glanced at her watch. It was 10:30. She knew at the very least she was risking her job, by leaving the house while Tammy was still out for the evening.

All the children were asleep when she left, but that status was always subject to change. Also, Dan was home. What if he wanted her? If she got caught, she knew it would cost her her job. In addition, if she incurred the wrath of Tammy, it might cost her more than her job.

Soon after the unwanted phone call, Jack flopped on top of his bed still fully clothed. All the lights in his room were on, and the TV picture was glowing with the sound on mute.

Aided by downing four beers in slightly more than an hour, Jack's hazy mind drifted into a deep sleep, just about the time Carmelita stepped onto a bus that would take her to his place in a matter of a few minutes.

A series of loud bangs on the door suddenly jolted Jack out of his slumber. He jumped up and scrambled across the room. He was still not fully awake and he fought to gather his thoughts. Jack wasn't expecting any visitors especially at this time of night. When he opened the door, Carol, a very pretty blond woman marched into his room with fire burning in her ice blue eyes.

"So you don't want to have sex with me again!" Carol said, virtually assaulting Jack with the statement.

"Carol!" Jack exclaimed, startled, and not at all pleased by her unexpected intrusion.

Jack partially closed the door to his room to keep the cool night air outside, but he did not close it completely. He hoped to make Carol's unannounced visit a short one.

"I thought you got your money's worth the other night," Carol stated, in an almost business like manner.

Carol was a chiselled faced beauty in her late thirties. She was casually dressed, and slightly disheveled. She still wore her blond hair long, and she constantly ran her fingers through it in an effort to keep it from covering her finely sculptured face.

In spite of years of continuous hard partying, Carol still managed to project a modicum of the air that had once made her one of the most successful high fashion models in the business.

Carol muttered something Jack didn't quite hear as she noisily rumaged through her hand bag in search of a cigarette.

"Shit, I forgot my cigarettes,…an' I can't stand those damn things you smoke,…"

"Carol, I,…" Jack tried to interject.

"We had a pretty good time fucking, didn't we? I love it when I make you scream. Don't you?" Carol said, reminding Jack of their last encounter.

"Now I suppose you've got a new fuck, haven't you?" Carol demanded. "Does she suck your dick better than me? Does she make you scream?"

"Look, I don't want to deal with you when you're,…"

"When I'm what?" Carol said, as she nervously grabbed one of Jack's cigarettes out of an open pack on the night stand.

The man outside in the truck was about to make his move, now that he noticed the open door. He took a sip that finished the half pint of liquor he'd been nursing during his wait.

As Carol lit the cigarette with her slightly shaking hand, Jack heard a soft knock on his partially open door.

"Hey, are you gonna talk to me?" Carol continued, as Jack firmly grabbed the handle and yanked the door wide open. To his surprise, Carmelita was shyly standing in the open doorway.

"Oh, now I see. There she is. Is that your new whore?" Carol questioned, as she crushed out her freshly lit cigarette on the carpet with her foot. Jack subtly ushered Carmelita into his room.

"Lo siento, Jack," Carmelita said, employing a low voice as she apologized for her presence and obvious intrusion.

"No, es bien, Carmelita," Jack responded, then took a deep breath. "Carmelita, esta es mi ultima esposa," Jack continued, in an effort to explain Carol's presence to Carmelita.

"Oh, how cute. Habla espanol." Carol offered mockingly.

"Carmelita, this is Carol. She's my last ex-wife." Jack said, repeating in English what he had just said in Spanish for Carol's benefit.

"I hear beaner chicks rock? Does she make you scream when she sucks your cock?"

"Carol!" Jack snapped.

"Dumbest thing I ever did was marry you, Jack!" Carol said, as she shoved Jack out of the way and stormed out of the room.

"I'm sorry," Carmelita told Jack, thinking her appearance had triggered the problem.

"That's okay, Carmelita. Es bien," Jack assured her as Carol turned back into the doorway to take one more verbal shot at her ex-husband.

"Have fun with your little Señorita. Better check her ID. I think there's some kind law, no Green Card, no nookie."

A moment later, Jack and Carmelita heard the sound of a car door opening then slamming shut, announcing what Jack hoped was Carol's emanate departure. Jack noticed that Carmelita's mood was very serious. Her beautiful dark eyes glowed with intensity.

"I have to speak with you," Carmelita said, in determined, but halting English.

"Have you been studing English?" Jack asked, pronouncing his words slowly. Jack knew speaking slowly was helpful when someone is learning to speak and understand a new language.

"Yes. My sister help me. Now, I study English every day."

Jack was impressed by her progress, but wondered about her sudden interest in learning English after living in this country for over five years. Could he be the reason?

Outside, Carol's car roared to life and tore out of the lot leaving a thin trail of rubber in her wake. Jack picked up the discarded cigarette on the floor, then approached the open door as he kept his attention focused on Carmelita. He flicked the butt outside. He knew Carmelita didn't smoke. Since he surmised that his room probably reeked with the smell of stale cigarette smoke, Jack left the door slightly open.

"Sientese, por favor," Jack said, and Carmelita carefully sat down on the edge of the bed. "¿Quieres alguna cosa? Lo siento, tengo solamente cervezas, y agua."

After Jack asked her to sit down, he had asked her if he could get her anything, then lamented that he only had beer and water to offer.

"No gracias," Carmelita replied.

"Okay," Jack said, then he joined her and sat on the edge of the bed. "¿Quieres mi amiga?"

Carmelita's demeanor was really serious. Sensing this, Jack gently took her hand. She responded and put her other hand over his.

"I, …"

"En espanol," Jack advised, when he realized she was having trouble remembering a word.

"Tengo un problema," Carmelita said, solemnly.

"¿Que es el problema?" Jack inquired.

"Señora Tammy," Carmelita replied.

"¿Tammy? ¿Esposa de Dan?" Jack asked.

"Si. She want kill Dan, or maybe you, or somebody. I don't know, but she going to kill somebody."

"¿Como?" Jack questioned.

"Yo pienso mi jefa va a matar alguien."

Jack responded to her statement with surprise and almost total disbelief. He wondered if he understood her correctly?

"What? Are you sure? ¿Segura? ¿Tammy va a matar alguien?"

"Si, si," Carmelita replied seriously. "I am sure."

"Oh, boy," Jack said, as he tried to digest this strange bit of unexpected information. "Tammy's going to kill somebody?"

"Si. Yes."

"And you're sure? Jack asked again. "¿Segura?"

"Si. Absolutamente," Carmelita stated, saying that she was absolutely sure.

"How do you know? Did you overhear something? ¿Tu escucha alguna cosa?"

"Si. Escucho dos veses. I hear two times."

"Wow," Jack said. "So that's what Tammy's up to."

"¿Como?"

Then Jack wondered when this was supposed to happen?

"Ah,… ¿Cuando?" Jack inquired.

"No se. I don't know," she replied. "Y no se quien."

"You don't know when, and you don't know who?"

"No. Se."

"¿Tienes mas informacion?" Jack asked if she knew anything else about the plan.

"No. No mas," she answered.

After learning that she didn't have any more information, his attention turned to the large bruise on her face. He reached over and gently touched the nasty abrasion on her cheek.

"Who hit you? Jack asked. "¿Quien te pego tu cara?"

Again, Carmelita looked slightly embarrassed by his inquiry, but before she had a chance to answer, the door to Jack's room was suddenly and violently kicked wide open, literally breaking it loose from its hinges.

The man from the truck, a large young tough looking Latino dressed in a dirty tee shirt, jeans, and steel toed construction boots, burst into the room with murderous intent in his alcohol glazed eyes.

Jack was caught totally off guard as the man from the pick up truck attacked him with vengeance.

Carmelita screamed, and Jack was suddenly in a brutal hand to hand fight for his life.

Jack and the large Latino proceeded to tear the room apart as the vicious fight increased in violent intensity. It had been years since Jack had been in a serious melee, and he knew if he didn't get the upper hand soon, it was going to cost him his ass, or maybe even his life.

The strong young Latino was much bigger than Jack, and it was apparent that he worked as a laborer. His body was lean and hard. His hands were calloused and his arms were very muscular. He was also good with his fists, Jack learned, as he caught a hard left on the chin and his mouth began to fill with blood.

After the chin punch, Jack caught his barrings, and started to hold his own. He was used to getting hurt, he'd been a stuntman, and soon Jack was landing some good blows. Although he connected with a couple of hard punches to the Latino's face, he found it almost impossible to stop the man's onslaught, and take his tough opponent down.

Jack had a lot of hand to hand combat training in the Marines, both in the infantry, and as an M.P. He tried to draw on that experience as the violent encounter accelerated. As the two men continued to exchange brutal blows, blood started to fly and the combatants soon crashed into a large mirror on the wall shattering glass everywhere.

Blood splattered on Carmelita as the two fighters bounced off the walls and furniture, before the battle crossed the room and then eventually worked its way outside through the open broken door.

Carmelita was horrified as she grabbed the phone to call 911. At this point she feared for Jack's life, but apparently someone else at the motel had heard the commotion and called the cops, because before the 911 operator answered, Carmelita saw the red reflection of bright flashing lights from a series of arriving Sheriff's cars, as the wild fight continued to rage outside.

Carmelita dropped the telephone as the noisy crackle of police chatter coming over the cop's radios cut through the night.

Carmelita was frightened when she heard the Deputies outside sternly order Jack and his assailant to stop fighting. The cops isussed the commands in both English and Spanish. Immediately after the terse verbal commands she heard the cops take physical action.

Carmelita furtively peeked out the door and saw at least four Sheriff's Deputies separate Jack and the Latino with their night sticks and pepper spray. Some more Deputies stood nearby with their guns drawn ready to shoot. She was horrified by the brutal way the peace officers subdued their prey. Both men were handcuffed and beaten unconscious.

A long line of trees and an open field abutted the parking lot near Jack's room. The area beyond the trees was totally cloaked in darkness. Carmelita saw her chance.

A crowd of twelve to fifteen motel guests had quickly gathered to watch the action. Carmelita slipped into the small crowd, then quickly escaped into the darkness without anyone noticing her.

XX

Tammy was seated in a chair next to her bed having a serious conversation on the phone.

"Well, I didn't know there was a fifteen day waiting period when you buy a gun," Tammy said, then listened for a moment.

"Yeah, I'm finally getting it this afternoon. Then I have to go someplace and practice with it."

Again, Tammy listened for a few moments.

"Yeah, I'll be ready in time. I just hope you are."

A slight noise outside Tammy's bedroom caught her attention.

"Ah, no. I got a three-fifty-seven magnum revolver with a snub nosed barrel. Listen, I gotta go, bye."

Before she hung up, the person on the other end said something else, prompting Tammy's final comment.

"Yeah, I love you too, bye."

Outside the bedroom door, Carmelita had been listening to the conversation. As she cautiously backed away from the door, she stepped on a skateboard that belonged to one of the kids, and fell backwards crashing noisily down the staircase to the bottom. The bedroom door flew open and Tammy stepped into the hallway.

Carmelita's little sister, Angela, had started her new job in The Donut Shop at 3:30 in the morning. It wasn't exactly what she wanted to be doing, but as always, she was grateful that she had some employment. The payments on her new Saturn didn't stop when she was out of work.

Angela's most recent boyfriend Carlos, whom she met during her brief one night stand as a bus person at the fancy French bistro, got her the new job. His uncle was a baker there.

Angela's duties included working at the counter. The Donut Shop was close to her home, so the commute was only a matter of minutes. The hours however, 3:30 am to noon, were not much to her liking.

The immediate area was mostly Latino, but Angela's bilingual talents did come into play because the shop also had a steady influx of English speaking customers. The establishment was located on busy Van Nuys Boulevard, a main artery through the San Fernando Valley.

She also noticed that the myth about cops frequenting doughnut shops was not without substance. Police seemed to come in and out of the place all morning during her first day on the job.

Because her shift basically began in the middle of the night, Angela had absolutely no sleep the night before. Although somewhat fueled by coffee, she was fighting staying awake as that first long morning seemed like it would never end. As the time dragged by, she wondered if she would make it til noon?

At 10:30 she still had an hour and a half to go when a cop she recognized walked into the shop. It was the old LAPD Sergeant who had stopped Angela and Carmelita for not wearing their seat belts. Sergeant Stack always walked with a bit of a swagger, but he smiled broadly when he saw Angela standing behind the counter.

Jack was standing outside Dan's office on the parkway smoking a cigarette. He felt like shit, and was sporting a bandage over his left eye, and his swollen face showed bruised evidence of the violence that occurred the previous night. His entire body ached with pain, but he took some solace in the fact that his opponent was still hospitalized with a severe concussion and a broken jaw.

Jack's last blow had really connected and hit the mark. He heard the guy's jaw crack just before the cops piled on and ended the fight.

Jack's eyes still burned from the pepper spray, and he thought the police had behaved like absolute pigs throughout the whole affair. Even after it was ascertained that Jack had acted in self defense, no apology was forthcoming from the Sheriff's Deputies, who engaged in what Jack felt was excessive force. His wrists still hurt from the tight cutting way he was cuffed, and half his injuries had been sustained after the fight was finished, at the hands of the arresting officers.

Just as Jack finished his cigarette, Brad what's his name, pulled his SUV into his parking space, Brad was at least fifteen feet away from the offending smoke, yet Jack noticed a look of disapproval cross his pussy face.

Everything seemed to irritate Jack today. He got out of the hospital and eventually out of custody a scant half hour before he had to report to work. The only thing that had gone right in recent memory, Jack thought, was that Carmelita was able to sneak away the night before completely unnoticed.

He spoke to her for about a second that morning just before Dan came down the stairs. She was happy that Jack was still in one piece, and safely out of jail.

Jack responded to Dan's inquiries about his obvious injuries, by saying he'd snagged another stunt job, and was up all night staging a fight scene.

Jack knew Dan didn't believe his story, but his boss quickly dropped the subject, probably due to lack of interest.

Jack fired up another cigarette as he watched Brad virtually ignore the two Latino gardeners he almost crashed into while he was yakking on his head set cell phone, and looking down at the open lap top in his hands as he made his way toward the office door. Brad's grousing and contemptible condescending attitude toward those who actually worked for a living, galled Jack to the core.

In his tight white shirt and too long tie, Brad's body looked fairly buff. His physique was acquired, Jack presumed, from his often announced after work visits to the gym.

Tales of Brad's many and varied athletic activities were always shared with anyone who would listen, and even those who would not. As usual, just the sight of this punk made Jack want to puke.

Jack had spent some time in Third World countries during his Marine Corps days, which caused him to think about social unrest, and classisum. Over the centuries, poor folks have fought bloody revolutions just for the chance to kill filth like Brad.

Jack concluded that his mood wasn't improving. He also began to wonder if he could possibly last a whole year working for Dan, without kicking Brad's ass. He seriously doubted he could.

Soon, his two friends, the gardeners Juan and Diego, approached to inquire about the bandage on his face. It was difficult to explain in Spanish, but Jack did the best he could trying to speak through his painfully swollen mouth.

It seems that Maria the maid's husband somehow found out about the kiss, and from what Jack could gather from his brief visit the night before, he wasn't too happy about it.

Jack's two friends got a kick out of his tale of woe, but they cautioned him about the danger of messing around with another man's wife. Jack tried to explain the innocence of his mistake, but their little chat was suddenly cut short when Tammy pulled into the parking lot. Tammy rolled right up to where Jack was standing. Juan and Diego walked away as Tammy's window came down, and she addressed Jack in a plaintiff voice.

"I've got to meet you alone, Jack. Tonight, if possible. It's really important to me. Please," Tammy pleaded.

Jack thought about it for a moment. He didn't know if she wanted to hit on him, or kill him, or set him up, or what? But he figured he'd better go along with the meeting and find out what the hell was going on.

"Okay, meet me at my place at eight," Jack said.

"Great. Thanks, Jack," Tammy said, then hit the gas and sped out of the parking lot, without asking about his obvious injury.

Sergeant Stack also remembered Angela. After he got a cup of coffee and a glazed doughnut, he exchanged some small talk with the owner of the shop, Mr. Park. The elderly proprietor was from Korea, and Angela was a little surprised that the old Sergeant was able to carry on a conversation in her boss' native tongue.

Sergeant Stack then took a seat near where Angela was standing behind the counter.

"Remember me?" Angela asked, in her usual cheerful manner.

"Si. Yo recuerdo. Yo nuca olivido una cara bonita," Sergeant Stack replied, in serviceable Spanish.

Angela was slightly flattered when he told her that he never forgot a pretty face.

"¿Usted habla español?" Angela said.

"Si. Yo hablo alguno español."

"Bravo," Angela complimented.

"It's pretty much a requirement now in LAPD. I also speak a little Korean, Vietnamese, and Armenian."

"Wow, that's impressive," Angela stated.

"Well, not really. I was stationed in Korea and Vietnam when I was in the Army."

"Hey, thanks again for not writing me a ticket that day."

"De nada. I try not to be a hard ass. An' I'm a Sergeant, so nobody gets on my case if I don't write any," Sergeant Stack said.

Despite his military type demeanor, his Sergeant stripes, and the ladder of seven hash marks on his left sleeve, Sergeant Stack also displayed a disarming sense of charm, Angela thought.

"How long have you been a police officer?" Angela asked.

"In about ten minutes, it'll be thirty-six years," he said, as he glanced at his wristwatch.

"¿Como?" Angela didn't quite understand.

The old Sergeant chuckled, then took a slow sip of his coffee.

"Thirty-six years ago today, at 11 am, I joined LAPD."

"Feliz aniversario," Angela said.

"Gracias," Stack replied. "It's probably time for me to retire, but police work kind of gets into your blood."

"Are you married?" Angela asked.

"No. I'm divorced. How 'bout you?"

"No. Soy soltera," she replied. "I'm still single."

"Usted habla ingles muy bien," he complimented.

"Thank you," she replied.

"¿Cuanto tiempo en Estados Unidos?"

Just as he asked her how long she had been in the United States, some noisy horn blowing commotion outside caused Stack to look out the window.

A homeless man, who was apparently drunk, had wandered out into traffic. The Sergeant watched as the man fell down right in the middle of the busy intersection.

"Oops, looks like it's time to serve and protect. Hasta luego, Señorita."

"Si. Hasta luego. Cuidado, Señor Sergento." She advised him to be careful.

"Si, por supuesto, sempre. See ya later," Stack said, as he headed out the door into the morning sun to save the man in the middle of traffic.

Like the other cops she'd served that morning, Sergeant Stack apparently felt no obligation to pay for his fare. Very much like Mexico, Angela thought. Then suddenly she realized she was wrong when she picked up his empty coffee cup, and found a neatly folded five dollar bill.

She rang up $1.76 for a glazed doughnut and coffee, then put the rest of the change, a generous propina, in her little tip jar.

XXI

Tammy parked her SUV not far from Jack's room. She was a half hour early. She was wearing a short sheer sun dress and sandals, and by her own appraisal was looking very sexy that evening. She clipped off the few steps to Jack's room, then gently rapped on his newly replaced door.

Jack was slightly startled by the knock. He was still a bit jumpy from the incident the previous night. He cautiously peeked out the window, and saw Tammy nervously twitching around waiting for him to answer the door. She really looked sexy, he thought, as he went to the door and let Tammy into his room.

She was wearing some great smelling fuck me perfume, and she milked the little outfit she was wearing to the hilt. No wonder Dan was always on edge, Tammy was a handful even when she wasn't doing anything.

"Hi, Jack. Sorry I'm early," she purred.

"That's okay, Tammy. I don't mind."

"I know," Tammy said, as she filled the small room with her presence.

Flora Sanchez, the gal from the sandwich shop hadn't seen or heard from Jack in quite a while. She'd left any number of voice mail messages, that Jack never returned. She was still mad about the night he said he had to go back to work, but she was also horny. They only had sex once, but it had lasted all night, and she found herself thinking about that encounter almost constantly.

The same thing happened the last time she slept with another Gringo. He too, had fucked her, then she never heard from him again. Men, sometimes Flora wondered if the world would be a better place without them.

Carmelita was quietly watching something in Spanish on her small TV when she heard a soft rap on her door.
"¿Si?"
"It's Dan."
She reached over and turned off her television.
"Un momenta, Señor," she said.

Jack was sitting in his chair by the table. Tammy was seated on the edge of the bed.
"Dan and I haven't had sex in six months," Tammy informed Jack, as she coyly played with the hem of her short dress.
Tammy leaned back on the bed as she glanced around Jack's tiny room.
"I think you can help me out, Jack."
Suddenly there was a loud rap at Jack's door.
"Are you expecting company?" Tammy said, obviously irritated by the interruption.
"No," Jack replied.
He got up and went to the door. He didn't answer it, he just yelled out, "Who is it?"
"Motel maintenance," came the reply from the other side of the door. The accent was thick and Hispanic.
Jack stepped to the window and peeked out through a corner of the closed curtain. He saw a Latino man he did not recognize.

Jack stepped away from the window.

"What's wrong?". Tammy asked.

"Something just doesn't click. I don't recognize this guy."

"Do you need something fixed?" Tammy inquired.

"No, I don't think so. Besides, it's almost eight, an I I've never seen this guy before in my life," Jack said. "The regular maintenance guy, Raul, is a friend of mine, and he always alone."

Jack then pulled a Smith and Wesson .38 revolver with a four inch barrel out from under his untucked Hawaiian shirt. Tammy was a bit startled at the sight of the gun. Jack cocked back the pistol's hammer and stepped away from being directly in line with the door.

"I don't need anything fixed," Jack said, in a strong voice.

Tammy reached over and pulled her hand bag close to the side of her leg.

"I must have the wrong room," the man outside replied. "Sorry I bother you. Good night."

"You're pretty cute when you carry a gun," Tammy commented.

"I've had some trouble lately."

"I heard. Dan told me."

"About the stunt job?"

"He didn't believe you. I think he checked with the cops. I hear you put a guy in the hospital? Congratulations."

"Thanks."

Jack quickly and carefully peeked out the window again, but he also never really took his eyes off Tammy for more than a second.

"Is he gone?" Tammy asked.

"Yeah, I think so," Jack answered, as he uncocked his weapon and set it on the table.

"You got anything to drink around here?" Tammy said, as she crossed her bare tan legs letting the skirt part of her dress slip up a little higher on her thigh.

"Yeah. I have a little beer, and I think I've got some good Gold tequila."

"Ole," Tammy said, with a purr.

Flora Vasquez looked at her nude body in the bathroom mirror and admired the way she had kept her curves. At almost thirty-six she was still a hot little Señorita, she thought.

She let her long black hair fall over her shoulders. The tips touched her ample firm tits right at the nipple level. Once again, Flora wondered why her luck with men was so awful? She looked at her full lips, her dark intense eyes, and her shapely hips.

"Shit, they all suck," she said, aloud in English. She thought of the names of some of the guys who had fucked her over. They were all the same, these men.

Next, she slipped into a sexy black bra and matching panties. She admired herself some more in the mirror, then donned her work clothes.

Mentally, the years at the sandwich shop were starting to take their toll. Between rude customers, low pay, lousy hours, and dictatorial management, simply driving the short distance to work had become debilitating.

She thought about Jack again, and decided to drive past his motel before going to work.

There was something very theatrical about Tammy, Jack thought, but he couldn't quite put his finger on it.

"So what will it be, beer or tequila?" Jack asked.

"Oh, how about one of each," Tammy replied, then flashed a naughty little smile.

Hum, a two fisted drinker, Jack thought, as he fetched her a beer from the fridge. Then he fished out a half empty bottle of Cuervo Gold that was stored in his sock drawer.

"How's your face feeling?" Tammy inquired sincerely.

"Ah, it's still a little sore."

"I'll bet. I'm sorry."

Jack poured some tequila into one of the motel's plastic cups and handed it to Tammy.

"Thanks," she said.

Sometimes there was something strangely sweet about Tammy, Jack mused, as he watched the sexy woman sitting on his bed take a healthy sip of straight tequila, then chase it with a swig of beer.

Outside, the guy who claimed to be a maintenance man lingered in the shadows, until a cop car cruised slowly through the parking lot, causing him to change his plans for the evening.

Flora was horny, and she thought about the way Jack had given her head, as she neared the motel driveway. She hated the 8:30 2:30 am shift she was required to work one night a week. Too few hours, six, at $6.50 an hour, so not much money, but still an evening of the same bullshit. The thought of quitting crossed her mind.

Then a little dose of reality struck her. How would she pay her bills? Could she find a better job? Probably not. Damn! Then her thoughts returned to sex.

Well, if she could corral Jack into the sack, maybe she'd just call in sick. She knew sex would make her feel better. Again, the recollection of Jack's talent in the oral sex department made her thighs and vaginal area tingle.

As she turned the back corner of the motel, she noticed a cop car stop just before it reached Jack's door. Flora was afraid of the cops and suddenly she wondered if this was a good time to make a surprise visit?

She seriously weighed her options, and sex still managed to make the top of the list. Damn. When she was really horny, lust usually won.

Flora watched as the cop car slowly moved forward a little. Did this have something to do with Jack, or were the police just on the prowl?

XXII

Dan was standing on the porch when Jack pulled into the driveway the next morning. A number of things crossed Jack's mind as he watched Dan descend the steps briefcase in hand.

"I'm ready to go, Jack," Dan stated, as he climbed into the Lincoln.

"I need to use the head," Jack said.

"We're going straight ot the office. You can hold it that far," Dan said, closing the subject.

Jack was disappointed he didn't get to go inside and speak to Carmelita. He'd showed up a little early especially for that reason, but Dan had managed to fuck up the plan.

On the way to the office, Dan seemed tense as he opened the morning's conversation with a revelation.

"I've been having this affair for six months, and I feel terrible about it. I think Tammy's about to do something desperate,…and I don't think I want to lose her," Dan said.

Dan paused, but Jack failed to respond, not knowing exactly what to say. A couple of moments passed, then Dan went on with what was on his mind.

"If she had an affair, I'd probably have the guy killed. And the funny thing is, I feel the same way about my girlfriend."

On a moral level, Jack found Dan's logic a little shaky. As Jack listened, he thought about what happened the previous night with Tammy, until his thoughts were interrupted when Dan mentioned that the next day was Carmelita's birthday.

"After you drop me at the office, an' take a piss, I want you to go out and find me a birthday card for Carmelita in Spanish. I think that Hallmark place next to Ralph's has cards in foreign languages," Dan said.

"Sure," Jack replied.

"I already took care of the gift. I gave her some cash."

Knowing how terribly tight fisted Dan was with every penny, Jack wondered how much his cheapskate boss actually gave her?

"Boy, I wish she'd learn to speak English," Dan added.

Finding out that the next day was Carmelita's birthday, gave Jack an idea. He thought about what he'd like to give her, as Dan continued his self indulgent chatter until they reached the office.

That afternoon, Jack not only got a card for Dan to give to her, he went to a jewelry store and found the perfect gift for Carmelita.

Jack had been told to report to work at ten the next morning. He arrived a half hour early. When he pulled into the driveway, much to his delight, he found Carmelita working in the flower bed picking some posies.

Jack parked the big Lincoln so the view of the flower bed from the house was somewhat obstructed. He got out of the car and approached Carmelita holding a tiny nicely gift wrapped package and a small card.

"Buenos dias, Carmelita."

"Buenos dias," Carmelita replied, as she continued gathering her flowers.

"I'm glad you got away okay the other night," Jack said, in a very low voice.

"Si. Me too," she replied. "¿Como esta su ojo?"

"It's okay. It's getting better. Bien, es major. Mi ojo es major, gracias."

His eye still hurt, but he didn't want to cop to it.

"Feliz cumpleanos," Jack said.

"¿Como?" Carmelita questioned.

"It's your birthday today, isn't it? ¿Tu cumpleanos hoy, no?"

"Si," Carmelita answered, somewhat surprised that Jack knew about her birthday.

Jack held out the tiny gift wrapped birthday present and card.

"Esto regalo es por tu cumpleanos," Jack said.

After a moment, she accepted the little package and card.

"Gracias," she said, as she slipped the items into one of the large pockets of the cute light green overalls she was wearing for her gardening chores.

"De nada," Jack replied.

A moment passed and Jack thought Carmelita was going to say something else, but she just returned to her work.

Jack didn't hesitate too long before he turned and started to walk away. Suddenly, he sensed something and turned back in her direction. She was looking at him. When he caught her staring at him, he smiled, and she turned her face away.

"Well,...pase buen dia," Jack said, as he turned and started to leave. He had just learned the phrase for, have a nice day.

"Jack," Carmelita said, causing him to turn back toward her again.

"Si," he replied.

At this point Carmelita offered Jack a beautiful red rose she had just snipped. Jack stepped forward and accepted the flower.

The feeling he had at that moment was one of the most romantic experiences of his life. Carmelita cast her eyes down shyly as the rose passed between them. She too, was starting to feel something for Jack.

"Gracias," Jack said.

"De nada," Carmelita answered, with a tiny smile. Then she returned to her work, as he smelled the lovely freshly cut rose, and continued to watch Carmelita go about her gardening.

Just looking at this woman made him feel all warm inside. The way the sun hit her face that morning made Jack even more aware of her incredible beauty. Her skin was absolutely flawless, and her thick ebony hair glistened in the natural light. Even from a few feet away, he sensed he felt the intense sexuality of her body heat.

His enrapture was abruptly interrupted when he heard Dan yell from the porch, where he had been standing watching the two for the last minute or so. Jack felt stupid that he hadn't noticed Dan step out of the house.

"Hey, Jack, you can take off now. I've decided I don't need you today," Dan said. He then turned and reentered the house without further comment.

"I think he play golf with Al today," Carmelita offered.

"Oh?" Jack replied. "Ah,…Feliz cumpleaños, de nuevo." Jack again wished her Happy Birthday.

"Thank you," she said, in a very soft voice as she touched the top of the pocket containing her gift. "Y gracias por mi regalo."

"De nada." Jack said. "Hasta mañana."

"Si. Hasta mañana. Gracias, de nuevo, Jack."

Jack got back into the Lincoln and left, wondering again if Dan was somehow involved with Carmelita?

Later that day, when Carmelita was alone in her room, she carefully opened the little gift box Jack had given her.

To her delight, it contained a beautiful delicate petite pair of gold earrings cut in the shape of a flower, with a very tiny diamond mounted in their center.

Carmelita was very pleased with her gift, and she immediately removed the hooped earrings she was wearing, then slipped the new flower earring's little pegs into her pierced ears. She brushed her hair back with her hands, and looked at her gift using the small mirror on her wall.

As she stood there admiring her new earrings, many thoughts raced through Carmelita's mind. She was starting to like Jack, and she knew that presented many problems. She also wasn't sure he was sincere in his amorous overtones.

She also pondered the Tammy problem. She wasn't totally sure if Jack believed her story about Tammy hatching a plot to kill somebody.

Her little sister Angela had mentioned that she had struck up a friendship with a cop, and Carmelita wondered if she should go to him with her problem? What if she was wrong? What if she had misunderstood what Tammy said in English? Carmelita had much on her mind when she heard a loud rap on her door.

"Carmelita, I need you to do some laundry, right now," Tammy said, from the other side of the closed door.

"Si, Señora," Carmelita instantly responded.

Then, just as Carmelita was about to leave her bedroom, she remembered that she hadn't opened the card that accompanied the gift. She opened the small envelope and removed a card that had a host of colorful flowers splashed across its cover along with the Spanish birthday greeting, Feliz Cumpleanos. Inside, she found a simple hand written note that read, I love you, Jack.

She thought twice about leaving the card in her room in open view, and tucked it into her pocket before she left to attend to Tammy's needs.

XXIII

The day after Jack gave Carmelita her birthday gift, Dan had him report for work at 9 am. Jack saw Carmelita briefly in the kitchen as she busied herself cleaning up the after breakfast mess.

Jack was pleased to see she was wearing the earrings he gave her. They exchanged a few words in Spanish. She thanked him again for her gift, and stated that she thought the tiny delicate flowers were both beautiful and appropriate, since her love of gardening was rooted in her deep passion for lovely flowers. She also informed him that her name, Carmelita, meant the little girl of the garden.

Their time alone only lasted a minute or two, before Dan came in and immediately broke the mood by snapping at Tammy who had just entered through the door from the garage.

"I just saw the bill from Nordstrom's!" Dan said, tersely.

"You know how much I saved you by buying that stuff on sale?"

"How can you spent $4,000 in an afternoon, then tell me you saved me money?" Dan responded, as he glared at his wife who was wearing a new white outfit that strongly reflected a Moroccan theme. "Come on Jack, we gotta get goin'."

Dan stormed out of the kitchen followed by Jack, who noticed a glow of true hurt emanating from Tammy's ice blue eyes.

When they arrived at the office, Dan promptly sequestered himself behind his closed door.

Jack went outside to have a smoke and encountered Diego who was tackling a maintenance task. He was replacing a burned out bulb in one of the antique looking parking lot lamps located next to where Jack parked the Lincoln.

Diego and his compadre Juan worked as gardeners and general handymen at the large well kept office complex. The grounds were lush with greens and trees and flowers. The California Spanish architecture blended tastefully with the rolling green mountains and the multi-cultured history of the area.

Jack liked Diego. He always had a cheerful attitude, he worked hard, and he seemed very eager to learn. His buddy Juan was more reclusive. Juan was the plumber of the two, while Diego handled most of the maintenance chores. They shared the gardening, painting, and clean up duties.

Jack liked the Spanish name Diego. It reminded him of the party town to the south, San Diego, that he knew well as a young Marine, and it was also the true identity of Zorro whose legend had its roots in these parts.

From time to time Jack liked to let his imagination drift back to thoughts of what this area was like during Zorro's era, the early 19th Century when California was under Spanish rule.

Before the Mexican revolution against Spain, California was a Colonial outpost of the Spanish Empire, very much like Colonial Connecticut was to the British Monarchy.

Diego was a handsome young Mexican man who had been in the United States for only six months. Jack often thought when he looked at Diego's classically Mexican face, that this man truly represented much of the heritage of Southern California.

In his pursuit of the Spanish language, during his down time with Dan, Jack had read a few history books concerning the rich background of California's evolution.

Jack was born and raised in the L.A. suburb of Culver City, so he too was a native of sorts to this land that had passed through many transitions. Whenever Jack drove past Chumash Park just off Thousand Oaks Boulevard in nearby Oak Park, he was always reminded of the Native Americans who inhabited this land long ago, and who chose to call the earth their mother, and didn't view property in a monetary sense.

Interesting history, Jack thought, the confluence and collision of cultures, here in sunny Southern California.

Soon into his conversation with Diego, Jack learned that his friend had a problem. The guy who managed the office complex, a real jerk in Jack's opinion, hadn't paid Juan and Diego on time. The paychecks were five days past due.

Diego asked Jack if he would translate and speak with the manager on their behalf. Diego was studying English in night school, but was only a couple of months into the course.

His hours of work at the complex were long, but he always took time to stop and chat with Jack. They helped each other with English and Spanish respectively.

Jack was flattered, but felt that using him as a translator in espanol was almost akin to using Hellen Keller as a forward artillery spotter.

However, Jack agreed, and had a word with Diego and Juan's boss and got the paycheck problem solved in a jiffy.

The manager offered some kind of lame explanation, and Jack just suggested, rather strongly, that handing over the late checks immediately would negate the need for further explanation, or conversation.

The man promptly complied, and Jack hoped he hadn't actually created a problem for his friends by intervening in a way that fell just short of intimidation. Jack's contempt for this type of irrogant asshole literally bordered on homicidal. He didn't much care for any kind of authority figure, especially those who exploited their employees.

This was the second labor issue Jack had resolved in as many days. After Maria the maid's husband was arrested the night of fight, the cops turned him over to the INS, who put him on a bus and deported him back to Mexico. Then Maria was fired from her job at the motel the next day.

When Jack heard about what happened, he quickly resolved the matter by threatening to sue the motel for his injuries if Maria wasn't immediately reinstated. She was, and further discussion of the lawsuit was dropped.

Following social ills had always interested Jack. He really hated injustice, and yet he seemed to see it everywhere. In the newspapers, on TV, and in particular against the Latinos he had come to know over the last few months. In this modern society, greed, pure avarice were the order of the day, and those who did actual labor were really getting the short end of the stick.

When Jack returned to the office area after talking with the manager, Dan was waiting in the car. Dan had needed him during his absence, and Jack's boss was not at all pleased when he heard that Jack had been involved in a labor issue.

Jack didn't really give a shit, but refrained from saying as much, as he slipped into the waiting Lincoln.

"Where to, boss?"

"San Diego," Dan said.

Damn, the name Diego just won't go away today, Jack thought.

"You can buy some underwear and toiletries down there. We're going to be gone for two or three days, Dan added.

Great! Jack thought. Three or four hours of sports radio each way, and a few days away from Carmelita.

Then another thought occurred to Jack. Would Dan fire his sorry ass when they returned from San Diego?

No job, no dough. No Carmelita? These grim thoughts caused Jack a great deal of stress as he pointed the Lincoln toward the 101 and the first leg of their San Diego journey.

Carmelita slept little that night. She had a dream about Jack, then was unable to go back to sleep.

She seldom had dreams about sex, but the one she had about Jack was really something.

She found him handsome, charming, intelligent, funny, and she knew he possessed real courage. The way he handled himself in the fight, the fact that he worked in the movies as a stuntman, and she knew he was also an ex-Marine.

He told her once how much Dan paid him, so she knew he'd spent maybe a couple of weeks salary on her birthday gift. Jack had signed the card, I love you. Saying te quiero was one thing, but putting it in writing was another.

Flora thought about Jack that night, too. On the evening she'd decided to pay him a visit, she'd become so angry she never wanted to speak to him again.

After the cops cruised out of the lot, Flora had doubled back.

She had approached Jack's door, but just as she was about to knock, she heard two voices laughing and talking inside. Jack was entertaining a Gringa.

She listened for awhile, then hid in the shadows until she saw the pretty blond woman leave.

Flora was horny, but she wasn't about to give Jack a double header that night. She laughed, then really got mad, when she heard herself use that term.

She'd dated a Gringo years ago when she first came to the U.S. who bragged one night about fucking two women in one day, doing a double header.

Flora had been number two on his lineup, and the thought of it made her want to slit his lousy throat.

The question now was, would she give Jack another chance? Her mind then returned to thinking about Jack's particular talent for pleasing her in a certain area, an area that she now noticed was becoming increasingly wet.

It was three in the morning when Flora reached for the phone, only to get Jack's motel voice mail.

XXIV

Jesus Hernandez understood few words in English, but "Where are you from?" were four words he knew. Deadly words in gang territory. When he answered incorrectly, it cost him his life.

Jesus's short life, seventeen years n Mexico, and one year in the United States had been a hard one. He had been forced to work since the age of nine. Most recently he had worked with his older brother Carlos as a busboy in the fancy French restaurant.

Angela and Carlos attended the funeral together. That night, when Carlos vowed revenge, Angela made her exit from his life.

Gang activity repulsed her, and she swore she'd never be a party to it. Pacoima, North Hollywood, Van Nuys, Panarama City, Arleta, the City of San Fernando in the North Valley, were all plagued by gang life. This tended to divide the Latino community.

Decent hard working Hispanics tried to distance themselves from it, but this was often impossible. The chasm between this violence and a better life, sometimes seemed hopelessly narrow in the North San Fernando Valley.

When Angela returned home that night, she was surprised not to find Carmelita there. Carmelita always came home on her days off, and Angela was worried by her absence.

The atmosphere in Al's den that early evening was thick with cigar smoke and male hubris. Dan's cadre of cohorts had also been drinking all afternoon.

"Hey, Al. How would you describe Tammy?" Dan asked.

"Honestly?"

"Yeah."

"Beautiful, sexy, and a world class, self indulgent Conejo Valley cunt," Al replied.

Then Burt chimed in with, "Bingo."

"I have a quorum," Al stated.

"What about the girlfriend?" Burt inquired.

"I'm just about to solve that problem," Dan confirmed.

"What's that gonna cost ya?" Burt asked.

"Plenty," Dan replied.

"Hey, it'll be worth it to have her out of your life," Al said. "An' remember, you did hire an expert to handle it."

"Yeah," Dan agreed. "Hey, I gotta get goin'. Can you give me a ride home?"

Once again, Flora was entertaining the idea of calling in sick. She hated the night shift.

Maybe I'll call Jack, she thought? Then decided against it. Then she changed her mind again. She hadn't been laid in weeks. Weeks!

Sergeant Stack had rolled on the call within seconds after the violent gang related shooting occurred. Stack generally didn't work nights. Friday was his usual day off, but that night he was on the second watch filling in for an old buddy of his.

Three people had died in the shooting. Two were gang bangers, the intended targets, and the other was an innocent bystander.

The term bystander struck Stack as odd when he was writing his report, since the victim was a fourteen month old boy.

The little boy couldn't really stand on his own, he was just barely a toddler. He died in the arms of his mother, who had no other direct relation to the incident. Even after thirty-six years as a cop, this sad collateral aspect of gang violence always seemed to break the old Sergeant's heart.

The police had quickly apprehended five suspects, four of whom were armed with automatic weapons. None showed the smallest sign of remorse as they hung tough, handcuffed and defiant, during the initial sidewalk interrogation.

The kids were driving Dan crazy. They seemed to be everywhere in the big house. Tonight, there were the five that lived there plus two more boys, eight year old twins visiting from the house next door. They were all screaming, and playing, and just completely raising hell in general.

In Carmelita's absence, Tammy had borrowed Rosarita, the older Latina who worked for the family next door. Rosarita was pushing fifty, very pleasant, a little on the plump side, and she spoke rather good English.

However, aside from these attributes, she quickly proved to be a hopeless disciplinarian. Dan felt leaving the kids with only Rosarita in charge would inevitably led to some kind of trouble.

He thought Tammy was having dinner with Annie Horwitz. This meant when she finally got home, she would probably be drunk.

The night was very dark outside Jack's room, his lights were off, and the sounds of love making mixed with soft music. Inside, the couple in bed were busily engaged in passionate sex.

After a few long moments of loud moaning and groaning, she screamed out with an unintelligible cry of pleasure, then moaned for another full minute. Once her moaning subsided somewhat, Jack spoke to her in Spanish.

"Estoy muy serio, y muy sincaro."

"¿Si?" She replied, in a low breathy tone.

Allen Horwitz parked his new black Porsche close to Westlake High School's dark football stadium. He was there to have some fantasy fulfilling sex.

Tammy and Annie Horwitz always drank too much when they had dinner together.

Annie, Allen's wife, was Tammy's best girlfriend. Annie was a professional consultant, and she made frequent trips out of town. She had just returned from two days in Philadelphia and New York, cutting her planned trip short by one day.

During dinner they completed their murder plot.

"Well, I'm glad that's all settled," Tammy said. "God, I just love your dress."

"Thanks," Annie said. "How are the kids?"

"Oh, just great," Tammy confided.

While having dinner, Tammy and Annie had consumed several tall glasses of wine. The meal and wine had been proceeded by pink martinis. Too much wine, and three pink martinis, had made Annie a little more than tipsy. Tammy, too, was starting to feel the booze.

All was quiet as Allen Horwitz stealthly jumped the chain link fence and made his way to the middle of the dark football field.

Once Allen was exactly in the center and on the fifty yard line, he dropped to the ground and rolled over onto his back. He was barefoot and wearing only an expensive two piece running suit. He slipped out of the top and pants, then folded them neatly and put the garments under his head like a pillow.

Allen looked up at the black star studded sky, then glanced at his gold Rolex. He took a deep breath. The night was quite chilly and Allen's naked body shivered on the cold damp ground.

Allen contended with the cold because he knew he was exactly four minutes away from a wonderful warmth that would cover his trembling naked body. He closed his eyes and waited, as he started to count down the seconds in his mind.

Allen Horwitz thought about how much he loved a certain type of danger. He was well known and respected in the commumity, both as a successful businessman, and on a social level.

After Annie Horwitz said good night to Tammy, and left the busy resturant in Westlake Village, she drove her silver Mercedes SUV south on Thousand Oaks Boulevard. She noticed her husband's new Porsche parked in a dark area on the street near Westlake High.

By the time Allen counted down to the number twenty, he was really starting to get cold. He shivered as he kept his eyes closed and counted down through the teens to the number eleven.

Ten, nine, eight, seven, six, five, four, three, two, one. A few seconds passed and Allen began to wonder if something had gone wrong. Then he felt her warm naked body press down hard on his, creating a wonderful sort of nirvana.

Allen opened his eyes as they kissed, and he wrapped his arms around her naked black body. Thus, their love making began, on the fifty yard line in the middle of Westlake High School's big football stadium.

Their hot sexual bout was short in duration, but when Allen Horwitz came, he had fulfilled yet another childhood fantasy. He had fucked a beautiful black chick on the fifty yard line of his old alma mater. The only thing missing was having his mother in the stands.

Outside Jack's room the night was cool and the crickets were singing their usual song. The music inside Jack's room was still playing softly, but the passion in bed was about to reach another loud crescendo.

"¿Verdad?" She said, asking Jack if he was telling her the truth.

"Si, verdad," he said, passionately. "Estoy muy serio."

"¿Si?" She replied, with a groan.

"Si, mucho. Te quiero, mucho. Para mucho tiempo," Jack said.

"¿Si?" She questioned again, as their love making moved toward a heated climax.

"Si, si," he replied, as he felt the sexual release coming that he was so desperately trying to hold back, so he could savor what seemed like the greatest sexual pleasure he'd ever known.

He held back as long as he could, and when Jack finally came deep inside her, she twisted and made her canal even tighter, as she moaned and drew him down hard against her warm wet body. She trembled as she continued to hold him in a firm embrace that seemed to fuse the couple's naked bodies into one solid enity. The intensity of the moment was incredible.

This round of sex had lasted perhaps thirty minutes, Jack thought, as he held her tight. He reveled in the realization that tonight he was having absolutely the most exciting sexual experience of his life.

After a few long wonderful moments, she reached over and flipped on the light on the nightstand.

Carmelita was indeed a mysterious woman. Jack was convinced that he truly loved her, but Carmelita had somewhat taken him by surprise, when she said she wanted to stop by his place on the way home. A mere month before, Jack had thought he didn't stand in hell of ever being with Carmelita.

Women, I'll never understand them in any language, he thought, as he looked at the beautiful naked Señorita laying next to him. Jack kissed Carmelita tenderly on the forehead, then thought back to their encounter that morning in the garage.

The large garage door was closed and Jack had entered from the kitchen door. Carmelita was up on top of a ladder trying to put a box on a high shelf. Wearing a short pretty blue sun dress, she was perched precariously atop the ladder.

"Buenos dias, Carmelita," Jack said, as he approached the ladder unseen by Carmelita.

Jack's voice startled her, and caused her to lose her balance. As she started to fall from the ladder, Jack had quickly jumped to her aid.

When she fell into his arms, he too lost his balance, and they both crashed to the cement floor caught in a tight embrace.

Suddenly, as if in an answer to a prayer, he was holding the woman of his dreams in his arms. He noticed that she was still wearing the earrings that he had given her for her birthday.

She looked up at him in a quizzical way that Jack was unable to read initially. Was she angry, or bemused, or just happy she was unhurt by the fall? Jack wasn't sure, but he did know that she sure felt good breathing heavily wrapped in his arms.

"You okay? ¿Tu bien?" Jack asked.

"Si," she replied.

"I'm sorry I scared you. Lo siento. Ah,…soy idiota,…or is it idioto?" Jack said, again fumbling with his Spanish.

He was relieved when she cracked a warm smile, and didn't try to escape his embrace.

"You funny," she said.

"I'm funny? ¿Gracioso?"

"Si. Sometimes," she said, with a note of whimsy in her soft voice.

"Sometimes? ¿Aveses?" He said.

"Si. Gracias de nuevo por los aretes," she whispered, as she touched one of her tiny earrings.

"De nada," Jack replied.

Their faces were very close. After a moment, Jack started to kiss her. At first, she slightly turned her lips away.

"I may be funny,…but I'm also serious," he said. "Yo muy serio."

"I know," she said. "It's,…"

Seizing the moment he cut her sentence short by kissing her. Their lips parted slightly as the kiss began. It was a gentle tender kiss that didn't last too long. Her lips were moist and he felt the slight insertion and withdrawal of her wet tongue several times during the duration of the kiss.

Carmelita controlled the kiss, as she lightly touched his lips and tongue with hers until she decided it was time to terminate the contact.

When the kiss was finished, she turned her face slightly away. Jack felt his lips brush across her soft cheek. He couldn't believe the warm glow that engulfed his entire body.

"Oh, my God. I've wanted to do that for a long time," Jack said, as he lifted his head just enough so he could see her face.

"Yo se, pero,…" Carmelita answered hesitantly.

"But what?" Jack whispered. "¿Pero porque?"

"I no want to talk about it now," she replied.

"¿Porque?" Jack said, as he again moved his face close to hers.

"Because I,…"

"Carmelita!" Tammy's voice rang out from the open door between the kitchen and the garage. "I need you immediately!"

"Oh, no!" Carmelita cried. "Jack, get up!"

She pushed Jack away and quickly scrambled to get up off the floor.

"Carmelita!" Tammy screamed again.

"Si, Señora." Carmelita said, as she grabbed the box she had dropped.

Jack too, quickly jumped to his feet. The mood of the very romantic moment was suddenly shattered by Tammy's unwelcome intrusion. Fortunately, she didn't step into the garage and see the couple entangled on the floor kissing. Both Carmelita and Jack knew that would have meant big trouble.

Carmelita tossed the box to Jack. It was fairly heavy and he almost dropped it, as Carmelita frantically tried to dust the dirt from the garage floor off her dress.

"We talk when you take me home today," Carmelita said, just before she dashed into the house to answer Tammy's command.

Jack completed Carmelita's task by carefully climbing the ladder and sliding the box onto the shelf. He smiled as he ran his tongue across his lips. He could still taste Carmelita's tender kiss.

Jack looked at Carmelita next to him in his bed, and he still couldn't believe his eyes. Sometimes dreams do come true, he thought.
They made love again, and Jack knew he wanted to spend the rest of his life with this wonderful woman.

Jack had been taken a little by surprise, but he was also pleased beyond belief, when he had asked her if she wanted to stop at his place, when they left Dan's house earlier. Jack figured she'd probably say she wanted to go straight to her family's house in the Valley.
"Si," she said.
Dan's house was less than ten minutes from Jack's motel. When they stepped into Jack's room the daylight from the open door had illuminated Carmelita in the blue sun dress, and Jack was once again struck by her incredible beauty.
She smiled as Jack closed the door and flipped on the light simultaneously.
Jack looked at her and just wanted to grab her and kiss her. Carmelita' s straight black hair was behind her shoulders and the spaghetti strapped sun dress accentuated her firm pointed breasts in a manner that Jack found irresistible. The way her long black hair framed her face made her look almost angelic.
"¿Quieres alguna cosa?" Jack asked.
"No, gracias," she replied.

After he asked her if he could get her something, and she said no thank you, she looked down at the floor, as Jack tried to read her mood. Just when he decided to walk over and kiss her, she spoke lifting her eyes almost shyly.

"Me gusta tu beso esta mañana," she said.

When she told him that she had liked it when he kissed her that morning, Jack had trouble formulating his thoughts.

"Me too, ah, yo tambien," Jack responded.

"¿Si?" She said, in a soft voice.

"Si," he replied, sincerely.

She looked him in the eyes as he stepped forward and took her in his arms. After looking at each other for a long moment, they kissed.

Carmelita had fought her attraction to Jack, even though he was always nice and seemed to go out of his way to flirt with her. His persistence she found flattering, and he was a handsome macho kind of guy. Especially for a Gringo.

She had fought her feelings until Jack gave her the birthday gift that day in the garden. That day, for some reason, she felt his eyes had touched her soul with a sincerity that seemed real. Pleased that he had given her a thoughtful regalo, she had rather impulsively given him a rose.

Later, when she unwrapped the gift and saw the little flowered earrings, she thought back to that romantic moment in the garden.

All these things passed through Carmelita's mind as they now shared a long tender kiss.

The long kiss eventually made Jack a little dizzy. She was so enchanting, and her kiss was so sweet, that Jack almost felt like he was in a trance. Eventually, they fell over onto the bed, and within a short time they were making love.

XXV

Jack reasoned, and rightfully so, that Carmelita had probably had some bad experiences with men in the loyalty department. Of course, all of Jack's experiences with women and love, had turned out badly in one way or another.

The tragic death of his first wife, whom he had loved very deeply, was never fully forgotten. No woman, and there were many, ever came close to filling that void until he met Carol.

He had loved Carol in a most passionate way. She was also one of the most beautiful women in physical terms that he had ever known. Aside from her astonishing beauty, she was bright, sexy, and possessed a marvelous sense of humor, and the sex with Carol was always incredible. It was her lapses in sanity that made her absolutely impossible to live with.

Jack always feared the potential of another suicide with Carol, which he felt he probably would not survive. Somehow, Carmelita just seemed like the perfect woman.

As they were relaxing after their last round of love making, Carmelita reached over an touched the last remnant of the bruise Jack had incurred during the fight with Maria's husband.

"¿Como esta tu cara?" She asked.

"Bien. Es major, gracias," Jack replied, saying it was much better.

Jack still couldn't believe how incredibly beautiful Carmelita was, especially naked and within his grasp. He had trouble not staring at her perfectly pointed breasts with large dark nipples that almost screamed, suck me.

He was starting to get aroused again, and was on the verge of surrendering to her screaming nipples when she slipped out of bed and walked to the sink area.

Her long hair fell loosely on her back as she crossed the tiny room. Her buttocks was firm and incredibly shaped. Jack was completely mesmerized by her every movement. She poured a glass of water from the tap and turned back toward Jack.

Next, she leaned against the sink and put her foot on top of one of Jack's nearby suitcases causing her legs to separate, slightly exposing the wet pink lips of her love canal. This very sexy move caused Jack's eyes to somewhat focus on that area.

"I've really been waiting for you," Jack said. "Yo espero para te. Solamente para te. The reason I started learning Spanish was so I could communicate with you. Yo aprende espanol solamente por comunicacion contigo. Carmelita, yo muy sincero, y tambien mi intencion contigo es honorable."

"¿Si?" She questioned.

"Si. Please believe me. Do you? ¿Crea me?"

"Maybe. Maybe I believe you," she said, noting his eye line.

"I'm not sure I know what that means?" He said, as he looked her in the eye.

"Good," she replied, rather impishly. "¿Listo para mas?"

Jack smiled when she asked him if he was ready for more, and he said. "Si, listo."

She finished her water and returned to his bed. The passion resumed, and this time Jack satisfied her orally, something he had wanted to do since the first time he saw her wearing shorts.

When he finished, they shared a long loving kiss. They seemed to have an easy manner together. He touched her hair and ran his hands over her smooth skin. Then they cuddled like a couple who'd been lovers for years. So far, it had been a perfect evening, he thought, as he silently thanked God for the woman next to him.

Suddenly the romantic atmosphere was rudely interrupted by a loud rap on Jack's door.

Damn, Jack thought, I forgot to put up the Do Not Disturb sign!

"Señor Jack," Nancy called, from the other side of the door.

Damn it, Jack thought.

"Jack? Soy Nancy," Nancy continued, identifying herself.

"¿Quien Nancy?" Carmelita asked, who's Nancy?

"Ah,…ella trabajo aqui." She works here, Jack explained.

Carmelita looked at her wristwatch, noting that it was eight o'clock in the evening.

"Es a las ocho," Carmelita said, pointing out the time.

There was another rap. This time louder.

"Señor Jack? ¿Estas aqui?" Are you there, Nancy asked?

Carmelita just glared at Jack, as Nancy rapped again, hard.

Jack's mind raced a mile a minute, before he grabbed his robe and went to the door. He opened it just a crack, as Carmelita covered herself with a sheet.

"Hola, Nancy. No necesita toallas," Jack said.

"No tengo toallas, Jack," Nancy answered, saying she didn't have any towels.

"Estoy ocupado, ahora," Jack said, stating that he was busy at the moment.

"¿Si? Nancy said, as she peeked through the cracked door and saw Carmelita sitting on Jack's bed.

"Oh, yes. Muy ocupado," Nancy said. "Very busy."

"Nancy,…"

"Yo regreso otra vez," Nancy said, she'd come back at another time. "Bye," she added, directing the comment toward Carmelita.

Jack closed the door, and looked over at Carmelita on the bed. Her intense dark eyes were demanding a further explanation.

"You have sex with Nancy?"

"No. No sexo con Nancy," Jack replied.

"You tell me truth about Nancy?"

"Si, ella es una de mis maestras en espanol.

"How many Spanish teachers you have?" Carmelita inquired, not at all convinced by Jack's explanation. "¿Cuantos maestras? Nancy, y Maria en la escuela. ¿Cuanto mas?"

Carmelita learned about the Maria mix up after the fight.

"¿No sexo con Nancy?" Carmelita asked, again.

"No. No sexo. I was paying Nancy to teach me Spanish," Jack said. "Solamente lecciones en espanol. She has a couple of kids, Nancy tiene dos ninos. Yo pago Nancy veinte dolars para leccion. I pay her twenty dollars per lesson, twice a week. Dos veces a la semana, to help me learn Spanish. Nancy ayuda me en espanol. Y no mas. ¿Entiende?"

"Si. Yo entiendo," Carmelita confirmed, that she understood.

"That's all. Y no sexo con Nancy," he reiterated.

"¿No? ¿Verdad? Carmelita again, questioned his truthfulness.

"Si, verdad."

"Okay," she said.

Jack finally sensed that she seemed satisfied with his answer, and rejoined her on the bed. She however, still harbored doubts.

"Now, what we do about Señora Tammy?" Carmelita asked.

"Nada ahora," Jack replied, grateful that she had changed the subject. "Because I think you're wrong."

"I think I no wrong," she said, just before he cut off further conversation with a long wet kiss that soon caused their love making to resume.

This time, including ample oral foreplay, their passion lasted twice as long as their previous sessions. Unbeknownst to her, Jack had popped a little blue pill, shortly after their first round.

The miracle drug Viagra brought Jack's sexual prowess to new heights. Even after four previous rounds, it gave him a hard on he could poll vault with for a week. He was with the woman he loved, and performing like an eighteen year old in heat.

On the fifth time around, they truly found their mutual sexual rhythm. They eventually came in unison, then held each other tight in the warm afterglow of complete sexual satisfaction.

After some tender moments entangled in each other's arms, their conversation again turned to the subject of Tammy. This topic was only briefly explored, because they were suddenly sidetracted when the telephone rang. Jack promptly retrieved the receiver from the nearby nightstand.

"Hello."

Jack then listened for a few moments to a woman who spoke to him in rapid Spanish.

"Ah,…I can't talk right now," he said.

Again he paused for a few seconds while he listened as the unwelcomed diatribe continued, now in both English and Spanish.

"No. I can't. I have company. Look, I gotta go," he said, then hung up the phone.

"Was that a girl?" Carmelita asked.

"What?"

"¿Una mujer?" Carmelita repeated, this time in Spanish.

"Ah,…si."

"You girlfriend?" Carmelita asked, employing a serious tone as she modestly covered her naked body with a sheet.

"No. No novia," he replied.

"¿Nancy?" She asked.

"No."

"You have other girlfriend?" She inquired.

"No. No tengo otra novia," Jack said, nervously.

"¿Verdad?"

"Si, verdad. I don't have a girlfriend," Jack repeated, this time in English.

"Is she Mexican?"

"Who?"

"Girl who call you."

"Ah, no." Jack was telling the truth. Flora was from El Salvador.

"¿No?"

"¿Por qué?" Jack asked.

"Why? Carmelita said, incredulously. "I want to know, that why! ¿Otra maestra en espanol?"

Jack now realized she had heard Flora speaking Spanish. The question was, how much did she hear?

"You have sex with her?" Carmelita demanded.

Oh, God, Jack thought. If I tell her the truth I might lose her. I told her earlier that I had'd had sex in a long time. And he also told her that she was his first Latina. Damn it, why did he lie? I wanted to make her feel special, that's why. Oh, God, what if she finds out about Flora, or the other Maria?

"¿Jack?"

"Si," Jack replied.

"¿Sexo?" Carmelita pressed further.

"Ah,…no." He said, rather unconvincingly. "No sexo."

Jack didn't want to lie to her. He was in love with her. But what if she finds out? She could. Either way he could lose her.

Jack immediately figured he'd better move out of the motel, and quick. Flora might come by. Shit, he thought. She might come by tonight! She has dropped by before unannounced.

"¿Jack? ¿Sexo o no?" Carmelita demanded, again.

Damn it, why did I lie to her? Because I'm an idiot, that's why, Jack thought.

"I no believe you, Jack." Carmelita said. "No me lo creo."

Jack let out a deep breath, and thought seriously about what he should say. He thought for a moment about what Flora was screaming over the phone. Some of the Spanish he didn't quite understand, she was speaking so rapidly. But he was sure Flora did say something about having sex with him. Carmelita must have heard that part, and she knows I'm lying, Jack thought. Damn it!

"¿Jack? ¿Sexo o no?"

"Si," he said, letting his head drop.

"¿Cuando? ¿Ayer?" She said, sarcastically.

"No, not yesterday," He replied, sheepishly.

Carmelita quickly got out of bed and started getting dressed. Jack's heart dropped into his stomach. Five minutes ago, he was the happiest man on earth, and now his life was suddenly turning to shit, and it all happened in a matter of seconds. Damn it! I should have lied, he thought.

"I, I can explain," he said, having no idea what he was going to say next.

"It no necessary. You lie to me. I no want hear more lie!"

Carmelita quickly finished getting dressed, and refused Jack's offer to let him drive her home.

"I go taxi, or take bus. I no want ride," she said, as she gathered her things and left, leaving Jack feeling worse then he ever imagined he could feel.

Then Jack remembered that her bags and her stereo were still in the Lincoln. He rushed out, jumped into the car, and caught up with her as she was trudging up the hill toward the bus stop.

Their conversation was short and tense, but he finally convinced Carmelita to at least let him drive her home.

She acquiesced to the ride, but refused to converse with him further during the long silent drive to her family's house in Pacoima.

XXVI

Jack stayed drunk for the next two days. When he went back to work on Monday morning, he had a terrible hangover.

Carmelita wasn't due back until Tuesday. He wouldn't have to deal with seeing her until the next day. He wanted to see her, but he also feared further rejection. His mood was foul that morning, and he wondered what the day would hold?

Dan was quiet during the short ride to the office. He had one quick conversation on his cell phone, then listened to sports crap the rest of the way.

Jack could only think about Carmelita, and how it was his fault that he had lost her. By lying to her, he had lost her. And what was really stupid was it all started by having sex with some women, he knew he shouldn't have been fucking.

The first person Jack saw when he pulled into the parking area at the office was Brad. The day did not get off to a good start, and Jack sort of felt like a fight.

Allen Horwitz lived in a big house, made a lot of money, and was a master manipulator. Allen was also a little like Santa Claus. Sometimes he was far too generous. Generous to a fault. His philanthropy and more than fair business deals, had earned him respect and lots of friends.

Allen had arranged to get a white Rolls Royce convertible that morning just for the occasion. It sported stolen license plates, so the car couldn't be traced back to him.

Allen was wearing sunglasses that were just a little bit too big, and silly looking knit golf cap with a tassel on top.

Albertsons Supermarket is the anchor store for a large and popular shopping center on Lindero Road just off the 101 Ventura Freeway. The area is known as Oak Park and it lies just a mile south of Westlake Village.

When Allen drove into the Albertsons parking lot that morning, he positioned the Rolls five spaces away from the big market's main entrance.

Allen looked at his watch. It was just after 10 am and the customer traffic was still rather light.

Allen got out of the car at exactly 10:07. He walked back to the trunk area where he was joined by a woman wearing a very short sheer sun dress and a huge straw hat. She too, was wearing larger than usual sunglasses. The high heels of her expensive stylish sandals had clicked on the pavement with anticipation as Allen approached.

He looked at her astonishingly beautiful African features, and smiled. God, how he loved having sex with this woman, Allen thought.

They embraced and kissed with wide open mouths and wet probing tongues. This quickly led to standing rear entry sex against the trunk of the white Rolls Royce.

In the glare of the morning light, a few people passed the busy couple, but either didn't notice, or couldn't believe what they were seeing.

The couple's moves had been quick and to the point. After the introductory kiss, she had laid face down against the trunk of the car, and Allen lifted up her short sun dress just enough to expose her naked behind. Her beautiful black buttocks and vagina were already wet from self stimulation, accomplished during the short drive to the supermarket.

Allen had quickly removed his penis from his sweat pants and finished the job in record time.

He came and they kissed good bye in less then two minutes.

Another major fantasy was achieved that day near the entrance of Albertsons market. Allen had always wanted to fuck a black chick on the trunk of a white Rolls Royce in front of Albertsons, where he'd worked as a box boy during his high school days.

They sped away in separate directions just as an alerted old security guard stepped out of the main entrance.

Angela looked at Sergeant Stack and she could see the sadness in his eyes. Gang warfare had touched them both recently.

Stack took a sip of coffee and noticed that some homeboys were walking slowly past The Donut Shop. There were four. A large enough group to initiate a shake down according to LAPD policy.

However, Stack was in no mood to shake down some punks, so he asked for another doughnut. He also didn't want to draw heat to Mr. Kim's little shop.

Before he swallowed the first bite of his fresh doughnut, he saw a squad car out of the corner of his eye stop next to the four chulos. Their shaved heads, their strut, and their baggy clothes basically gave the cops probable cause.

The two young buff gung ho cops who got out of the squad car, also had shaved heads. Rather than a strut, these two examples of LAPD's finest walked with a swagger.

As he watched, the similarity of the opposing cultures struck the old Sergeant rather hard that morning.

Angela had something on her mind that she wanted to share with sergeant Stack, but the commotion that erupted outside caused her to delay her conversation.

Stack charged outside, gun in hand, to help the two hot shot cops, who were now up to their young asses in a heated gun battle with four armed suspects. So much for a quiet morning, Sergeant Stack thought, as he fired off a couple of rounds of return fire.

After Jack had helped Dan carry some of his stuff into the office, he returned to the parkway to have a smoke.

He had encountered Brad inside who greeted him by saying, "Hey buddy," in his usual condescending tone, designed no doubt to remind Jack that he was only a driver.

Jack hated it when this yuppie piece of shit referred to him as buddy. Buddies they were not. Nothing wrong with Brad that four years in the Marine Corps wouldn't kill or cure. That maggot wouldn't have lasted a week in one of my platoons, Jack mused.

Jack was dealing with many issues that morning. At the moment, not hitting Brad and hanging on to his job was his most immediate concern, and of course Carmelita was the other.

Jack had known some highs and lows in his life. The loss of his child and his first wife. Seeing two hundred and seventy-one fellow Marines killed in Lebanon, was another. Both his parents died when he was in his twenties, the nasty divorce from Carol, and more brushes with poverty then he cared to recount.

Jack did his best to subjugate his anger, but at times the absolute absurdity of life just got to him.

Jack had loved and lost before, but this was the worst. He loved Carmelita so bad it hurt. He'd loved her since the first time he laid eyes on her. After months of thinking he didn't have a chance in hell of getting her, then he finally got her, then he lost her. All in one night.

Jack was certainly dealing with many conflicts. During the seventeen years since he left the service, he never seemed to really find his niche in life. A lot of failed relationships followed the death of his first wife. He could never quite bury the loss of Julie and his child, but somehow he had found renewed hope with Carmelita.

Carmelita and Angela had much to discuss that afternoon when Angela finally got home from The Donut Shop. Carmelita's dilemma over Jack, and Angela's recent brushes with gang life, gave them plenty of fodder for a long intense sister to sister talk.

Carmelita wanted to talk about her situation with Jack, and the Tammy problem. Angela was concerned about her ex-boyfriend Carlos. He had threatened her for breaking up with him.

Angela wanted to mention this to her cop friend, Sergeant Stack, but the shoot out had prevented her from doing so. Then, once Carmelita knew her little sister had made friends with a cop, she thought it might be time to take her concern about Tammy's murder plot to the police.

Doing this through her sister's friend would be far better than going through official channels, Carmelita reasoned. She had a fear of the police, and her tenuous immigration status made her even more cautious.

Angela offered to bring up the Tammy thing the next morning if she saw Sergeant Stack at work. She also counseled Carmelita about her hasty decision to dump Jack, for something that had happened before the two were ever intimate.

Angela sensed her sister really liked Jack, and she reminded Carmelita how her intense jealousy had caused her so many problems in the past. Angela also felt that Carmelita was truly afraid of making a serious commitment with a man.

Tammy and Annie Horwitz drove together into the hills just west of Westlake Village to practice with Tammy's new gun.

Tammy fired the big pistol first. The powerful .357 magnum produced a hell of a bang, and it packed a mighty kick. Tammy fired the gun twice, then gave it to Annie.

Annie Horwitz was a fairly delicate woman, and she held the pistol in both hands and pulled the trigger twice. The short barrel exploded with two loud fiery flashes. Both women immediately realized that the large caliber hand cannon was far too loud for their purpose.

"It's too loud," Annie said. Her ears were still ringing from the echo of the shots.

"You're right. You can hear this thing a mile away," Tammy concured.

"Shit," Annie said.

"We don't have time to get another one," Tammy lamented.

"I know," Annie agreed. "We'll just have to take a chance with the noise."

Sergeant Stack didn't come into Mr. Kim's Donut Shop the next morning.

Around noon, a uniformed cop Angela had never seen before approached her counter.

Eddie Williams had been with the Department for ten years. He was a cocky red headed honky who spoke fairly fluent Spanish.

"Hola," Eddie said.

"I speak English," Angela replied, almost defensively.

"Okay. A cup of joe and two glazed, please."

Eddie's light blue eyes flashed with interest as he spoke to the pretty young Señorita behind the counter.

"You got it." Angela retorted, proud of her acumen in English.

She quickly poured Eddie a cup of hot coffee, and fished a couple of fresh glazed doughnuts out of a tray.

"Where's Sergeant Stack today?" Angela asked.

"What's your name? ¿Como se llama?"

"Angela," she replied. "¿Usted?"

"Eddie Williams."

The cocky cop extended his hand. They politely shook hands.

"Mucho gusto, Señor," she said.

"El gusto es mio," Eddie replied.

"Ah,… ¿Donde es Sergeant Stack? ¿El es amigo de usted?" He inquired.

"Si. Is he hurt?" She asked.

"No, he's fine. After the shooting yesterday, they put him on desk duty. LAPD always takes cops off of field duty after an officer involved shooting. He won't be back until they finish their investigation, and clear the shooting."

"Oh, how long?" Angela questioned.

"It should be fairly quick. Three of the homeboys were wanted on felony warrents. They're all in critical condition, but so far nobody's died. He'll be back in a week or two."

"Oh," Angela replied.

"¿Casada?" Eddie asked, as he took a sip of his coffee.

"No, Señor," Angela answered. "¿Usted?"

"No. Soy soltero."

The cute cop was flirting, Angela concluded. Now that they both knew that the other was single, she wondered what he would say next?

"Ah, hasta luego, Angela." Eddie said. "Pase buen dia."

Some cop chatter coming over the radio Eddie had attached to his belt seemed to be summoning the officer to answer some sort of problem. Eddie quickly left the counter with his coffee in hand.

"Iqualmente," Angela replied, in answer to Eddie's wishing her a pleasant day. Then she noticed he forgot to take his two untouched doughnuts.

"Hey, you forgot your doughnuts," she said.

"Give 'em to the next cop that comes in, bye."

Eddie quickly walked out the door and got into a tan patrol car. Not quite undercover with Eddie in uniform, but low profile.

Angela wondered if Eddie was some kind of special cop? She watched him drive away, then returned to her duties as some loud construction workers wandered in for their morning coffee break.

XXVII

In the days that followed the Carmelita debacle, Jack only saw her at Dan's house a couple of times. She either avoided him, or ignored him. Jack was absolutely heart sick.

Also during this period, Maria Mendez, the Spanish teacher, called Jack several times. She wondered why he hadn't returned to class, and more importantly, why he hadn't returned any of her calls?

Flora also called a few times. Jack never wanted to see Flora again. Although her actions were unintentional, he held her responsible for losing Carmelita.

After Jack finally called Maria back, and explained the drama in his life, she offered to buy him dinner.

Comida and consolation sounded good to Jack. Maria was easy going, compared to all the other women in Jack's life, and they agreed to get together that night for some Chinese food.

Although Maria Mendez had been Jack's other mistake, in terms of making love to the wrong woman, she was also really nice, and not at all demanding beyond hooking up for a little recreational sex.

Despite her strict Catholic upbringing, Maria Mendez had been married and divorced two times. Like a lot of Latinas who grew up riding the cultural divide, Maria was comfortable with looser American mores. She was in no hurry to remarry, and truly enjoyed Jack's company on a physical level. She found him to be an exciting sex partner, especially when measured against some of the boring academic types she'd shared the sack with in recent history.

The day they'd had lunch together at Fin's, they both got very drunk by the time their meal was finished.

Maria was wearing a little low cut black outfit that somewhat revealed the shape of her well rounded breasts. Maria liked Jack's rugged good looks, his interesting military background, and' the fact that he'd been a stuntman. By comparison, he made the other males in her life look like a bunch of whimps.

During lunch she playfully exposed a little more of her tits as she leaned forward in a teasing way. Her actions did not go unnoticed by Jack, who switched to Stolie vodka and orange juice after they finished their wine.

Toward the end of lunch, she asked him if he smoked pot, then during the drive back to the motel, Maria fired up a joint and handed it to Jack.

He took a couple of long hits, and held the cannabis deep in his lungs until he felt the effect of the drug combining with the booze in his system.

Oh, what the hell, let's get ripped, Jack thought. Getting stoned on one thing or another had been an ongoing problem for Jack since his high school days. He'd been pretty good lately, confining his usage to beer and an occasional shot of tequila, but the frustration over getting nowhere with Carmelita, and Maria's sexy presence, caused him to want to really recidivate that afternoon.

Being intoxicated, he also soon initiated sexual contact with the all too willing Spanish teacher. They hugged and kissed and messed around once they got back to Jack's room. They also smoked some more dope and drank the rest of his beer and tequila stash.

Jack's ex-wife carol was truly without peer when it came to the area of living better through chemistry. She had laid some Viagra pills on Jack the night they had sex. Jack popped a tiny blue tablet the second he and Maria returned to his room.

The weed had gone straight to Jack's head and he stumbled as he made his way to the bathroom to eliminate some of the booze in his bladder.

While Jack was in the john, Maria removed her dress, and her bra and panties.

When Jack came out of the head, Maria was sitting naked and cross legged in the center of his bed.

Maria had a nice body, well shaped breasts, and a very neatly cauffed vagina. She had tied her fairly long dark hair into a tight bun atop her head, and was smoking another joint when Jack joined her on the bed.

His head was hazy as Maria moved closer to him after she had another hit off the joint, then dropped the remains into the ashtray on the nightstand. She reached over and groped Jack's dick with one hand and pulled his face to her lips with the other.

They exchanged a long wet sloppy kiss as Maria brought Jack down to a horizontal position on the bed. She quickly removed his shirt and opened his pants and got her hands on the organ she felt stiffening as she continued to massage it tenderly with much anticipation.

Damn, Jack thought, here I go again. His mind was really very foggy, but he wondered if fucking this woman might in some way cause him trouble in the future?

He liked Maria, and she had him pretty well on the hot road to the point of no return as she ran her rather long wet tongue down his chest toward the target area.

Next, he felt her tongue and mouth engulf him in a way that sent him into high sexual gear, and soon they were making love in Maria's preferred position, like a couple of cocker spaniels in heat.

Maria again looked sexy when she picked Jack up, and whisked him to her favorite Chinese restaurant in Calabasas.
They had some weed on the way, cocktails at the bar, then some more drinks during dinner.
Jack had sweet and sour prawns, and drank enough booze to sink a shrimp boat.
Maria was sympathetic, as Jack related his tail of woe.
"You just have too many women in your life, Jack."
"Not now I don't," he lamented.
"Maybe I can help you take your mind off your problems," Maria offered.
Her comment was greeted by silence. Jack knew he was in love with Carmelita, and nothing was going to change that any time soon. Not cocktails, or cannabis, or meaningless copulation.
By the time they finished dinner and returned to Jack's room, they were both totally blasted.
Again, just like dejavu, Jack went to the john, and when he returned he found Maria naked in the center of his bed smoking a joint. The second he saw Maria naked, Carmelita came to mind.

Carmelita wrestled with the idea of forgiving Jack. She was vacillating between giving him another chance, or continuing her stance of never speaking to him again. Men had always caused her nothing but grief.

She looked at the little alarm clock next to her bed, and wondered if she should give Jack a call. Then she entertained the idea of surprising him with a late night visit.

Why do men always lie, she wondered? And why were they all just a bunch of horny bastards?

This train of thought led her to think back to the wonderful sex she had experienced that night with Jack. Before Jack, she had only been with three men, and none had made her come as many times as Jack had during their first sexual encounter.

Oral sex was something somewhat new to her, at least on the receiving end of the deal. Jack was an unselfish lover, who seemed more interested in pleasing her than himself. This too, was a first with Carmelita.

She continued to toy with the idea of taking a bus to Jack's place once she was sure everyone in the house was asleep. A warm glow came over her body as she sat on the edge of her small cot and thought about Jack's hard throbbing cock.

Carmelita tried to switch her thoughts to something else, but a tingling sensation in her groin tested her continence and she continued to ponder the pleasure she had enjoyed having sex with Jack.

Was she losing the battle? She thought about a sexy black bra she had purchased a day before they made love.

The tingling increased as she imagined him penetrating her vagina again. She got up and removed the black bra from one of her bags, and also found a matching pair of panties. Holding the sexy under garments, she returned to her bed and pondered the prospect of surprising Jack with an unannounced knock on his door.

She took off the jeans and tee shirt she was wearing, and felt she should take a shower before deciding whether or not to give that lying lusty Gringo another chance.

Jack had joined Maria on the bed, and helped her finish the joint. Here we go, Jack thought. I'm totally stoned out of my mind, and about to make the same mistake again. Sex with the wrong woman.

His brain was hazy as Maria opened his trousers and started giving him some head.

What the fuck am I doing, Jack thought? I'm really in love with Carmelita.

As Maria continued her work she pulled his pants down to his knees. Her lips had brought him to a full erection, when he suddenly pulled out of her mouth, and rolled away, then reluctantly told her he didn't want to have sex.

"I can't Maria," he said. "I'm in love with Carmelita."

Maria's response was not a happy one. As Jack pulled up his pants and refastened his belt, she layed back with her hands behind her head, and pouted.

"I'm too loaded to drive, Jack. Do you mind if I sleep here tonight?" Maria said, slurring her words in a way that indicated that she was completely intoxicated. "Or are you expecting, what's her name, Carmelita?"

He wasn't expecting Carmelita, so he agreed to let her spend the night, after considering the idea of driving her home, then catching a cab back to the motel.

"I think I'm too loaded to drive, too," Jack said.

"You are too loaded to drive, Jack. Just let me spend the night, she said, as she rolled her pouting face into his pillow.

Half on her stomach, with her buttocks somewhat spread open and one leg pulled up under her, Maria had managed to pose herself in a rather provocative position exposing her wet and very available pubic area.

Jack found this exposure inviting, in spite of his intentions, and he wondered if he could make it through the night without succumbing to the temptation that was now laying on his bed so readily presenting itself.

"I just want you to fuck me a little bit, Jack," she whimpered as she twisted slightly revealing even more of her vagina as she humped her buttocks up a little in Jack's direction.

"I can't," Jack repeated, as he hunted for a cigarette, and tried to look the other way.

It was going to be a long night, but Jack felt good in his air of resolve. If only Carmelita knew what painful lengths he was going to in an effort not to get laid.

Carmelita decided to call Jack first, rather than just show up unannounced. She had a funny feeling that he might be with a woman, when she picked up the phone in the kitchen and dialed his number at the motel.

Carmelita only had one question on her mind, when he answered the phone on the second ring.

"Hola, Jack," Carmelita said.

Jack's heart jumped at the sound of her voice.

"Hola," he said, hesitantly.

"Are you alone?" She asked.

Jack looked at Maria as she turned over onto her back. Her nakedness somehow seemed to totally fill the room.

"Who is it?" Maria said loudly, closing Jack's option to lie to Carmelita.

Carmelita heard the female voice and hung up before Jack had a chance to respond.

"Shit!" He said, as the telephone went dead in his ear.

"Who was it, Honey?" Maria inquired again.

"Carmelita," Jack replied, as a cloud of depression descended on him that no amount of drink or drug could possibly remedy.

XXVIII

Eddie the cop returned to The Donut Shop the next day, and he flirted shamelessly with Angela.

At first she turned down his request for a date. Later, just before he left, she relented and agreed to have dinner with him that night.

Angela had never been out with a Gringo before, but she did have sex with one once.

Rape is actually the correct term. The price she had paid for entry into the United States.

The white Border Patrolman who had caught Angela and a couple of her friends sneaking across the border, had told her in perfect Spanish, that if she didn't cooperate he would charge her with one count of attempted drug smuggling, a lie, plus an additional charge of assaulting a peace officer, another lie. He said she'd end up doing five to ten years in prison, then be deported back to Mexico.

The forced copulation with this creep seemed like the only solution at the time. The actual act made her physically sick, but at least he kept his word and let her go afterwards. Angela managed to put the whole ugly matter behind her, but she wondered now, if she turned down Eddie for a date, would he arrest her on some phony trumped up charge?

Even worse, if she accepted, would he coerce her into having sex by employing the same tactic as the Border Patrolman? If he tried anything funny, she decided she'd immediately inform her friend Sergeant Stack. Somehow she trusted the old Sergeant, and she knew that Eddie was his subordinate.

That night, Angela and Eddie had dinner at a nice restaurant, and then went to a movie.

Eddie was a perfect gentleman on their date. He didn't even try to kiss her good night. The only low point in the evening was when he informed her that one of the homeboys Sergeant Stack had wounded in the gun fight, died earlier that day in the Jail Ward at the USC Medical Center. Now, it might be a few more days, or maybe even longer, before her friend returned to work.

She wondered if she should tell Eddie about her ex-boyfriend's threats, and about the Tammy problem? She wasn't sure. Although Eddie's manners were above reproach that evening, there was also something about him that she couldn't quite figure out. She got the odd feeling, that Eddie was hiding something. Was he dating her for lust, or love, or possibly in the line of duty?

The next day Jack again had a terrible hangover when he came to work. He didn't see Carmelita at the house that morning. He and Dan went straight to the office. There was a big brouhaha erupting when they arrived. It seemed that Diego had failed to change a burned out light bulb in the bathroom fast enough to suit Brad.

Brad was in an absolute tirade over Diego's inability to comprehend colloquial English and respond instantly to Brad's commands.

Brad's arrogance and condescending attitude toward Diego was almost beyond Jack's comprehension. Especially when Jack took into account that this shirt and tie collage boy had probably never done a day's worth of real work in his life. Jack wondered, if this fucking guy could be any more of an asshole if he went to school to study the subject?

The hangover, the incident with Carmelita the previous night, coupled with his disgust in general with everything and everybody, all came into play as Jack decided it was probably time to clean this clown Brad's clock. Brad started up the steps to his office.

Just as Jack was about to make his move, Dan rushed out of his office and announced they had to be in West Covina in forty-five minutes. West Covina was approximately sixty-five miles east of Westlake Village. Sixty-five miles through the traffic clogged arteries of Los Angeles' frustrating freeway system.

Jack's plan, such as it was with Brad, was to accost him in a verbal way, probably by saying something about wanting to make that faggot breeding whore he calls his momma, cry. Then let him make the first move. Fortunately for Brad, Dan's interruption possibly saved the day. Brad disappeared into his office, then as usual, Dan said he forgot something and retreated back into his lair.

Jack knew it was time to grab a quick smoke and stepped outside to wait for Dan.

Outside he ran into a guy he'd come to know from his time in the parking lot.

Lance was a dapper dressing guy with a very neatly trimmed gray beard. From their brief chats from time to time, Jack learned that Lance was an idealistic lawyer who had gone to Berkeley back in the Sixties. He'd also seen Lance on TV from time to time.

He certainly cut quite a handsome figure as a criminal defense attorney, and he always took time to stop and chat with Jack.

Today, Jack asked for his card. The way things were going, Jack knew he might need a good lawyer any second.

Lance was in a hurry, but he gave Jack his card and said, "If you ever have a problem, give me a call."

"You're probably too expensive for me Lance," Jack said.

"I defend people, not pocketbooks. If I like the person, or I find the case interesting, I'll defend 'em if they buy me a large pizza."

As Lance vanished down the pathway to his office, another buddy of Jack's joined him for a smoke.

Bob was one of the guys who worked next door with the cute red head. He too, thought Brad was a pompous ass.

"When you gonna kick Brad's butt?" Bob asked, as he lit a cigarette.

"I almost did this morning."

"I figured. I saw you take Lance's card."

Jack laughed. Brad had been the subject of a number of their conversations. Bob used to drive a big rig, before he got an office job.

"Lance always ends up on TV. Kill Brad and you'll be national news, and Lance'll probably get you off."

Just then, Dan emerged from the office running.

"Where you off to?" Bob inquired.

"West Covina," Jack replied.

"That's gonna be a mess."

"Tell me," Jack said, as he flipped his cigarette butt into the street.

"What's the deadline?"

"I think thirty-seven minutes, now."

"Good luck."

"Thanks," Jack said, as he jumped into the Lincoln.

On their way to West Covina, Dan asked Jack what he said to the guy next door about Brad?

"About Brad?" Jack replied, rhetorically.

"You don't like him, do you?" Dan asked, exercising a hint of authority in his voice.

"No." Jack replied, visibly irritated by Dan's inquiry.

"What'd you say to what's his name next door?"

"Oh, I don't know," Jack said, really not liking the tone of Dan's inquisition. "Something about wanting to rip off Brad's mother fucking pussy face and wipe his ass with it, I think."

"Oh," Dan replied. His utterance didn't reflect any feeling one way or the other. Dan was always very hard to read.

Jack was in a horrible mood, but he hoped he hadn't blown it with Dan. He needed to hang onto his job.

Jack still hadn't totally made up his mind about Dan. He just couldn't quite figure him out. And what the hell was he up to business wise? Secret meetings. Tough looking Middle Eastern types, up scale yuppies, and enough tension in the air to keep things on edge almost all the time.

It seemed like Dan worked every waking hour. He also juggled Tammy, five kids, a secret girlfriend, his business stuff, and he still managed to find time to play some golf. He also kept current on sports. Dan was sharp as a nail in most areas, and Jack also concluded, his boss was dangerously competitive.

Jack marveled at the guy's energy as he watched Dan shuffle through a maze of legal documents he had rifled out of his main briefcase shortly after they left the office. Whatever Dan was up to now, had something to do with airplanes.

After Dan's noncommittal, "Oh," they discontinued conversation for the rest of the drive. Sports radio, and a couple of phone calls occupied Dan's attention. For Jack, thoughts of Carmelita filled his head. How could things go so wrong?

Traffic turned out to be lighter than usual and Jack got to Dan's destination within the allotted time.

Later that night, when Jack finally dropped Dan off at home, he said he needed to use the bathroom before he headed for his motel.

Jack used the excuse to look for Carmelita. He found her in the garage doing the laundry. As he approached, she turned and focused her attention on the clothes she was loading into the big dryer.

"Carmelita, necesitamos hablar," Jack said. "I need to talk to you."

"No quiero hablar."

Jack's hangover was still plaguing his head, so he switched to English because summoning words in Spanish suddenly became very difficult for him.

"Are you ever going to speak to me again?"

"Posible nunca," she answered, without looking at him.

"Maybe never, huh? Hey, I'm sorry. Lo siento. Look, when you called I had a woman there, but I wasn't having sex. And I didn't have sex with her. We just had dinner together, that's all, and that's the truth, damn it!"

She finished putting the wet clothes in the dryer and hit the start button hard. Next, she turned and walked past him on her way out of the garage.

"Won't you just talk to me? Please, he begged.

"No, I'm busy," she said, as she passed through the door and reentered the house.

Jack followed her into the kitchen where he ran into Dan who was retrieving something from the refrigerator. Dan glared at Jack when he noticed he was pursuing Carmelita for some reason.

"I thought you went home?" Dan questioned.

"I had a Spanish question for Carmelita."

"Oh, yeah," Dan said. "Did you get an answer?"

"Yeah, I guess I did. See ya tomorrow."

"Okay, just make sure you're on time. We've got to be in Long Beach by nine."

"I'll be here."

"Six sharp."

"Yeah, six am sharp. See ya in the morning," Jack said, as he made his way out of the kitchen. By this time Carmelita had left the kitchen and vanished into the bowels of the big house.

XXIX

Exactly ten days after the shooting, Sergeant Stack returned to field duty. When he walked into The Donut Shop Angela greeted him warmly. He smiled in return.

After they exchanged pleasantries, she got right to the point. She explained the situation with her ex-boyfriend, and also the dilemma concerning Tammy and the murder plot.

Stack said he wanted to talk to Carmelita as soon as possible, and suggested that they meet sometime that day. He told her he would change into civilian clothes and pick Angela up as soon as she got off work. Stack checked his watch. It was 11:35, and Angela's shift ended at noon.

He quickly finished his coffee, left her the usual five, and said he'd be back in twenty minutes.

Sergeant Stack left The Donut Shop, and just as he was getting into his black and white, a series of loud shots from a military style assault rifle ripped across his chest, slamming him back against a nearby wall. After the violent volley of gunfire, he fell to the pavement in a motionless heap.

Angela screamed in horror as she witnessed the cold blooded shooting of her friend. She also saw a low white sedan with a bare headed gunman leaning out the back window speed away from the scene.

Mr. Kim, who also saw the shooting, ran to the phone and called 911. Algela rushed outside to help her fallen friend.

A curious crowd quickly gathered and the place was swarming with cops and paramedics within what seemed like only a matter of seconds.

They were all too late, however. Angela knew the moment she looked at Sergeant Stack's lifeless body laying on the ground, that the old cop was dead.

Angela was soon approached by a nice bilingual paramedic. His name tag identified him as Lopez. Angela was sitting on the pavement with her back against the shop's wall, crying. Although very upset, she still managed to maintain her composure. Angela was a strong young woman.

"Do you understand English?" Lopez asked.

"Yes."

"Was he a friend of yours?"

"Yes."

"¿Usted una Méxicana?"

"Si," Angela replied.

"Lo siento, Señorita," Lopez offered, saying that he was very sorry.

Angela could tell by his accent that Lopez was a Chincano who had learned Spanish as a second language. He did however possess a certain soothing manner.

Another younger paramedic approached the two and addressed Lopez in a tone that suggested that Lopez was the senor man in charge on the scene.

"It's funny. We didn't find any blood," the junior paramedic told his superior.

"I know. It looks like he died of a heart attack. His vest stopped the bullets," Lopez stated.

This news did not ease Angela's shock or pain. At this point she looked up and noticed Eddie making inquires. She hadn't talked to him since she learned from another cop that Eddie was married.

Once Eddie spotted Angela, he quickly came to her side.

"We got 'em," Eddie said. "How are you doin'?"

Angela just looked up and shook her head, then said softly, "Me siento muy mal."

"Si. Yo entiendo," Eddie said, sympathically. "Yo tambien."

Just then, Angela noticed that Mr. Kim was standing not too far away. No one was consoling him, and old Mr. Kim looked like he too had been crying.

Angela got up off the ground and went to her boss' side. She touched his arm with both hands, and tried to comfort the old gentleman.

"I'm sorry, Mr. Kim. He was your friend for a long time, no?" She asked in a very somber voice.

"Yes, for fifteen years. He was very nice man. Always pay. He remind me of GIs I knew during the War in Korea when I was a boy. And he die like GI," Mr. Kim said, sadly.

Mr. Kim turned and walked away. He wanted to be alone with his memories and his sorrow.

Later that day, Jack managed to corner Carmelita in the back yard. Their conversation was a short one.

"I no want to talk to you," she said.

"I know. That's why I wrote you a note."

Jack tried to hand her a neatly folded little note that he had painstakingly written in Spanish. She refused to take the note.

"No quiero, Jack," she said, as she turned her attention to the loud group of unruly children she was busy supervising.

Jack stuck the note in a crack in the fence, positioning it carefully at her eye level.

"I'll leave it here, just in case you change your mind."

"I no change my mind," she said.

Jack looked at his watch and knew Dan would be ready to hit the road again any second. That afternoon they were headed for Landcaster.

"Jack, I have to talk to you," Tammy said, catching Jack off guard.

He turned and saw Tammy approaching. She was dressed in hot pink shorts and a thin tank top that silhouetted the shape of her breasts in a very provocative way.

He saw Carmelita watching as Tammy led him away and engaged him in a private conversation. Carmelita watched Jack agree to Tammy's request, and something about the body language between the two made her suspect that maybe her boss was somehow using Jack in her murder plot. She also wondered if Jack and Tammy had ever had sex?

The next day, Saturday, was Jack's day off. It was also his birthday. No one in his present life knew it was his birthday, so he wasn't expecting any calls.

He wondered if maybe Carmelita had changed her mind and read his note. The note basically begged her to reconsider. He told her he loved her, that he wanted to marry her, and that he was so very sorry that he had lied to her. He also explained once again that when she had called, he wasn't having sex with the Spanish teacher. Then he promised that he would never lie to her again, ever, about anything, if only she would give him another chance.

Actually, he wasn't at all optimistic. Her attitude really indicated that whatever chance he had with her, had been lost. By noon, Jack decided that he would spend the day drinking.

He walked up to the store on the corner and bought some beer and a bottle of tequila.

By two-thirty that afternoon, Jack was about half in the bag. The phone rang, and his heart jumped. He grabbed the receiver before the end of the first ring, and much to his disappointment Tammy was on the other end.

The day before in the backyard, Tammy had alluded to him that she might be on the verge of asking him to do her a big favor.

She wasn't very specific, and Jack, totally consumed with the Carmelita problem, hadn't really speculated about her intentions. Tammy often talked in riddles.

Today, she had a rather strange request. Jack's depression, and state of intoxication caused him to readily agree to her odd proposal.

What the hell, it was his birthday. If Carmelita didn't call, the only other thing on his mind, was to maybe shoot himself.

Tammy said she'd come by within the hour. Jack had another drink, and waited for his boss' sexy wife to arrive.

Back at Dan's house, Carmelita had suddenly left after someone called. She said she had to attend to a family emergency. Tammy had left, but not before enlisting the aid of Rosarita from next door to help watch the kids.

Dan had secluded himself in his office upstairs, but he was concerned about the children running wild while poor Rosarita's negligible child wrangling skills were being put to the test downstairs.

The phone call Dan had been waiting for came and he snapped up the receiver the second it rang.

"Hello."

Dan listened for a few moments, thought about what he had just heard, then replied in a decisive voice.

"Well, it better happen quick!" Dan said, then he abruptly hung up the phone.

Jack ran his hands through her blond hair, then he laid back on his bed and enjoyed the wonderful fellatio she was so lovingly and expertly performing on his very erect penis. This was an activity in which she truly excelled.

Except for Tammy's brief visit, Jack had been drinking alone in his room all day.

When his ex-wife Carol called to wish him a Happy Birthday, and hit him up for a couple a hundred bucks, he said, "Sure, come on by."

Jack had recently picked up a slew of residual checks, and he actually had some dough for a change. He received his mail at a P.O. Box over in North Hollywood, and because of the odd and long hours working for Dan, sometimes he didn't get a chance to go by there for weeks at a time. During his career as a stuntman, Jack had doubled a number of major movie stars, but usually only once. Something always seemed to happen. Jack was never any good at kissing ass, an essential requirement in the movie business.

Jack was actually glad to see Carol today. He'd always had a certain weakness for her. Sexual passion had gotten them together in the first place, and kept them together long after the their relationship had soured. They were married a total of four years. Four of the most tumultuous, incredibly miserable years of Jack's life, except for the sex. Only his recent love making experience with Carmelita had exceeded the pleasure he'd known with Carol.

Jack had met Carol on a movie set while he was working as a stuntman. She was absolutely beautiful beyond belief.

Jack had remembered her from a series of shampoo commercials that had run constantly over a period of several years. At the time they met, Carol had recently turned years of lucrative work as a model and commercial actress, into a somewhat less than successful acting career.

When he met her she was in her late twenties, and she was in the process of destroying both her life and career with heavy and careless drug use. Cocaine was her drug of choice, but Carol would also use just about anything else that came down the pike.

She had watched Jack do a high fall off the top of a six story building, and introduced herself just as he was rolling out of the air bag that had broken his fall.

Jack had almost missed the bag, hitting it right on the edge, so at the moment he felt lucky just to be alive. The beautiful blond actress immediately took his mind off the near brush with death or crippling injury.

She cheerfully complimented him on his fall, causing him to ignore the disapproving glare of the stunt coordinator with whom he was certain he would never work again.

Carol had an incredible sexual appetite. She was also the most gorgeous woman Jack had ever seen. Her film career had never made it past the B movie straight to video stage, and at the time when she and Jack hooked up, even that work was becoming hard for her to find.

None of this mattered to Jack. She just flat turned him on. Once copulation occurred, she became the best sexual partner Jack had ever known. Carol was an incredible lover, and she had an alert sense of humor. She was the prettiest girl on earth, and was also esoterically intelligent. Jack fell in love with her instantly.

The first time they had sex was on the night they met, in the small set trailer that served as her dressing room. They went there immediately after work, and they kept it up, so to speak, for almost five hours.

They drank wine, smoked weed, Carol did some coke, and they playfully explored the many pleasures of their new found passion. At first they hit it off on every level.

Jack moved into her two story house in Studio City the following week. The intensity of their sex life demanded that they live together. In the beginning, their affair was hot and fun. Carol had wrapped on the picture the afternoon after their first sexual encounter, and she was able to devote all her time and energy to their romantic adventure.

Jack's work pattern at the time was sporadic at best. He'd sometimes go for weeks without working. Carol's house in the Valley was very cozy. It had hardwood floors, two fireplaces, a nice pool, and somewhat spacious grounds. Jack liked Studio City. It was a charming area, with all sorts of interesting shops and neat restaurants.

The residential streets were quiet and tree lined. Her house was on a street that offered a host of white picket fences, some nice Colonial houses, and several red tile roofed early California Spanish places like the one Carol owned. A white washed ivy covered seven foot wall surrounded the house. Her ample swimming pool occupied the center of the backyard, and their privacy was assured by a row of tall trees that lined the wall to her property in the back.

Jack had always thought that Studio City was one of the best locations in the San Fernando Valley. It was very close to Hollywood over either Laurel or Coldwater Canyon, and it was also close to the Ventura Freeway and the many Valley movie studios.

However, it didn't make a whole lot of difference how close Jack was to the movie studios during that period of underemployment. Jack just had a hard time making a living doing stunt work. He had never quite gotten into the clique.

When he was in the Marine Corps, he'd served with a guy named Charlie Smith, whose much older brother was a big time stuntman. Jack looked up his buddy Charlie, right after he got out of the Corps.

For almost five years Jack hung out with some stunt guys, and eventually after working a lot of extra jobs, and years of going to weekly stunt practice, he finally started occasionally working as a stuntman shortly after he turned thirty.

Over the next few years he eked out a modest living and had a really great time. When he worked he made good money, and he met a lot of pretty girls. He did plenty of partying, hung out with some interesting Hollywood types, and lived in a small apartment in Tarzana.

As far as stunt work was concerned, Jack always thought that it was very much like being back in the Marine Corps. It was all about blowing up stuff, jumping off of things, fighting, staying in good physical shape, and shooting guns.

The only real difference was in stunt work, when you fought, you tried not to hurt the other guy. It was a fun way to make a living. A man's job, not some whimpy ass kind of work.

When Jack and Carol got together, her unfortunate decline was already well underway. Jack tried his best to help her. Their love was strong, and for a short while in the beginning, Jack got just enough work to keep them afloat. Carol stopped hunting for work, because the rejection always seemed to send her off on a binge.

Aside from the house, Carol had very little to show for her ten years as a top model, and her few bumpy years in the acting field. The same erratic behavior that had caused Carol's career to decline, soon began to affect their relationship.

After Carol had one particularly ugly relapse into heavy drug use, they had a terrible fight. When they finally made up, they decided to go up to Las Vegas and get married. Logic had never been one of Jack's strong points when it came to love.

By the time their turbulent marriage was over, Jack had pretty much given up any hope of ever finding true happiness. However, even with all the drama and bitterness Jack and Carol had endured during their marriage, they almost always managed to stay somewhat in touch, and occasionally lust would draw them together for a little sexual tryst.

Carol was currently living in a tiny apartment in Sherman Oaks, and she constantly had trouble making the rent. She had lost her house shortly after both their careers dried up three years into their marriage.

When she came over that Saturday on his birthday, he offered little more than token resistance to her other request after he gave her some money to cover her rent.

A birthday blow job was the least she could do, considering he'd absolutely saved her ass from certain eviction, Carol told him.

In a moment of weakness, Jack agreed. Carol's talents may have eroded in other areas, but in oral sex, she was still at the top of her game.

Jack had gotten so drunk that afternoon, that he had totally given up hope of ever being with Carmelita. As Jack looked down at Carol, his mind drifted back to the first time she had taken him all the way home using her beautiful lips.

It was that first night on the set in her tiny dressing room trailer. As Carol was in the final stages of giving him the most incredible head he'd ever experienced, he complimented her on her beauty, and told her she was, on a Hollywood scale of one to ten, a quintessential TEN, in capital letters.

She protested the moment she finished the act by saying, "No, I'm actually an eleven. You know what an eleven is, Jack?"

"Ah, no," Jack admitted he didn't, almost inaudibly.

"It's a ten that swallows," Carol said, as she wiped a drop of fresh semen from the corner of her incredibly beautiful wet pouting mouth.

Again, Jack's head spun as Carol finished her work. He layed back on the bed, feeling both the effects of the booze, and the mind numbing ejaculation he had just experienced. Carol, however, quickly snapped him back into the reality of the present with her next unexpected comment.

"So what do you say when you want one of your little beaner chicks to suck your dick?" Carol asked.

Oh, God, here we go, Jack thought, pretty much stuck for an answer.

"Well?" Carol implored, as she grabbed his organ a little to hard.

"Ah,…please."

"No, tell me in Spanish," she demanded.

"Okay, please let go. You're hurting me, Carol."

"Good," she said, releasing her grip. "Now tell me in Spanish."

"Por favor," Jack answered.

"Oh, how cute. I've always wanted to fuck a beaner chick, I hear they're hot?"

"Carol, please."

"Say, por favor."

Carol always had a way of ending up being a pain in the ass. It was part of what Jack felt was her consistency.

Carol left shortly after giving Jack his birthday present. She had also managed to thoroughly piss him off. All his life, he had absolutely hated racist crap, and sometimes Carol could be a bit of a racist bitch.

Jack finished off what was left of his booze, and soon fell into a deep sleep. He had a dream about Carmelita, but it was not a very good dream. She had caught him in another lie. She asked him what Carol had given him for his birthday, and he told her a tie.

XXX

Esthetically the office complex Dan used in Westlake Village was very pleasing to the eye, Jack thought. Tasteful California Spanish architecture had always been Jack's favorite.

A guy named E. Dallas Farnsworth III ran the place. He was probably in his fifties, Jack figured. Jack heard that E. Dallas actually owned the place, but he looked more like a guy who made blue movies, or hung out a lot at the racetrack. Since the day Jack straightened out the problem with Juan and Diego's paychecks, E. Dallas had always cast him a jaundice eye.

His daughter Cindy, however, who was in her early twenties, was quite a fox. She worked in her dad's office.

Westlake Village certainly had an abundance of beautiful gals, Jack observed. His weakness in that area caused him to like good old Westlake Village on that level.

Jack watched Cindy Farnsworth approach on her way to deliver some missives addressed to their tenants. He had just fired up a smoke and taken his usual position on the parkway.

"Hi, Jack," Cindy said, cheerfully.

"Hi, Cindy."

Cindy was wearing a cute black mini skirt, a crisp sleeveless blouse, and heels. She also had a big smile on her pretty face.

"Beautiful day, isn't it?"

"Yeah," Jack replied. "I like your blouse. That color blue looks good on you."

"Thanks."

With her dark hair, light skin, and well shaped face, Cindy looked good in just about anything, Jack thought, as he watched her pass by.

"See ya later, Jack," Cindy said, as she looked back over her shoulder and continued on her mission.

"Bye, Cindy."

Jack's eyes followed Cindy as she walked away. She had very erect posture, big tits, a nice ass, and Jack knew instinctively that Cindy was probably nothing but trouble. He was sure that's why he found her appealing.

Suddenly Zorro appeared by the duck pond. Black hat, shirt, pants, boots, and mask, in full view of all the offices in that area. Zorro's outfit was complete except he didn't have a sword.

Jack did a double take, and wondered if he was seeing a ghost, or had he simply just lost his mind?

Then a woman suddenly appeared in a costume from the same era, except her face was covered with a grotesque Mexican Day of the Dead mask.

Then, Zorro, without a sword, suddenly whipped out his erect penis. The woman lifted her long skirt and dropped onto her back on the bench by the pond, and spread her legs.

Jack couldn't believe his eyes. Next, Zorro mounted the woman and humped her vigorously for about forty seconds. Once the sex act was done, they both disappeared in opposite directions.

Up to that point, Jack had always thought that the folks in this community were pretty boring. Just then Dan showed up.

"Come on, Jack. We gotta go."

"You won't believe what I just saw!"

"I saw it, too. Probably the same couple from Albertsons parking lot. They're the talk of the town," Dan said, seemingly unimpressed by it all.

If they're the talk of the town, how come I never heard about it? Jack wondered, as they walked to the Lincoln.

When they got back to the office about an hour later, Jack had to have a smoke, and check out how many office windows had a view of the duck pond.

Just as Jack was surveying the scene of the crime, he ran into Lance the lawyer who was leaving with a big box of briefs in hand. Jack knew that Lance's upstairs office overlooked the pond.

"Hey, Lance. Did you see,…"

"Oh, yeah. I'll tell ya, when they get caught, now there's an interesting case. Talk about freedom of expression."

"I hear they've been doin' it all over town," Jack said.

"Yeah. The ice rink, Albertsons, Home Depot. They're quite the traveling act. Gotta run, bye."

Lance, who was always in a hurry, jumped into a waiting car, driven by one of his assistants.

As Jack was finishing his cigarette and walking back towards his boss' office, Brad pulled up in his tank, effecting casting a dark cloud over the area.

Cindy was still busy running around visiting all the tenants in the complex. Jack figured they were probably raising the rent when he watched her hand a document to Brad as he exited his SUV.

He immediately got into a huff when he examined the contents of the papers she gave him. Cindy said something to the effect that Brad would have to discuss the matter with her father, then she left without further conversation. Obviously there was no love lost between these two, Jack thought, as Cindy passed him and smiled on her way back to her office.

Damn, she has a nice walk, Jack observed, as he watched Cindy until she reached her destination.

Jack decided to have another cigarette, rather than risk a run in with Brad by entering the office. He watched as Brad read the papers in his hands, while he continued a conversation on his ear piece cell phone, that even an earthquake was probably incapable of interrupting.

Jack was so sick of watching these self indulgent arrogant greedy assholes like Brad, trying to get something for nothing. Whatever happened to honest labor? Or at very least, peddling something tangible.

Jack also had the feeling the dot-com balloon was about to break. He read about unfolding dot-com debacles almost daily, and it didn't surprise him a bit. The Business section of the L.A. Times continued to be very entertaining reading.

Carmelita was beginning to have second thoughts about the way she had handled the situation with Jack. Even though she fought it, in her heart she felt that she was probably in love with him. It wasn't just the sex, although she did think about that often. There was something else about Jack. He was not the same as the other Gringos she had known. He tried to learn Spanish, and he also didn't seem to hold any kind of racial prejudice. Most Gringos felt they were superior just because they were white, but she never got that feeling from Jack.

It was the lying thing, but then again, all men lie. This was hammered home again when Angela told her that she found out from another policeman, that her friend Eddie the cop was married.

She had taken Jack's note out of the crack in the fence, but she still hadn't read its contents. It had remained folded up in her pocket since that day. Also, another problem had presented itself recently. Carmelita hadn't had her period since she and Jack had sex.

When Jack ran into Carmelita the next morning at Dan's house, she actually cracked a slight smile and spoke to him.

"Hola, Jack. ¿Como estas?"

"Hola," Jack replied. "Bien, gracias. ¿Y tu?"

"Bien. I look at note."

"Oh," he said, unable to mask his reaction to her change in attitude.

Just then, Dan walked in sporting a foul mood, and effectively ended Jack and Carmelita's conversation.

"Let's go Jack, I'm in a hurry."

"Hasta luego. Llama me."

"Si," she replied.

"There's some dirty shirts on my bed, Carmelita. We don't pay you to stand around and talk, we pay you to work."

Jack glared at Dan, and came within a breath of decking the son-of-a-bitch. *Before this little adventure is over, I'm really gonna kick Dan's ass bad for that comment,* Jack vowed.

Back at the office that afternoon Jack encountered Brad again. Brad, who was usually busy putting out fires or accomplishing something awesome, in his vernacular, was unusually sullen that afternoon.

This in no way interfered with his attitude of condescension, he just wasn't his normal upbeat sickening self, Jack noticed.

The dot-com world was taking a dive, and Jack wondered if this self styled genius of cyberspace was losing his ass. *Gee, what a shame,* Jack thought.

Jack had been downstairs speaking Spanish with Diego the nice maintenance man, who had come by to replace a cracked mirror in the bathroom. While they were chatting outside the john, Brad entered the office in a huff.

Brad charged up the stairs and got on his hard line phone in his office. He left the door to his office open. Why couldn't Brad close the door? Jack knew he often left it open so others would hear him wheel and deal.

It always irritated Jack when he had to listen to his dick's one sided verbal dribble. Jack was no grammarian, but the way this clown mangled English syntax, he wondered how Brad ever completed four years of college? His mommy and daddy sure wasted a bunch of money there.

On the phone Brad was apparently dealing with a dissatisfied investor. After the conversation ended Brad came running back down the stairs with a look of absolute distress on his pussy face.

"Good afternoon, sir," Diego said, to Brad.

Brad of course was too busy or too important to reply in any language. He hastily went to a stack of mail on the counter by the coffee machine and starting separating his mail from Dan's.

"Aveses estoy muy avergonzado porque soy un Gringo," Jack said.

This comment in Spanish elicited only a nasty glare from Brad. Diego wondered why Jack had just said, that sometimes he was very ashamed to be a Gringo.

Inside his office, Dan was having a serious conversation on the phone.

"Well, I'll tell ya, it better happen pretty quick! I'm gettin' God damned tired of waiting!"

Dan listened for a few moments.

"No. It has to happen now!" Dan said, in a very decisive tone.

Jack stepped outside and walked over to the parkway to have a smoke. Within moments Brad rushed off in his SUV undoubtedly on his way to put out a fire somewhere. Whenever he saw Brad leave, Jack was always relieved. Hanging on to his sense of decorum was becoming increasingly difficult. Also, he swore if Dan ever made another disrespectful comment to Carmelita in his presence, it would cost his boss a couple of rows of teeth.

Jack figured he'd really better watch it today, his fuse was getting far too short.

No sooner then Jack crushed out his cigarette, a big Fed Ex truck pulled up in front of the office. He knew their regular Fed Ex guy, but today there was a different driver. As Jack got near the office door he heard the new driver yell at him.

"Hey, do you work in 107?"

"Yeah," Jack replied.

The driver held out a package to Jack. Jack usually signed for Dan's stuff, although he didn't recognize the company name on the package.

"It's also addressed to a Mr. Brad Rodriguez," the driver said.

Jack looked at the label and was absolutely astounded when he learned that Brad's last name was Rodriguez.

Brad didn't particularly look Latino, but he did have dark hair and dark eyes. His skin was somewhat light, and his extreme arrogance toward Hispanics made this revelation all the more astounding. What a piece of shit, Jack thought, as he refused to sign for the package.

About twenty minutes later, Jack spirits suddenly soared when an unexpected chance to see Carmelita arose. Dan stepped outside and told Jack that the kids needed a ride home from school.

Once he arrived at the middle school Jack was greeted by a daisy chain of gas guzzlers lined up the length of the block in front of the school.

Look at all these spoiled white folks, Jack thought. Almost all the faces were caucasian, with a smattering of Asians here and there. Jack didn't see any blacks or Latinos.

Certainly a lot of these kids were in immanent danger of leg atrophy. Tammy and Dan lived a good three blocks from the school.

Now, as a child Jack didn't exactly walk sixteen miles in the snow to get to school, but he did walk a mile or so like everybody else. These yuppie kids were spoiled and pampered beyond belief, Jack thought. The idiocy of all these up scale people driving their precious offspring this short distance struck Jack as absolutely absurd, but it did offer him an opportunity to see Carmelita.

Jack concluded that he was probably being far too critical, and he quickly turned his thoughts again to Carmelita. God, she made him feel good again that morning. She'd read the note, and now he felt that maybe there was a chance of reconciliation with the beautiful Señorita.

Then, the slow moving cars caught Jack's attention again, as the creeping line slowly snaked its way toward the flag pole in front of the school. This is where he was instructed to meet the children. Jack watched the drivers, mostly women, yakking on their omnipresent cell phones.

What did their husbands do for a living, Jack wondered? They were probably all engaged in selling each other some kind of dumb service. He also figured most of the stuff these people owned was no where near being free and clear.

What's going to happen if the economy crashes? Look at history. It's 2001 for Christ's sake, we're overdue for a crash.

Finally Jack pulled up to the flag pole area and a phalanx of screaming children jumped into the Lincoln.

Minutes later, when he delivered the hoard of noisy kids, he was met in front of Dan's house by Rosarita, not Carmelita.

The car load of kids quickly disgorged and attacked the house like an army of avenging Huns.

"Where's Carmelita?" Jack asked. He knew Rosarita, and she insisted that they always speak English. She had been in this country for years, and her superb command of English was a point of pride with her.

"Carmelita was sick, so she went home to her family's place in the Valley. Her sister came and picked her up about an hour ago," Rosarita informed him.

"Oh," Jack replied. His disappointment was highly visible.

The kids suddenly came screaming back out of the house, all demanding to be taken various places. Their cries were deafening. What a price I paid, and with no payoff, Jack thought, as he prepared to counter the demands of the noisy impatient children.

"I'm sorry, I'm off duty," Jack told the clamoring crowd.

The resulting cacophony of complaining kids caused Jack to retreat into the car. He watched as the kids fell into Panzer formation in front of Rosarita. His heart went out to her as he gently hit the gas pedal and carefully backed out of the driveway.

Angela and Carmelita got stuck in heavy traffic, and it took them well over an hour to get to their place in Pacoima. Today the delay was okay, because Carmelita had much to discuss with her little sister.

Carmelita began their conversation by getting right to the point. She told Angela that she thought she was pregnant.

During the hour and twenty minute drive, they discussed the matter at great length.

Finally, Carmelita asked about the cop Angela had approached concerning the Tammy murder plot?

"El murio," Angela said, sadly, informing her sister that her policeman friend was dead.

"¿No?" Carmelita replied.

"Si, y estoy muy triste," Angela added, saying that his death made her very sad.

Angela then went on to describe the details, and also the possible motive.

Now, Carmelita was troubled in three areas. The cops still didn't know about Tammy, and Carmelita was certain that somebody was going to die. What should she do?

Secondly, she felt real compassion for poor Angela who had a big heart, and she knew her little sister was taking the death of her friend very hard. She had spoken highly of Sergeant Stack. She said he wasn't the least bit prejudice, and that he tried to do his job fairly.

He had treated Angela with respect, and indeed she said, he was that way with everyone. Carmelita felt bad for Angela, and she also felt bad about losing the opportunity to discuss the Tammy problem with a decent cop.

Thirdly. Was she pregnant? She would know the day after tomorrow. That was the earliest she could get an appointment.

"¿Cuando?" Angela asked.

"El dia después mañana."

"¿Si?"

"Si."

Carmelita was going to a clinic to see a doctor at nine in the morning that Thursday. What if the test turns out positive?

As Jack parked the Lincoln near his room, he immediately saw Tammy waiting for him in her car. She jumped out looking really foxy in a short skirt and an almost see through blouse.

"Hi, Tammy," Jack said. His words really asked a question.

"Hi, Jack," Tammy said, with a smile. "I need you."

"Oh, yeah?" Jack replied.

"Can we go inside?"

"I guess so."

Surely this was going to create some sort of dilemma. Jack was certain Tammy's visit spelled trouble.

He opened the door to his room, and Tammy quickly slid into his dark abode. Jack followed her inside and flipped the light switch. Nothing happened. The room remained dark.

"How romantic," Tammy offered, in a cute voice.

"Yeah, it's a nice feature. It's been broken for a week," he said, as he switched on the light over his table and closed the door behind him.

"Got any tequila?" She asked.

"Of course," Jack said, as he fished a fresh bottle out of his sock drawer. "Straight with a beer chaser?"

"You got it."

"May I?" She asked, as she sat on the edge of his bed.

"Be my guest."

Outside, Nancy, with a stack of clean towels in hand, quickly approached Jack's door.

The flow of female traffic in and out of Jack's room was a constant source of fascination and gossip among the motel staff.

The other blond woman's back, Nancy noted, as she paused for a moment, then rapped on Jack's door.

Nancy's unexpected knock abruptly interrupted Tammy and Jack's conversation. He had just handed her a shot of tequila, and she had just asked him a question.

"What?" Jack said.

"I want to borrow your gun. And there's something in it for you I don't think you can refuse," Tammy said, as she cracked an impish smile and crossed her naked legs.

"My what?"

"Your little gun," Tammy intoned, as she let her expensive gold lame flip flops fall from her feet.

Nancy rapped on the door again, and firmly announced, "Hello, Housekeeping."

Jack answered the door and was greeted with an arm full of clean towels, and a curious look.

"Gracias," Jack said, politely.

"De nada, Señor Jack." Nancy replied. "¿Ocupado?"

"Si," Señor Jack answered. Nancy could be a little playful at times. That's why he liked her.

"You are very busy man, lately. ¿No?"

"Si," Jack replied.

"Okay, bye." Nancy said, as she turned and quickly vanished from view.

"Now, where were we?" Tammy asked, as Jack shut the door.

He knew he was in a bind. Tammy was the kind of woman who always got what she wanted.

Jack went to his little fridge and retrieved a couple of beers and popped the caps. He set one bottle on the table next to his bed by Tammy.

"Thanks," she said.

At this point, Jack thought, why does life have to be so damn complicated? Why can't Carmelita and I just ride off into the sunset?

"You really like those little Spanish broads, don't you?" Tammy said, as she took a healthy sip of tequila.

"Huh?" Jack responded. He always played dumb, poorly.

"Jack, I'm going to tell you a secret," Tammy said, seriously.

Oh, no, Jack thought.

Tammy's short skirt slipped up her leg a tad, as her body became tense with passion concerning the subject she was about to discuss.

XXXI

It was just after sunset and the ritzy Westlake Hyatt Plaza Hotel was alive with activity.

Allen Horwitz parked his Porsche some distance from the main entrance. On this occasion, Allen was completely and accurately dressed as a circus clown. His costume was replete with big red shoes, bright yellow outfit, large red wig, and a huge round red nose affixed to his expertly made-up face.

The Hyatt Plaza Hotel was a popular gathering spot for all types of business and social events. Its main lobby was large with comfortable sofas, a grand piano, and a bar at the far end. Just inside the main entrance there was a large lovely fountain.

Allen entered the lobby were he was immediately joined by a female clown who had entered the hotel through another door.

She was dressed in an almost matching outfit, except she was wearing a short red skirt and bright yellow tights. Her wig, her nose, and large floppy shoes mirrored Allen's outfit.

The girl clown quickly sat on the edge of the large fountain in the center of the foyer and leaned back and lifted her little red skirt. The crotch of her yellow tights had been neatly cut out revealing her shiny black smoothly shaved vagina, with its exposed pink wet lips, ready. As usual, she had primed herself well during the short drive to the hotel rendezvous.

Allen was always primed. He needed little more than the hot anticipation of their brazen public sexual encounters to turn him on. He quickly whipped out his tool and went to work penetrating her deeply, and causing her to squeal with delight.

"Hey, there are a couple of clowns fucking in the foyer," an indignant guest said, catching the attention of a fat security guard, who was on duty not far from the fountain in question.

The slow moving corpulent guard suspected the complaining man had just come from the nearby bar.

"You mean a couple of fucking clowns?" The guard inquired, with a chuckle.

The guard had seen the female clown on her way to the fountain, and he thought she was part of one of the parties in progress. He was also slightly offended by the bar patron's unusually vulgar reference to the two folks dressed as clowns.

"No, I mean there are a couple of clowns over there fucking on the fountain!" The indignant patron reiterated.

"Oh, my God!" The guard said incredulously, when he looked at the fountain and saw the couple in action.

Alarmed, the fat guard waddled off in the direction of the big fountain followed closely by the complainer.

The guard approached the fountain just as Allen ejaculated deep inside his fellow clown's sexual cavity. She screamed with glee as they quickly separated and dashed off in opposite directions. Another fantasy fulfilled followed by a clean get a way.

Life was good, Allen thought, as he punched his Porsche and ploughed past a bunch of cars patiently waiting for a light to change at the intersection of Townsgate and Westlake Boulevard.

Carmelita showed her little sister the short note in crudely written Spanish that Jack had given her. It basically said, he was so very very sorry he had lied, and that he would never lie to her again under any circumstances. It stated how much he loved her, that he wanted to marry her, and he begged Carmelita to forgive him and give him another chance. It seemed sincere.

Upon reading the note, Angela came up with an idea. Carmelita agreed, and their plan was swiftly put into motion. Jack had never met Angela, but he was about to, and the sisters were going to put him to the test.

The next morning, Angela slipped into her sexiest low cut sun dress, and drove alone to Westlake Village. Using the ruse of having the wrong address for a job interview, Angela was going to try and seduce Jack. If he accepted the sexy Señorita's bate, it was going to cost him his ass. No second chance. If he rebuffed the tempting little beauty, Carmelita would give him another opportunity to prove his worth.

What if he failed the test? What if he failed the test, and she was pregnant? Carmelita decided she would cross that bridge later, when the results of the two tests were known.

While sitting in the outer office, Jack found some interesting reading in the police blotter section of one of the local papers, The Acorn. In an article titled, Costumes and Public Copulation, Zorro had finally made it into the press.

The first known incident had occurred just before Christmas. Dressed as Santa Claus, he had hammered a masked female helper elf in the garden section of Home Depot. The skating rink offered a conjoined couple of turns around the ice, and attested to their athletic prowess in terms of winter sports. Albertsons, the new Barnes and Noble Book Store, the steps of a local Temple, the duck pond, and the Hyatt Hotel were all mentioned.

A group of high moral minded concerned citizens were now going to offer a $25,000 reward, for the couple's apprehension and conviction.

Next to this article, on the blotter page, was a story about someone stealing $2.00 worth of petunias from somebody's garden.

Yes, Westlake Village is certainly proving to be a hot bed of criminal activity. The sooner they catch the petunia bandit and the copulating couple, the safer we'll all be, Jack thought.

When Angela drove past Dan's office she was relieved to see that the Lincoln was parked in the lot. She knew from what her sister had told her, that it was only a matter of time before the target of their plot would step out to the parkway to have a smoke.

Sure enough, within minutes Jack strode outside and fired up a cigarette on his way to the smoking zone.

Angela drove into the parking lot and pulled up next to the Lincoln. She noticed, that Jack noticed her immediately.

Dressed in her sexy little summer dress and stylish high heel sandals, Angela stepped out of her Saturn and approached Jack. She was holding a piece of paper in her hand with the address of her bogus job interview written on it in bold ink.

Angela actually went a little overboard with the flirting. She wasn't wearing a bra, and she bent down several times to give him a good glimpse of her firm pointed breasts beneath her low cut sun dress.

They switched back and forth between English and Spanish, as she ruefully confided that she was late for her interview, and had apparently written the address down incorrectly.

Next, she bummed a cigarette from Jack and almost choked when she tried to smoke it. She complained about being bored, how late it was in the day, and that she didn't want to be stuck in heavy traffic for hours driving back to East L.A. She also asked if there was a good place nearby where she could get a drink?

Jack was unresponsive to the point that sexy little Angela was actually hurt by the fact that this middle aged honky didn't go ape shit over her. She was happy for Carmelita, but it was also an ego thing. Maybe he's a little bit queer, she thought, as she slid back into her Saturn and left Jack standing where she found him.

Jack lit another cigarette as he watched the beautiful young Señorita drive away. She's really cute. I guess it must run in the family, Jack mused. He had never met Carmelita's little sister, but he recognized the Saturn sedan from the driveway at Carmelita's house in the Valley. The tiny soccer ball hanging in a small net that was dangling from the rear view mirror was a dead give away. Also, there was an uncanny resemblance between the two girls that was remarkable.

Jack felt he had passed some kind of test with flying colors. He hoped that he would hear from Carmelita that night.

That evening, Jack was alone in his room working on his third beer when he heard a gentle rap on his door.

"Yes," Jack said, just before he opened his door.

"Hola, Jack." Came the soft feminine Spanish accented voice from the other side.

Jack's heart jumped as he flung open the door that separated them.

To Jack's surprise, Flora was standing there with her hands on her hips, and a smile on her face.

"Flora?" Jack said, his high hopes dashed at the sight of the wrong Señorita. "What do you want?"

"Posible sexo," she said "¿Quieres?"

Just then the phone rang. As Jack went to answer the phone, Flora stepped into his room.

"Hello," he said, into the phone.

Flora was quickly making herself comfortable, much to Jack's discomfort. Carmelita had just identified herself, and asked if he was alone?

I can't believe this is happening again, Jack thought.

"Am I alone? ¿Solo ahora?" Jack said, as he looked at Flora, who appeared as if she'd been drinking.

Flora flopped down on the bed face first with her skirt riding high enough on her thigh to expose some of her naked buttocks. She was obviously ready for some action.

"No, Carmelita. Yo no solo. Es una Senorita agui, ahora," he said. Jack told her the truth this time as he had promised.

Flora looked up at Jack from the bed and wondered who he was talking to on the telephone?

"¿Quien es Carmelita?" Flora asked.

"Un momenta," Jack said, to Flora, a second before the phone went dead in his ear. "Damn it!"

Jack slammed the receiver back into its cradle. It's like a horrible nightmare that keeps reoccurring, Jack though. My bad luck just won't go away!

"¿Quien es Carmelita?" Flora asked, again. Then she rolled over onto her back exposing what she assumed would be of interest to Jack.

Annie Horwitz dialed Tammy's number as she tapped her fingers impatiently on her kitchen table. Tammy answered on the second ring.

"Did you get another gun?" Annie asked.

When Annie got an affirmative answer, a broad smile crossed her face. Their timetable couldn't be interrupted, and now the noisy gun problem had been solved.

Dan got a ride with his buddy Al to the apartment he kept in nearby Agoura Hills to rendezvous with the woman he had been seeing for the last six months.

The furnished apartment was in the back of the large complex, where anyone coming or going would hardly be noticed.

As they pulled into the apartment complex they watched a taxi leaving the back area. The woman didn't drive, and she had just arrived at exactly the appointed time.

With Al's help, Dan planned to end the affair later that night, permanently.

XXXII

Jack's room was dark and the loud noise of passionate amor was emanating from between his sheets.

"Ah,…me gusta, me gusta, duro, duro," she pleaded, and moaned in Spanish.

Their hot naked sweating bodies writhed in unison as their very intense love making began to reach a climax.

"Mas, mas, mas, quiero mas," she cried, begging him for more.

Jack gave her more, and said, "Te quiero, te quiero mucho."

"¿Verdad?" She said, her voice panting as he drove his organ deep inside her.

She screamed out when he came, and they clung to each other as their bodies and souls united as one.

"Gracias, Dios, Jack said, as he held her tight.

Angela was driving along Van Nuys Boulevard less than a mile from her home, when she noticed that she was being followed.

Her heart started to race. Was Carlos going to try to kill her? Her cop friend was dead. Did anyone else know, she now began to wonder?

The vehicle behind her moved up closer. This stretch of Van Nuys Boulevard was not well lighted, and it would be a good place for an armed assault. That car could easily whip around her, and open fire and kill her.

Angela was scared as she started to increase her speed. Her heart jumped again when the car following her flipped on its red lights and tweaked its siren.

"Caramba." The cops!" Angela said, out loud.

She pulled over to the curb and parked under a dimly lit street light. As she set the brake, she looked back and saw Eddie approaching.

"Not you?" She said, as Eddie stepped up to her window.

"Si, soy yo."

"Speak English. I heard you were married?"

"What? Who told you that?"

"Officer Levitz," Angela replied.

"She's a bitch. I've been divorced for four years."

"What?"

"I'm not married. She's lying."

"You're kidding?"

"No, Officer Levitz lied. She hates me."

"Why?"

"I popped her once, and didn't go back for seconds."

"¿Mande?"

"A woman scorned, or something like that. Look, I pulled you over 'cause I've got some good news," Eddie stated.

"What?" Angela responded.

"Carlos. We just got Carlos on a string of felony raps, and he won't be back on the street for about seventy-five years."

"That is good news. Thanks," she said.

"Wanna have a drink with me in about an hour?" Eddied asked.

"Ah,…si," Angela said.

"Great," Eddie replied.

Angela had still not fully recovered from the Jack rejection thing earlier. Even though it turned out right for her sister, the fact that an older white guy wouldn't just kill to be with her, hurt to the core. Having Eddie hit on her helped Angela's wounded ego.

Also, Eddie had apparently solved the Carlos problem. Was he married, that was the big question?

Angela figured she'd probably just tease him a little tonight, then look into the married matter later.

If Eddie was unattached, she could actually like him. He was cute, but if he was a liar, she knew as a cop Eddie could be a very dangerous man. She also wondered if she should bring up the Tammy thing with him?

"I'll meet you at Stella's in about an hour, okay?" Eddie continued.

She noticed he was dressed in civilian clothes.

"Where's your uniform?" Angela questioned.

"At home in my closet, I hope."

She laughed. What kind of cop was Eddie, she wondered?

"Is Stella's that place we went to last time?" She asked.

"Yeah, on Foothill next to the car wash."

"Okay, see ya at Stella's in an hour," Angela confirmed.

After Carmelita hung up on him, Jack had forced Flora to leave. This was not an easy task. She'd been drinking, and was dead set on getting laid. She caused a bit of a scene, but Jack clearly explained that he was in love with Carmelita, and that no amount of sexual enticement was going to work.

After Flora finally left almost in tears, Jack immediately called Carmelita back. Only twenty-five minutes had passed. He explained the situation with Flora honestly. I didn't ask her to come over, I didn't have sex with her, and I made her leave, he told Carmelita, as he pleaded for another chance.

Carmelita eventually acquiesced. Jack drove hell bent to the Valley and picked up the woman he loved.

When they got back to his room, things were somewhat awkward at first. Jack was awash with contrition, and Carmelita played the role of appellate judge to the hilt. She was dressed in a killer little red outfit.

As Jack pleaded his case, Carmelita tossed her mane of thick black hair back behind her shoulders and stared at him with a set of dark eyes that could have penetrated the soul of the devil.

Jack shamelessly begged; he pleaded, and he fell just short of cajoling, as Carmelita continued to firmly stand her ground, as she watched the desperate Gringo grovel during her very critical evaluation process.

Her eventual forgiveness was hard won, but followed by a long deep kiss that sent shivers through Jack's body. More kisses followed as they slowly undressed each other then slipped onto the bed.

Carmelita's soft skin, the pleasant fragrance of her perfume, and the pleasure of her sensuous kisses gave Jack an experience that was nothing short of spiritual. Also, once the beautiful Señorita was in full love making mode, she developed an almost unmatched appetite for more.

"Quiero mas," was her oft repeated love making mantra, and he did his best to give her more. Jack was in heaven. The sweet combination of indescribably great sex with this beautiful woman, and absolute true love, left Jack feeling like the luckiest man in the world.

Her sexy ability to get him to rise to the occasion, time and time again, caused him to forgo the viagra he'd used. The lovely lips of Carmelita's constantly wet love canal, was a place Jack visited often that night. The secred area was visited visually, manually, orally, and copulatively.

He was completely on cloud nine with Carmelita. This time nothing would ever separate them, he thought, nothing.

"Gracias Dios," Jack said, again and again. "Thank you, God."

Later that night she shared with him the possibility that she might be pregnant. The thought of possible procreation with Carmelita overjoyed Jack beyond his wildest dreams.

Carmelita had been concerned about how he would react, and the fact that Jack wanted a child with her somehow confirmed he was sincere, and not just after sex.

Tengo amor, in Spanish means to have love. To the Anglo ear, it also sounds a little bit like a dance. Love is somewhat like a very delicate dance, Jack thought. In a metaphoric sense, love is almost akin to an intricate 17th Century minuet, except this delicate little mating minuet was set to Mariachi music.

With the revelation of Carmelita's possible pregnancy, Jack felt it was time to tell her about the loss of his son. Talking about T.J.'s tragic death was always troubling, but Jack thought this was an appropriate time to re-visit the subject.

Jack pulled T.J.'s photo out of the drawer; and told her what had happened. Carmelita was truly touched with sorrow when Jack related his sad tale. She also realized the significance of her possible impregnation, and she now knew that she absolutely wanted to bear Jack's child.

Next, Carmelita mentioned the other problem that was preying on her mind.

"What we do about Tammy?"

"Nada, ahora. Nothing right now," he said, as he pulled out a stack of other photographs he wanted to share with the woman he loved. "Because I think you're wrong."

"I think I no wrong!"

"I think you are."

"How you know?"

"I know," Jack replied.

"How you know for sure?"

"I can't tell you, but it's okay. You're just wrong."

"Why you no tell me?"

"Carmelita, trust me. And please don't go to the police."

"Why no police?"

"Because, Tammy isn't going to kill anybody. Believe me. You misunderstood what you heard, and you'll just get us both in big trouble. Trust me, okay? It's under control. Don't worry."

"Okay," Carmelita said, not totally convinced.

He showed her some stills from his stunt career, and then she came upon an old photograph of Jack wearing his dress blues.

"You were soldier?"

"Si. I was a Marine," he replied. "Por ocho anos."

"Eight years?"

"Yes," he said.

She found another photo where Jack is wearing battle dress, complete with helmet, flak jacket, and an assault rifle.

"¿Donde estaba?" She asked, then repeated the question in English. "Where was this?"

"In Lebanon," he answered.

"¿Donde es Lebanon?"

"It's in the middle east," he replied. "Acerca de Israel."

Next, she pointed at what looked like a bandage on his hand in the photo.

"You hurt hand?"

"Si."

"Why?" She asked.

A this point he dug out a yellowing newspaper clipping from 1983.

"Some terrorists blew up the Marine barracks, and two hundred and forty-one Marines were killed, and seventy more were hurt. I survived, but I got wounded. A lot of my friends died."

Carmelita flashed Jack a serious look like she didn't quite understand what he was saying.

"Una bomba de las terroristas mataron dos cientos cuarenta y uno Marineros, y sententa heridos. Yo estaba herido en la mano," Jack said, hoping he'd related what happened to him in Lebanon correctly in Spanish. "Yo estaba muy suerte.," he added, stating that he was very lucky.

This news caused Carmelita to gasp slightly as she looked at the newspaper clipping, with some photographs of many wounded and dead Marines.

Jack, as a soldier, had narrowly escaped death, in what looked like a horrible scene. Carmelita realized her friend Jack had seen a lot of tragedy in his life, and also faced danger on many fronts. She had also long been fascinated with the subject of death. Why some people lived, and others died far before their time.

God had wanted Jack to live, she thought. She also felt a little proud of herself, having conceived the foregoing thoughts in English.

"Yo estaba adentro en un hospital par dos semanas," he said.

"You in hospital for two weeks?"

"Yes," he confirmed, as he also took note on how well her English skills were improving. Her vocabulary, and comprension seemed to be growing in leaps and bounds.

"¿Agarste una medalla?" She asked, as she pointed at one of the photos where he's wearing his dress blues and sporting a few colorful medals on his chest.

"Did I get a medal?"

"Medal, is medalla in English?" She asked.

"Si," he said.

"You get one medal for your hand?"

"Si. Una Corazon Murado," he told her.

"A Purple Heart?" She asked.

"Si. A Purple Heart," he said, pointing at the medal in the photograph.

"Do they give medal if you die?" She inquired.

"Si. Mismo medalla. The same medal. A Purple Heart."

"¿Mismo? The same? You get same medal to die?"

"Si," he said. "Same medal."

"Better to get medal your way," she concluded.

"Si. Yo estaba muy suerte. I'm very lucky to be alive," he said, remembering how 241 of his fellow Marines weren't so lucky.

The word lucky really stuck in his mind as he looked over at Carmelita sitting on the edge of his bed, naked beneath an unbuttoned shirt of his that she had borrowed after their last love making round.

Her breasts even became more exposed as she leaned back on the bed and looked at Jack. Her nipples always screamed suck me, and Jack submitted to their summoning call as she uncrossed her lovely brown legs in a most inviting manner. Their love making resumed, and lasted until well past dawn.

With little sleep, they left the next morning at eight, for her doctor's appointment in Pacoima. They also both called in sick, much to Tammy's and Dan's dismay.

XXXIII

Jack always had women problems, and Jack always had women. With his rugged good looks, his sparkling blue eyes, and his cocky independent air, Jack perpetually seemed to have a lot of ladies in his life.

The stunt world had been absolute heaven, to Jack. Movie sets attract the best looking most romantic people on earth.

In the movie biz, lots of pretty girls were an everyday fact of life.

Being a young Marine abroad, meant he also saw more than his share of action, in both Denmark and sunny Italy. Even in high school, his surfer boy persona served him well with the young ladies.

However, with all the ladies in all the lands, Jack had only been in love three times in his life. His first wife Julie, who committed suicide after the death of their son, then Carol, and now Carmelita.

Jack and Carmelita pulled up in front of the Clinica a few minutes before nine.

They soon found out the doctor had an emergency early that morning, and wasn't expected back until about noon.

With three hours to kill, Jack and Carmelita took a little walk, then stopped at Denny's restaurant for a bite to eat.

After an exhausting night of amor, their appetites proved to be huge. Almost everything about Carmelita, Jack observed, was femine and delicate, except she ate like a horse.

They both had the grand slam Spanish omelet breakfast, and Carmelita also had a side of pancakes as well as some toast.

After they finished their meal they started to walk back in the direction of the Clinica. Instead of taking the same route back, they detoured slightly and leisurely strolled down a quiet residential street. They still had about an hour to kill.

While walking hand in hand and enjoying each others company, they came upon a cute little house that was for sale. A white picket fence surrounded its tiny neatly kept yard.

The couple decided to have a closer look. The older wood frame house was freshly painted a light brown with white trim. A brochure in a slot attached to the For Sale sign in the front yard provided information on the place and listed its asking price at, $189,000.

The happy couple discovered that the front door was unlocked and they decided to go in and have a look around. No one seemed to be in attendance as they toured the tiny two bedroom abode.

They found that the house had a cute little remodeled kitchen, a wood burning fireplace, and fine thick newly laid wall to wall carpet.

Jack and Carmelita both noticed the chain lock on the inside of the front door. Having just inspected the house, they knew that they were alone. They glanced at each other devilishly as the same idea occurred to them simultaneously.

Jack locked the bolt on the door, and hooked the chain lock. Within a matter of moments they were having tengo amor on the floor. They returned to the Clinica just before noon.

Jack often thought back to the first time he saw Carmelita. How beautiful she looked, mad, and all covered with mud.

He remembered her hair, her skin, her eyes, her lips. In the glare of the morning sunshine she was stunning. Absolutely breathtakingly beautiful. It was like Jack was instantly hit by a bolt of lightning. The lightning bolt of love.

Jack looked at Carmelita sitting next to him in the Clinica waiting room. She turned and smiled at him. He sensed that she was a little nervous. He wondered what they would learn today?

She smiled at him again, and gently pushed her hair back a bit revealing one of her delicate flowered earrings. Earlier that day she had told him again how much she loved the litte gold earrings he'd given her for her birthday, and he told her again how much he loved her.

The Dockside Terrace was one of several charming restaurants that sat on the edge of the little lake that gave Westlake its name. Set against the beautiful Santa Monica Mountains to the west, the small lake shimmered in the midday sun. It was another perfect California day in the Conejo Valley.

Allen Horwitz was dressed in a black three piece suit with a matching fedora hat that made him look like an elegant Forties gangster. He was seated at the bar, and had just finished his forth scotch and soda. He set his empty glass on the mahogany bar, as the attentive bartender served him a fresh drink, along with a pink lady cocktail for his soon to arrive lunch date.

Allen liked Chivas scotch, and drinking it during the day made him feel slightly decadent. It was just past 2:30, the last of the lunch crowd was thinning out, and Allen was starting to worry because his sexy partner was never ever late for a date.

Just as Allen looked toward the door, he saw her step into the restaurant and stand near the hostess' podium for a moment. She scanned the near empty room and almost immediately spotted Allen sitting alone at the bar. Neither one of them had ever been in the newly reopened and renamed Dockside Terrace before today. It was their virgin appearance in the establishment, so to speak.

She looked incredibly stunning dressed in an exquisite white linin mini skirted suit. The finely tailored coat was a man's cut, with her cleavage slightly exposed in the V of her tightly tailored jacket.

Shirtless under the coat, her diamond choker sparkled against her black naked neck. She was wearing a pair of elegant white high heeled shoes, and no hose. Her legs were tone and they looked very sexy during her momentary stance by the front door.

Her black hair was hidden beneath a huge white hat that almost totally obscured her classically beautiful African face. She continued to wear her diamond dotted stylish dark glasses as she crossed the room and joined Allen at the bar.

The on duty hostess who failed to approach her in a timely manner, watched as Allen handed his lunch date her favorite cocktail.

"I got us a table outside on the terrace," Allen Horwitz said, immediately feeling her intense body heat.

"You got here early?" She replied, with a sexy smile, then took a sip of her cocktail.

"Yeah, an' I'm smashed," Allen informed her.

She laughed, flashing a glimpse of her perfect white teeth, then she took another sip of her drink as they headed for their table outside overlooking the lake.

Only two other tables were still occupied on the wide terrace. Allen had selected a table in a quiet area off to the side away from the other remaining patrons.

A few small boats were cruising the placid water of the man made lake. It was an absolutely lovely afternoon, Allen mused, as he watched the incredibly sexy woman sitting next to him, as she touched his thigh with one of her bare black legs.

Carmelita had left Angela a message the night before, letting her little sister know that Jack was driving her to the Clinica, for her doctor's appointment the next day. Angela thought that sounded right.

Angela had met Eddie the cop at Stella's Steak House where she had far too much to drink. Stella's was a not too chic cop hangout that had been around for close to fifty years.

The surrounding neighborhood in the North San Fernando Valley had completely changed, and was now almost totally Latino, but the place remained a favorite with off duty policemen. The neighborhood may have changed, but the watering hole Stella Kelly had opened in the early Fifties, seemed like it was caught in a time warp. The place was dark and most of the patrons were white.

Eddie and Angela had found a cozy booth in a dimly lit corner of the busy restaurant. At first they talked about old Sergeant Stack. Eddie had known him during his entire career as a cop. They had met when Eddie was still a rookie. Seems that Stack was somewhat of a legend within LAPD.

"Usually cops will go thirty years without ever firing their gun," Eddie told her. "However, that wasn't the case with old Sergeant Stack."

"Oh?" Angela questioned.

"He got his first kill in Korea, while he was serving as an MP in the Army."

Angela had listened attentively as Eddie continued to drink and pour forth about their dead friend's past. He digressed from time to time to include tales of his misadventures, which Angela found quite intriguing. What exciting lives these cops led, she thought, as Eddie skipped back and forth between stories about himself and Sergeant Stack.

"The last one out in front of your doughnut shop was probably his seventh kill," Eddie said, as he ordered another round of drinks with a wave of his hand.

"Seven?" Angela said, as she swollowed the last of her third vodka and tonic. Seven, that's a lot, she thought, and he seemed like such a gentle man.

Eddie went on to detail some of Sergeant Stack's more notorious exploits, including the day back in 1973 when he killed four in a heated gun battle with some bank robbers, who killed his partner early in the gunfight.

Because Eddie used slang, Angela had a some trouble following the story. Also, the drinks were starting to go to her head.

"They gave him the Medal of Valor for that one. But you know what? He never wore it."

As she started on her forth drink, she interrupted Eddie by saying, why, when she meant to say, what?

"He was kind of a modest guy, I guess," Eddie answered. "The last couple of guys he killed were gangbangers."

Angela ended up sleeping with Eddie at the end of the evening. She figured he probably was married, since they went to a motel instead of his place.

She also figured she'd probably never hear from him again. She had a terrible hangover. She felt like shit, she thought, using a new colloquial phrase she'd recently learned. She also felt a little slutty, again employing in thought, a randy piece of newly acquired American patois. She had never had sex that quickly with a man before, never on the first date.

Language skills aside, Angela wondered if she was becoming a bit too Americanized? She'd heard that Gringas were infamous for jumping into bed with men early in the game.

Allen Horwitz and his lovely lunch date looked very perplexed as they conversed with the police in the parking lot near the Dockside Terrace. The cops responded quickly in this community, and four black and white squad cars were in attendance, as well as two motorcycle cops.

Tammy was supposed to meet a designer alone at the Westlake Yacht Club a hundred yards from the Dockside Terrace Restaurant.

She was stunned when she saw Allen arguing with the police as she drove through the lot looking for a parking space.

Tammy knew she'd better stay out of it. Also, she thought Annie Horwitz was out of town, and she knew her best girlfriend would not approve of her hiring a new designer.

Unnoticed by Allen, who was totally occupied in an animated confrontation with the group of lawmen, Tammy parked her car in a space marked, Reserved for the Commodore, then marched straight to the Yacht Club.

XXXIV

The evening air was slightly chilly outside Jack's room as the sun set behind the nearby Santa Monica Mountains. Jack and Carmelita had returned that afternoon, had a late lunch, and made love again. They decided against having dinner, since they'd already had two hearty meals that day.

Jack's libido really required little sustenance. The only thing he cared to put in his mouth at that moment was Carmelita's lovely left breast which was peeking out of the unbuttoned shirt she'd slipped into shortly after their last round of amor.

He'd told her how sexy he thought she looked wearing nothing but one of his shirts, and from that point on, one of Jack's open shirts became Carmelita's post conjugal costume of choice.

Her beautiful dark nipple was again screaming, suck me, and he reached out to touch the source of the call.

"You want to make sex with me all the time!"

Jack laughed. Carmelita was just so damned cute.

"¿No?" She said impishly. "You want make sex with me every minute."

"Okay, it's time for a little English lesson. It's either make love to me, or have sex with me. "¿Entiende?"

"¿Como?" She questioned.

"Make sex with me, is incorrect English," he instructed.

"Oh. ¿Es incorrecto?" She said, cracking a devilish little smile as she let the shirt fall open, and reclined on the bed exposing her incredibly beautiful body.

"Actually, making sex with you is never, incorrecto," he said, as he joined her on the bed.

"¿No?" She said, playfully.

"No," he replied, as he began this session by answering the call of the screaming nipple. Then his lips soon journeyed south in search of the delicious sacred area.

Their passionate love making could only be defined as devine. It was like they'd been lovers all their lives. Their sexual rhythm was truly remarkable. It far exceeded all of his previous experiences, even with Carol, something Jack had never dreamed possible.

With Carmelita there was an absolute spiritual quality about their sexual union. Jack couldn't put it into words, but when he put it in her, their little world became a state of total sexual nirvana.

After a many minutes of sizzling bliss, they climaxed together, for the third time that day.

"Wow! I guess that pretty well puts to rest the rumor that mutual orgasms are rare."

"¿Como?"

"That's the third time we've climaxed together, today."

"¿Que?"

"This morning on the floor of the vacant house, and two more times since we returned here. Nosotros tenemos tres climaxes en junto, hoy."

"Si," she concurred, not bothering to correct his Spanish.

While holding the woman he loved in his arms, Jack thought, what a wonderful day they were having, vacillating between making love, and exchanging their life stories.

Jack learned that Carmelita grew up in a very poor suburb of Mexico City. She told him that life was hard in the huge teaming metropolis with a population that exceeded 10 million people.

She was one of seven children. Her father was illiterate, and worked sporadically as a day laborer. Her mother was a maid, who worked steadily enough to keep simple food on the table. Their casa was a crowded two room apartment, that lacked accouterments such as running water, and reliable electricity.

Carmelita and Angela were the youngest, and the only girls in the brood. The oldest brother Martin, was the first to journey to El Norte. He left Mexico in 1980, the year Angela was born.

Martin was soon followed by two more brothers, Juan and Jose. With money from the United States sent by the three brothers, the family's standard of living in Mexico City improved.

Carmelita, and later Angela were both able to finish Mexico's equivalent of high school. They were the first in their family to achieve that level of education.

Her two other brothers, Fernando and Francisco, joined their father working as day laborers who sought jobs by gathering on the streets of Mexico City before dawn each morning.

Francisco later died in a terrible construction site accident, and Fernando eventually drifted away from the family and found a new life among the criminal element that flourished in Mexico's capital city. The last time they had heard from Frenando, he was serving a lengthy sentence in prison for armed robbery and murder.

Jack also found out that Carmelita too, had once lost a child. A fetus actually. Her first boyfriend, who promised to marry her, but only if she had sex with him first, beat her severely when he learned of her pregnancy.

Carmelita was eighteen at the time, and after the beating, she never heard from the boyfriend again.

During the time between the brutal boyfriend, and when she meant Jack, Carmelita had only been to bed with one other man, and he too, had lied to her.

Shortly after Carmelita moved to California, she fell in love with an handsome young Latino, who failed to tell her about his wife and two kids in El Salvador. This second experience almost totally soured her opinion of men.

At this point, Carmelita made it very clear, once again, that she would not tolerate lies, even small ones. She also had little patience with any intentions that were less than honorable.

"The last man I like was a Gringo. I like him, until he tell me, he want to pay me for sex."

"¿Por qué tu vino a los Estados Unidos?" He said, asking her why she came to the United States?

"Trabajo," she replied. "I want to escape being poor."

"That's a good reason."

"Es por qué todos Mexicanos son aqui. We come here to work, and for a better life."

Carmelita didn't venture North until she was twenty-three. Her little sister Angela made the trip at nineteen. Carmelita also related what happened to Angela with the Border Patrolmen, and Jack was revolted by the man's behavior. Again, for a moment he was ashamed that he was a Gringo.

He also realized how lucky he was to get another chance with her. The things that had shaped Carmelita's view of the world, would certainly be hard for anyone to overcome. Jack was now more determined than ever, to give her a better life, and to love her always.

Carmelita's father died a year after she came to California. Her mother, whom she loved dearly, passed away suddenly last year. Carmelita suffered a certain amount of torment because she didn't get to see her mother again before she died.

In the course of the conversation, Carmelita learned that Jack too, had lost both of his parents. They shared an area of sad commonality. They were both adult orphans.

Jack continued to stumble between English and Spanish, as he told her about marrying his high school sweetheart, Julie. He was only seventeen at the time. Julie was pregnant, and they were very much in love.

Jack told her about growing up in a working class neighborhood in Culver City, a small town on the west side of L.A. His father worked in a machine shop, and his mom was a housewife. Jack was an only child.

His parents met and got married during the Korean War, while his father was serving in the Marine Corps. Soon after his dad survived the war, he returned to the States to pursue the American dream. Jack said he was very lucky, and that he grew up during a period of great prosperity. In the Fifties, this was especially true for working people.

Jack surfed, was a poor student, and mostly screwed around in school. His main interests were basically the beach, partying, and girls. He somewhat down played the part about the girls.

Then, when he was in the eleventh grade in high school, he fell in love with the prettiest girl in the senor class, Julie Peterson.

Then in a coup that sent the school's gossip mill abuzz, Julie dumped her football player boyfriend for Jack. In high school, Jack never cared much for the butt sucking jock types, so stealing Julie Peterson, head cheerleader, from this jerk, became one of Jack's proudest accomplishments.

Julie Peterson was by no means Jack's first sexual partner. His high school days took place during the swinging Seventies and Jack had been getting laid since he was thirteen. He was sixteen when he hooked up with Julie, and she became, at that point in his life, the best sex he'd ever had.

She was blond, cute beyond belief, had a body built for the beach, and was a real little hottie in the hay. Jack absolutely loved the shit out of her sexually. Although Jack though of all these sexual things while he recounted what happened, he only told Carmelita the core story.

Julie got pregnant the summer after she graduated from high school. Jack, who was fifteen months younger, still had another year to go in school, but the responsibly of having a child on the way caused him to drop out of high school after his junior year. He followed in his father's footsteps and enlisted in the Marine Corps so he could support his family.

Also, at that time, Jack had a sense of idealism about his country. The fact that his father, his uncles, and all the older men he'd known, had done their duty in the military as a matter of honor, before they went on with their lives and their civilian careers. Jack was seventeen when he got married and joined the Marine Corps.

The Marine Corps was a good job for a young man. A man's job. He also got extra money for his dependents, and free medical care.

Jack excelled in his duties and rose to the rank of Sergeant toward the end of his first enlistment. Then the T.J. tragedy occurred.

After he explained how his little son died, he told Carmelita that his wife went crazy with grief. Jack felt horrible, worse than he could imagine, he loved his son, but poor Julie just went crazy. There was no consoling her. She had killed her little baby. She slashed her wrists in the bathtub, and had completely bleed out by the time Jack made the gruesome discovery.

In the course of a couple of weeks, Jack had tragically lost the two people he loved the most in the world. Also, from that time on, he'd harbored a horrible fear about backing a car over a child. That fear had struck home again, Carmelita realized, that day she screamed when he almost backed the Lincoln over her stereo. Although totally unintentional on her part, Carmelita now felt horrible about having triggered that awful memory.

She looked at the sadness in Jack's eyes as he related this story that he still found very difficult to retell. He went on to say, that after Julie killed herself, he decided to reenlist for another four year tour in the Marine Corps.

He wanted to die, but he chose to live. Besides, the Marines always presented the potential of danger, and he was comfortable with that aspect of the Corps. The service became kind of an escape from his terrible experience. He told Carmelita that he was pretty much numb for the next few years.

Strangely, coming so close to getting killed in Lebanon, made him want to live again. That brush with death, when so many others died, became a serious life changing experience for Jack.

He looked over at the beautiful woman sitting on his bed, and he thought about how much he loved her. He loved her more than words could describe. Carmelita, the quintessential Latina, was the absolute physical antithesis of the other two women Jack had loved. Yet, in his heart, he felt he loved her more. The very thought of having a child with Carmelita made him feel like his life was taking on a new beginning.

The last twenty-four hours, had been perhaps the best twenty-four hours Jack had ever spent. The sex, the love, and the fact that Carmelita gave him another chance, after he was certain he had lost her, made him feel like the luckiest man on the face of the earth. Even her penchant for jealousy he found flattering.

He knew that the subject of Carol would come up soon, and he dreaded dealing with the question he knew Carmelita would surely ask.

"¿Tienes sexo con Carol recientemente?"

The troubling question came up sooner, rather than later, when Carmelita asked if he'd had sex with Carol recently?

There was no getting around this one. If he lied to her, and she found out, he would lose her. But, if he told her the truth, what would she do?

"Have you had sex with Carol, recently?" She asked again, this time in perfect English.

"Ah,…not according to former President Clinton," he said, groping for a way to deal with the touchy matter.

"¿Como Presidente Clinton?" She inquired, apparently ignorant of the scandal that had rocked the Oval Office.

"Ah,…" Jack stammered.

"¿Jack? ¿Sexo con Carol?"

"Ah,…no se."

"¿Como no sabes?" Carmelita said, giving no indication that she was going to let the subject go unanswered. "¿Sexo o no?"

"Ella chupa me varga," he answered truthfully.

XXXV

There was an awkwardness that immediately followed his honest admission. Carmelita rolled over on the bed and covered her face for a few moments.

Jack knew the confession would hurt her, but he pointed out that he promised he would never lie to her again. He went on to explain that he was drunk and lonely on his birthday. He also gingerly reminded her, that at the time, he thought that she would never, ever speak to him again. He did however, fall short of actually blaming her for his indiscretion. He emphasized that he had once loved Carol, and that she could be very persuasive. He told Carmelita how sorry he was, and he begged her to forgive him.

She rolled over on her back and stared at Jack with her dark penetrating eyes.

God, how he loved her, Jack thought. What sentence would this beautiful judge impose, now that the damaging evidence was before her court?

"Lo siento," Jack said, again. "I'm truly truly sorry."

"You like to have sex with Carol, don't you?" Carmelita said, employing perfect English.

"Yeah, I used to," Jack admitted. "But not as much as with you, Carmelita. Look, I'm really sorry I lied the first time. I didn't want to lose you. I love you more than I've ever loved a woman, and I never want to be with another woman as long as I live, and that's the truth. Please, believe me."

Carmelita looked him long and hard in the eye. He wondered what was going on in that mind of hers?

God, she was beautiful, spread out on his bed, weighing their future, and his fate.

"If you marry me, I promise I'll never look at another woman, for as long as I live. I only want to be with you. Only you, solamente tu, and that's the truth. The honest truth," he said.

"¿Verdad?" She questioned.

"Si. Verdad," Jack replied.

Carmelita continued to stare at Jack. Still laying on her back, the shirt now fell slightly open as she adjusted her body on the bed.

After a couple of moments, she reclined into a sexy position and let the shirt fall completely open, exposing the vital areas of her lovely body.

Jack cracked a slight smile, as he looked over at this sexy inviting Venus on his bed. Apparently the verdict was in.

He approached her slowly, then fell gently onto the bed beside her. Next, he rolled onto her and felt her wonderful full warm breasts touch his naked chest, as he let his lips and tongue find hers.

They shared a long wet loving kiss that Jack found absolutely intoxicating. The kiss lasted for several minutes, before his lips and tongue traveled north to caress her delicate ear. After a few moments of probing this orifice with his wet tongue, his lips ran down her face and neck and came upon her waiting firm breasts. He paused there and tenderly kissed and sucked both of them for what seemed like a very long while.

She moaned and moved her body sensuously as he left her lovely hardened breasts and worked his way down her tasty body. Soon, he spread her open and slipped his fingers inside as he licked, and then sucked on the delicious wet lips of her ever expanding precious entrance.

Their passionate love making ended an hour later with a climax that left them both completely numb. Early on, they developed a practice that prolonged their pleasure, but also left them pretty well spent.

God, this is wonderful, Jack thought. The pure satisfaction he felt with Carmelita surpassed anything he had ever known. The magnitude of his love for her was almost incomprehensible. The sex and love created by their union was the strongest emotional sensation Jack could imagine. What had it been before, when now there was this?

They laid there quietly for awhile as love struck Jack Hardin stared at his bonita Señorita and gently stroked her beautiful black hair with his hand.

"Te quiero. Te quiero mucho," he said, then he kissed her tenderly on the forehead.

"I love you, too," she replied. "You're doing very good with your Spanish," she added, using a sexy voice that dripped with double entendre.

"¿Si?"

"Si," she responded, as she rolled out of bed. "Tengo sed. ¿Quieres agua?"

"No, gracias."

Just after she asked him if he was thirsty, she bumped into the nightstand next to the bed almost knocking it over. She flipped on the light and saw that the hard bump had caused its single drawer to pop open.

Carmelita was slightly taken aback when she spotted Jack's other pistol, an ominous looking .45 caliber Army Colt automatic laying in the open drawer.

"¿Tienes una pistola?"

"Si."

"¿Por qué?"

"Por protección," Jack replied, saying he kept the pistol for protection.

"Oh," she said, then she made her way to the sink to get a glass of water.

Jack gently closed the drawer, and the subject as well, when he asked, "¿Tu cansada?"

"Si," Carmelita said.

She quickly downed the glass of water and returned to bed, as Jack watched her every move.

"¿Tu cansado?" She asked, as she curled up next to him.

"Si, muy."

They both agreed that they were tired. Indeed, it had been a long long day on several levels, and deep sleep soon overtook the tired loving couple.

The alarm clock went off early the next morning, and Jack hit the kill button a second after it first sounded. Next, he turned on his side and looked at Carmelita in the dim morning light. She was laying on her back, and her eyes were still closed.

Jack looked at her lovingly for a few moments, then he gently ran the two forfingers of his right hand along the ridge of her nose and the edge of her cheek. Her skin was warm and soft, and oh so very sensuous to touch, Jack thought.

She smiled a little smile, but her eyes remained shut as his hand followed the contour of her face, then down her neck until his hand finally reached her left breast. He touched it with the whole of his hand, then let his fingers find the nipple which was hard and erect.

He let his hand roam down across her flat stomach until it slipped over her very warm public area. His fingers soon found the soft wet lips of her wonderfully inviting vigina.

Jack was erect before her hand reached his organ. She rolled onto her left side as she gripped his hard throbbing penis and guided it inside her from behind so his hand was free to continue clitoral stimulation, which eventually would cause her to come, hopefully again in unison with his ejaculation.

Their passion increased until they brought themselves to near climaxes, a series of times, by stopping just short of reaching their zenith, then starting again. They both discovered early, that this was one of their favorite ways to make love.

When they finally finished, in unison, she moaned loudly and they held each other tight. Jack couldn't imagine a better way to start the day.

After a quick breakfast of instant coffee and a couple of day old croissants, Jack dropped Carmelita at Dan's place just before daybreak.

XXXVI

Jack returned later hat morning and picked up Dan at nine. As was often the case, his boss was fairly quiet, and listened to one of his sports radio stations during the short journey to the office. Jack wondered if Dan had seen him drop Carmelita off at the house before dawn? Dan was often up early.

Then, just as Jack parked in front of the office, Dan spoke to him in a somewhat conciliatory tone.

"I apologized to Carmelita this morning, and I also want to apologize to you," Dan said. "I shouldn't have spoken to her the way I did the other day. I'm under a lot of pressure right now, and sometimes that spills over. Also, I don't understand you two when you speak Spanish, and to be honest, sometimes I find that irritating, but I apologize."

Jack was surprised by Dan's low key apology. It seemed very uncharacteristic. Maybe his boss realized he came within a knat's ass of gettin' his butt kicked, Jack reasoned.

The rest of the morning at the office was quiet. Dan remained behind the closed door of his office all morning. Jack read the newspaper, and drifted outside to smoke from time to time.

Brad showed up just before noon to retrieve a bag of soccer balls for a kid's team he coached.

Brad's arrival caused Jack's romantic thoughts of Carmelita to cease as he watched this clown load soccer equiptment into his SUV. Now, there's a role model for kids, Jack thought. Truly a shinning example of everything Jack didn't want his next child to be, a butt sucking yuppie punk.

Jack fired up another cigarette for Brad's benefit, and said, "Buenos dias, Rodriguez," in reply to Brad's usual, grammatically grating salutation, "Hey, man, what's up?"

Brad just glared back at Jack, and said nothing in response to the Spanish greeting.

Brad soon left, leaving Jack to return to his thoughts of love, and how he looked forward to Carmelita's three days off, which would commence the next day. This time they could spent the entire time together.

At 12:30 Dan emerged from his office and announced that he had an important meeting in the Valley. They took off for Sherman Oaks immediately. Again, thirty-five minutes of silence from Dan, and sports radio all the way.

Jim Rome came on the air and offered a couple of intelligent comments, which made him somewhat of an anomaly in the sports radio world. Jack could never understand the proliferate interest in spectator sports. He liked to play sports as a kid, but failed to find any amusement in watching them. And sports talk, how inane. It was either pure speculation, or just history after the fact. That intelligent adults could invest their time and energy in this moronic pursuit, was beyond Jack's comprehension.

Jack dropped Dan off for his meeting at an office building on Ventura Boulevard just west of Woodman Avenue. Dan gave Jack a couple of errands to run, and told him to be back in three hours.

While cruising down Moorpark Street Jack ran into an old stunt buddy of his standing on a street corner. Jack had just passed a movie location shoot, when he saw Billy Hancock having a smoke and chatting with a couple of pretty extra girls.

Seeing this, Jack had a flash about having to do stunt work again. The job with Dan would end in a few months, and Jack knew he would soon be faced with having to find a new means of support. He quickly pulled over and parked next to where Billy was standing. Jack jumped out of the car, and they greeted each other and hugged. Stunt guys always hug.

"What's going on?" Jack asked.

"I'm doin' a little burn," Billy replied.

Burns were Billy's specialty. He went on to tell Jack that he was getting set on fire in about an hour.

"Barbecue time."

"You got it," Billy responded enthusiastically. "Then they're shoving me off the roof of that building over there," Billy added, pointing to a four story apartment complex.

"Cool," Jack commented.

"Long paycheck today," Billy bragged.

"Hey, I'm kinda lookin' for some work," Jack said.

"Oh, yeah," Billy replied, glancing at the shiny new Lincoln.

"It's not mine. I'm the driver."

"Bummer."

"Yeah," Jack confirmed.

"I'm coordinating a show next month, some piece of shit called, Riot City. I've got some falls, a couple of burns, some fights, an' a lot of N/D stuff. Give me a call."

Then suddenly, for the first time, the thought of doing a stunt gig kind of scared Jack. It was a young man's game, and at his age, he was starting to worry about his reflexes, and his nerve. Also, he now had a reason to live.

Jack looked at Billy, who was probably in his early thirties, and still eager to test the limits of this dangerous line of work.

"Hey, did ya hear that Paul Raines got killed doin' a high fall out at the big DWP plant?"

"Yeah, I heard. Bob told me," Jack answered.

"Missed the bag by a foot."

"That's as good as a mile," Jack offered.

"Tell me."

Jack thought about the last couple of times he fucked up doing a fall, and almost ate it. Paul Raines had taught Jack how to do high falls. Paul must have had a couple of thousand falls under his belt. Then Jack thought about the money. Stunt work paid better than anything he'd ever done for a living.

"Yeah, I'd like to work," Jack said. "You still at the same number?"

"Yeah," Billy affirmed, then turned his attention back to the two honeys he'd been chatting up before Jack arrived.

Over the last two years, counting Paul, three of Jack's buddies had gotten killed doing stunt work. This crossed his mind, before his thoughts returned to Carmelita.

It was Angela's last day at The Donut Shop. Her charm and her language skills had landed her a job as a service rep at Sears.

She had applied for the job on the same day she visited Jack at Dan's office. She had actually answered an ad in the Thousand Oaks area, so she wouldn't be totally lying.

The new job had come up rather suddenly, and she fortunately was able to find Mr. Kim a replacement, and he agreed to let her go immediately.

Today she was training her girlfriend Ana, acquainting her with the duties at The Donut Shop.

She had first asked Carmelita if she wanted the job, but her sister had no interest in taking a job where the shift started in the middle of the night. Angela worried about Carmelita working where there was some kind of murder plot in play, but her older sister wanted to stay near Jack, who had assured her that she was wrong about there being a plan to kill somebody. Carmelita said, she also felt quite safe with Jack around.

Angela wasn't totally secure with Carmelita's assessment of the situation, but she was happy that her sister's relationship with the handsome Gringo was going well. She had also more or less gotten over the sting of his rejection, once she figured he probably knew it was a set up. That conclusion satisfied her, and it was great to see Carmelita in love with a man who seemed to truly love her.

Angela was really excited about her new job. She was starting at $9.85 an hour. A salary that included a bonus because she was bilingual. More money then she had ever made in her life. The United States of America was truly the land of opportunity, she thought.

Johnny Lopez walked in and surprised her when he called her by name.

"Hola, Angela," Johnny said, flashing a big smile.

Angela immediately remembered the nice paramedic who assisted her the day Sergeant Stack died.

"Hi," Angela said. "You're Lopez, right?"

"Yeah. You remembered?"

"I never forget a pretty face," she said, borrowing a line from the late Sergeant Stack.

"You're also very funny," Lopez retorted. "Muy graciosa."

"¿Si? Y usted estaba muy simpatico. Gracias."

"De nada," Lopez replied.

"You were very nice to me that day." Angela said, basically repeating what she had just said in Spanish. The good looking paramedic made her nervous, and she wanted to impress him with her English.

"Well, that's my job."

"Yes, but you also save lives."

"I try to," Lopez responded, modestly.

"Did you come in for some doughnuts?" Angela asked, in a slightly coquettish manner.

"No. I came in to see you."

"Good thing you came today," Angela offered. "It's my last day."

"I guess I'm lucky, aren't I?"

"Lucky Lopez," she said, aware of the fact that she'd just turned a cleaver phrase.

"Yeah, I guess that's me," he answered, as he cracked a broad smile. "Lucky Lopez."

Angela returned the smile as she continued to be a little bit nervous in the presence of this charming man, whom she found very attractive.

XXXVII

Soft Mariachi music was gently flowing from the speakers of Carmelita's small stereo on Jack's nightstand.

He ran his hands through her thick raven hair as he rode up inside her as far as he could go. Feeling the hot slippery walls of her amazingly tight love canal, he savored the movements of her love making until he came deep inside her.

Carmelita sighed and moaned as she moved her thighs in a way that seemed to suck every last drop out of Jack. After they finished, he didn't withdraw from her for almost an hour as they laid together tight in a fusion of one.

Finally, when they kissed and separated, Carmelita switched her stereo off and soon found a documentary on Irving Berlin on the TV's History Channel.

"I like to watch television in English. It help me learn," she cooed, as she resettled on the bed next to Jack.

"Oh, yeah," he replied, as he adjusted the pillows behind their heads.

"I see this before. It very interesting. Irving Berlin come to the United States. He no speak English when he come, but he make very beautiful music," she said.

"Excuse me?" Jack replied.

"I like Irving Berlin music," she restated. "Very much."

Aside from her beauty, Jack loved the fact that Carmelita had an open inquisitive mind. As he watched her, he wondered how many Mexicans were truly big Irving Berlin fans?

"He make song I like very much. Listen, they play now," she said, as she focused intently on the TV.

The song Carmelita liked was the tune, ALWAYS, that Berlin wrote as a love song to his first wife.

Carmelita's reaction as she listened to this lovely rendition struck Jack's heart as he too listened to the words, 'I'll be loving you, always. With a love that's true, always.' He looked at Carmelita, and all the words rang true.

After they watched the whole documentary, she turned to him and said, "Would you like to meet my family?"

"Really?"

"Si."

Jack knew this was a big step in their relationship. Carmelita wanted to take him home and introduce him to her family. Wow!

"Yeah, I'd like that very much."

"Okay," she said, offering a warm smile.

"¿Cuando?" Jack asked.

"Mañana noche."

At that point, Jack realized he'd heard a car idling outside his room for the last couple of minutes. He got up, went to the window, and cautiously peeked outside.

"¿Que?" Carmelita asked.

Jack saw a Sheriff's black and white sitting outside his room. It looked like the cop was checking license plates in the lot.

"La policia," Jack answered.

"¿Por qué?" Carmelita inquired.

"No se. La policia en todos partes en esta area," he offered, saying the cops were everywhere in this area.

"¿Un problema?" She questioned.

"I don't think so," Jack said, remembering that within these environs you couldn't go five minutes without seeing a bunch of cops. Between Calabasas and Westlake Village the police presence was absolutely ubiquitous.

Tammy was alone in the workshop area of her garage. She was fiddling with the pistol Jack had given her. As she held this one, she looked satisfied with its size. It fit easily inside her fashionable little hand bag. She removed it several times, and pretended to take aim. A smile crossed her pretty face.

Jack watched as the cop slowly pulled away. He returned to the bed where Carmelita was waiting. Her look was one of very serious apprehension.

"¿Mañana noche?"

"Si. Tomorrow night. Police leave?" She asked.

"Yeah, they're gone. Don't worry," he said, in a reassuring tone.

"Why police here?"

"They're always here. We live in a police state. They're everywhere," Jack said, tired of seeing a cop on every corner.

"¿Como?"

"Tomorrow night? You want me to meet your family tomorrow en la noche?"

"Si," she said. "Mariana noche es una fiesta grande en la casa de mi familia."

"Okay, bien," Jack said.

"¿Por que una fiesta?" Jack asked, why they were having a party?

"Por mi tio. You meet my uncle. El dia deje bicicleta?"

"Oh, he was the guy when I dropped off the bicycle."

"He come recently from Mexico."

"He didn't understand any of my Spanish. El no entiende mi espanol."

"He no hear good," she informed Jack, then she glanced at her watch.

"You in a hurry?" Jack asked.

"You must take me home."

"¿Por qué? ¿Yo pienso tienes tres dias de libre?"

"Si. I have three days off, but I no can stay here."

"¿Por qué?" Jack again, asked her why?

"Es imposible," she replied.

"¿Por qué es imposible?"

"Mi familia." Carmelita answered.

"Oh,… Yo entiendo," Jack replied, stating that he understood.

He started to get up, but she playfully pulled him back onto the bed.

"We go in one hour. Okay?" Carmelita said, in a most inviting way.

Jack smiled as he cuddled back into her arms and felt her warm naked body, under the open shirt that she was wearing.

"Si. Vamos en una hora," he said, repeating in Spanish what Carmelita had just said in English. Jack just loved the way their conversations shifted between English and Spanish. It was sure a long ways from those no comprendo crap days.

As they began kissing again, Carmelita reached over and turned out the light. She also hit the switch on her stereo, and once again the small room filled with soft Mariachi music.

After almost an hour of wonderful love making, they both got dressed and prepared to leave.

"I gotta hit the head, first," Jack said.

"Why you say, hit the head, for going to the bathroom?"

"Because English is a really silly language," he answered, as he vanished into the john.

Curiosity drove Carmelita to peek into the drawer of Jack's nightstand. Again, she saw the Army Colt automatic. The sight of the big pistol made her nervous.

"¿Por qué tienes una pistola?" Carmelita asked, again. Her voice was rather tentative.

"I told you, I have it for protection," Jack said, from inside the bathroom. "Solamente por protección. I have two of 'em."

"Oh?" She replied, as she gently closed the drawer.

He neglected to tell her that Tammy had possession of his other gun, the .38 revolver.

"¿Lista por vamos?" He said, as he returned from the head. "Si," she replied, confirming that she was ready to go.

Tammy heard Dan open the door from the kitchen, and enter the fairly dark garage. At the moment she heard his hand start to open the door, she had switched off the light above the workbench.

Dan was surprised to see that his wife's car was still in the garage. He thought she had left long ago to have dinner with her girlfriend Annie Horwitz.

Jack and Carmelita left his room and walked hand and hand to the Lincoln which was parked nearby. The night was still and very dark. The clear black sky was dotted with a thousand stars that sparkled like little diamonds.

The perfect night with the perfect woman, Jack thought, as they paused beside the car and shared a long kiss beneath the star studded sky.

At that moment, Jack vowed to himself that nothing would ever interfere with their spending the rest of their lives together.

Tengo amor, he thought, as he held her tight. The term still sounded like a dance to him, and what a wonderful dance they were having.

When their kiss was finished, he looked at her beautiful face, and almost lamented the fact that he had ever loved anyone else. Jack knew in his heart that he would love Carmelita, always.

Also, the topic of Tammy's alleged murder plot had surfaced once again during the course of the evening, and Jack had very carefully reasured Carmelita that she had misunderstood what Tammy had said on the telephone.

Carmelita still didn't know about Tammy's clandestine visits with Jack. He was sworn to secrecy, and he knew that violating Tammy's trust would mean serious trouble for everyone. He also felt Tammy was somehow using him.

Jack and Carmelita held hands in the car all the way back to her family's house in the Valley. He pulled into the driveway just after 1 a.m.

"Estamos aqui," Jack said, as he put the Lincoln in park, then leaned over to kiss Carmelita.

"No me beses aqui," she protested, as she gently pushed him away.

"¿Por qué?" Jack questioned, why she didn't want him to kiss her here?

"Porque, mi familia. Lentamente, Jack," she said, because of my family, slow down.

"Oh, okay. Yo entiendo." He said, understanding her reason, and feeling slightly embarrassed by his faux pas.

Next, Jack extended his hand for a polite handshake. Carmelita smiled as she took his hand in hers.

"Buenas noches, Señorita Sanchez," Jack said, very formally.

"Good night, Mr. Hardin. Thank you, for a wonderful evening."

"You're welcome. It was indeed my pleasure."

Next, they shared a little laugh, then he walked her to the front door. She glanced around furtively, then gave Jack a very quick kiss on the cheek.

"Buenas noches, Señor."

"Buenas noches, Señorita."

It was the end of the best evening imaginable and Jack just glowed in the memory of her ardor as he drove back to Calabasas alone.

He tried listening to some Mexican music on the radio, but that just made him miss her more.

He hit another button which produced one of Dan's sports talk stations. The idiot on the air was muttering something about an important game, prompting Jack to think, that dumb phrase was probably the sports world most often repeated oxymoron.

Jack hit another button that instantly filled the Lincoln with lively rock and roll. Next, The Righteous Brothers, Unchained Melody, flowed from the speakers. The line, I've longed for and hungered for your touch, struck Jack like a bolt of lightning, as he remembered how he had hungered for Carmelita for so long.

Strange how a song can sometimes really hit home. Then he thought about her affection for the Irving Berlin tune, Always. I guess things do work out right sometimes, he thought.

When he returned to and entered his room, he flipped on the light switch just inside his door. Nothing happened, he had forgotten that the switch was still broken. He left the door wide open until he found another lamp that lit up the room around his unmade bed.

Next, he closed and locked the door, then he let out a large sigh. Carmelita's sexy scent was still hanging heavy in his room.

Jack removed his clothes and plopped down on his messy bed, but sleep that night would allude him. His pleasant thoughts of Carmelita kept him awake most of the night. These sexy thoughts, however, were better company than sleep.

He eventually drifted off into a deep slumber around dawn, and didn't come back to life until a rap at the door awakened him at 11 a.m.

"Who is it?" Jack shouted, at the closed door.

"Raul. I came to fix your light switch," Raul announced, from the other side of the door.

"Can you come back in twenty minutes," Jack replied.

"Sure."

Damn it, I forgot to put the Do Not Disturb sign on the door, Jack thought, as he turned on the hot water tap in the sink, and fumbled around with an almost empty jar of instant coffee.

He lit a cigarette as he waited for the water to get hot. He had just enough coffee left to make one weak cup, but that was better than nothing.

After downing the cup of tepid coffee in two gulps, he reached for the phone, deciding he was going to call Carmelita before he did anything else.

The phone line was dead, then he remembered he'd unpluged the phone the previous night, as a precaution against anybody calling and interrupting his evening of amor. He quickly reconnected the wire, and the red message light immediately began flashing.

He only had one message, and it was from Dan. His boss had left the message early in the evening. He wanted Jack to work Sunday, which was the next day, and he absolutely wanted him at 5 a.m.

"Shit, tonight's Carmelita's party, and that asshole wants me at five tomorrow morning," Jack said, as he hung up the phone.

Again, there was a rap at the door, announcing the return of Raul, Jack presumed.

Nancy the maid, was sneaking a smoke just around the corner from Jack's room. She was soon joined by her co-worker Maria, who was pulling duty as the towel runner that day.

Maria told Nancy, that lately Jack had been seeing a beautiful Mexican girl. Nancy took a drag off her cigarette while Maria unharnessed the full dirty towel bag on Nancy's cart.

"¿Si?" Nancy said.

"Si. Una Méxicana bonita," Maria repeated, as she fastened a new empty towel bag to the side of Nancy's cart.

"Y dos Gringas," Nancy added, letting Maria know about Carol and Tammy's recent visits.

"El es muy vigoroso,.." they said, in unison with a laugh, eluding to Jack's lusty sexual appetite.

Meanwhile, Raul stepped into Jack's room proudly carrying a shiny new light switch fixture. He was also accompanied by the Hispanic man who had come to Jack's room the night after the big fight.

"Have you met Salvador?" Raul said. "He works here two nights a week, then helps me on Saturday and Sunday when we're really busy. He also works as a maintenance man at Home Depot."

Another mystery solved, Jack thought, as he shook hands with Salvador, who was now wearing a tee shirt embroidered with the motel's logo.

After the introduction, and the, 'mucho gustos,' were exchanged, Jack left Raul and Salvador to work on the switch, while he went in search of some more coffee.

I'm just not worth a shit in the morning until I've had two or three cups of strong coffee, and smoked about a half a dozen cigarettes. Man, I'm certainly a stickler for heathy living, Jack joked to himself.

They kept coffee for the guests in the foyer near the front office, but usually the coffee was all gone by this late in the morning.

Just as Jack approached the coffee dispensers, he saw two cop cars roll into the parking lot. Boy, there everywhere, he thought, as he watched the black and whites head for the back of the motel. Then some more pulled into the lot.

XXXVIII

That afternoon, there was much activity at Carmelita's house in preparation for the party that night. Ricardo, Carmelita's newly arrived uncle from Mexico, and his cousin Carlita were busy working in the back yard, while the women were all gathered in the house cooking and cleaning.

Carmelita and Angela were hard at work in the kitchen, being supervised in part, by a group of older women who were members of their extended family here in the States.

From time to time, when Carmelita and Angela were alone, they were able to catch up on each others love life. Angela was very anxious to tell her sister all about her new male friend, Johnny Lopez. He would be coming tonight, and Angela was pleased to say, she thought he was the most decent guy she'd met in years.

Carmelita brought her up to date on Jack, and Angela reveled in hearing all the sexy details.

The term Gringo turned up in the conversation just as one of the older women reentered the kitchen. The girl's discussion quickly turned to food as the woman looked at them quizzically. Carmelita and Angela kind of giggled girlishly as they continued their work.

That night, the convivial crowd that gathered at Carmelita's house was in full party mode by 8 p.m. By 8:30 Carmelita started to worry, when Jack didn't show up at the appointed time.

Johnny Lopez, the paramedic, was also late. He had wittnessed a fiery three car crash on the freeway, in route to Carmelita and Angela's party. Although off duty, he had immediately stopped to render aid. He called 911 as he rushed to a burning vehicle, in which a woman and child were apparently trapped.

By the time the L.A. City Fire Department and paramedics got to the scene, Johnny had pulled two victims out of the wreckage and administered immediate first aid, and probably saved the lives of the terrified mother and her eight year old daughter.

Help arrived within five minutes, and Lopez was soon treated for second degree burns on his hands and arms, and also a series of minor lacerations in the same area. He severely damaged the clothes he was wearing, and decided to return home and change, before once again heading for the fiesta.

He called Angela, and told her what had happened, and she was overwhelmed with pride, when she related to the assembled guests, that her new beau had been sidetracted saving lives on his way to the party.

There had also been a lot of action at the motel that Saturday. Sheriff's Deputies had surrounded the place in force, in order to affect a felony arrest.

Plainclothed, uniformed, SWAT, and officers from the Highway Patrol, had all participated in the apprehension of their suspect.

The motel had been cordoned off for hours, while the long arm of the law went about its work.

The object of this mass police operation was a felony parole violator. It took over a dozen Deputies to take her into custody, even though she offered no resistance.

Jack couldn't get back into his room for several hours, because the cops completely cordoned off the back part of the motel with bright yellow tape.

He expected to see nothing less than a machine gun toting Ma Barker type, but the woman turned out to be a fragile looking middle aged drug offender.

God, if they could only nail that petunia bandit, Jack thought, then I'd truly feel safe.

When Jack finally got back into his room late in the afternoon, he immediately fell asleep. The stress of what had transpired in the last few days, plus the sexy sleepless night with Carmelita, had left Jack absolutely spent.

Exhausted, he fell into an unexpected deep sleep, and didn't wake up until a little before eight. Embarrassed by oversleeping, he thought about calling Carmelita, but instead decided to quickly get dressed and just haul ass over to the party.

When Jack reached Carmelita's house, he could hear the sounds of the party when he got out of the car. The fiesta was not too noisy, the party goers were being considerate neighbors.

As Jack walked inside, he noticed that the well kept home as truly alive with people. More than he anticipated. Most were Latinos, and everyone seemed to be having a good time.

Carmelita spotted him right after he entered, and she pulled him aside and admonished him for being late.

Carmelita told him how worried she'd been, and Jack apologized profusely, but also offered a truthful explanation.

She accepted his apology, and his explanation, then took him by the hand and introduced him to various friends and members of her family.

Everyone was terribly nice, and Jack quickly felt completely at ease with the lively Spanish speaking crowd celebrating at Carmelita's house.

Once Carmelita was sure Jack was comfortable, she left him alone so she could continue her co-hosting duties. Jack soon encountered Angela and inquired about her recent job searching progress?

Angela handled the potentially embarrassing situation with her usual wit and grace, and quickly won Jack's approval employing her cute disarming charm. She also honestly added, that she had found a new job that day.

"Did you know all along that I was Carmelita's sister, or did you just think that I was a skag?" Angela said, relishing her nimble use of a new slang term.

"Skag? That's a surfer word for a butt ugly chick. Where'd you learn that?" Jack asked.

"¿Como?" Angela replied.

"Yeah, Angela's really knarly, isn't she?" Johnny Lopez said, as he joined the conversation.

"Yeah, a real two bagger," Jack added, with a laugh.

Angela, who suddenly found herself lost in this salty sea of surfer colloquialisms, simply decided to strike a sexy pose.

"Hi. I'm Johnny Lopez."

Jack started to extend his hand, then he noticed Johnny's bandages.

"I'm Jack Hardin."

Angela invited the two men to follow her to the nearby bar, as she proudly explained Johnny's injuries.

Johnny said his hands would be fine in about a week, and he didn't anticipate missing more than about ten days of work. He also didn't seem to have much trouble holding a bottle of beer.

"So I hear you and Angela's sister are pretty serious?" Johnny said, to Jack.

"That's what she tells me," Jack replied, flashing a big smile.

Jack spotted Carmelita who was not too far away. She smiled at the group.

"Yeah, talk about a couple of chicks who've been whooped by an ugly stick," Lopez said, in a parity of the old Bo Didily song.

"I leave you two alone. I think my feelings are very hurt. I think you say something bad about me," Angela said, impishly.

"Damn, she's cute, isn't she?" Lopez said, as he watched Angela leave the bar area to greet some newly arriving guests.

"Yeah, she is. They're quite a pair," Jack replied, as he watched the sisters hook up in the center of the room. They both glanced over at the men watching them from the bar.

Everyone at the party was nicely dressed, reflecting to some degree the prosperity they had found through hard work during their tenure in the United States. Jack and Johnny Lopez also noticed how many attractive Señoritas were in attendance.

Johnny Lopez was an athletically handsome Chicano, with short cropped hair, who had recently celebrated his thirtieth birthday.

After serving four years in the Navy, Lopez became a fireman, then a paramedic. He had just marked his eighth anniversary with the Los Angeles Fire Department when he met Angela. A consummate achiever, he was well on his way up the ladder of the Department's chain of command.

He confided to Jack that at thirty, he was finally at a stage in life where he had the urge to merge with the right woman. In the past, marriage was something that Johnny Lopez had assiduously avoided.

Lopez liked to travel on his days off and his vacations. Hang gliding, mountain climbing, and surfing were just a few of his sporting interests.

Johnny also found Jack's background in stunt work fascinating, and they both shared a strong interest in surfing. Although with Jack, surfing was now a thing of the distant past, he still truly enjoyed discussing the subject.

Jack liked Lopez. The two men hit it off well. They both had served their country, and Jack felt Johnny actually did something useful for a living. Here was a guy who was giving rather then taking, and he put his ass on the line every day to do it. Jack respected this aspect of Johnny's profession.

"Where'd you grow up?" Lopez asked.

"Culver City. How 'bout you?"

"El Monte."

Jack had recently learned that Chicano was a term used to describe a person of Mexican descent born here in the United States. El Monte had long been an L.A. Mexican American enclave.

Just then, Angela returned and grabbed Lopez by the hand.

"Come on, Lucky. Let's go dance," she said, undulating her body to the beat of the music.

At that point, Uncle Ricardo approached the bar, and Angela introduced him to Jack and Johnny.

Once the introductions were complete, Angela dragged Lopez by the hand to the patio just outside, where they joined some other dancing couples.

Jack remembered Ricardo from the day he dropped off the new bicycle for Carmelita. Tonight, Ricardo was in a cheerful mood, and he also understood Jack's Spanish perfectly. Soon Carmelita joined the two. The three chatted for a few minutes, before Tio Ricardo excused himself.

"Hasta luego," Ricardo said, then he headed for the dance area on the nearby patio outside the den's open sliding door.

"Tu tio entiende me todo esta noche," Jack said, once Ricardo was out of earshot.

After Jack proudly told Carmelita that her uncle completely understood his Spanish this time, she smiled and offered Jack an explanation.

"¿Si? ¿Tu sabes por qué?" She said, you know why?

"Si. Mi espanol es major." Jack replied, because my Spanish is much better.

"Es posible. My brother get him,…how you say?" Carmelita pointed at her ear. "Hearing ad,…"

Jack thought for a second, then said, "Oh, he got a hearing aid."

"Yes, a hearing aid. Now he hear everything. My uncle is very happy," Carmelita said.

They both glanced at Uncle Ricardo, who was smiling, sipping a cerveza, and dancing to the lively Mexican music.

"Tio Ricardo tiene felicidad," Jack said, concurring that her uncle seemed very happy.

"Si. Me too. I am very happy, too," Carmelita said, as she took one of Jack's hands and held it in both of hers.

A bold move that did not go unnoticed by some members of her family. They noticed, but their reactions were not overt, one way or the other.

Jack just felt a warm glow engulf his body as she clutched his hand.

"You know I want to marry you, and have about eight kids," he said.

"Oh, ocho? I think one is enough for now, don't you?" She replied.

They exchanged a loving look, as she squeezed his hand. Jack hadn't been this happy in years. I guess if you wait long enough, things sometimes do work out in this life, Jack thought.

As the evening progressed, Jack drank sparingly, knowing that he had to be up before dawn to pick up Dan. He wanted to stay at the party as long as possible, just to watch, and be around the woman he loved. Every moment with Carmelita was precious. His heart glowed, just being in her presence.

Later, as Jack was talking to a young man at the bar, he saw Carmelita closeby helping another woman clean up some paper cups and discarded party plates.

Suddenly she bumped into a table knocking over a nearly full glass of soda, then she dropped the dirty plates as she tried to save the soda from spilling onto the carpet. Carmelita recovered without missing much of a beat, as Jack watched her fumbling with fondness.

"¿Quieres ayuda, Carmelita? Do you want some help?" Jack asked.

"No, esta bien. Gracias," Carmelita answered, as she stoically juggled the various items of party debris.

Carmelita was incredibly beautiful, beautiful beyond belief, and he loved her more than life itself, Jack thought, but sometimes she was also just an absolute klutz. At times, Carmelita was the most accident prone person he had ever known. He watched as she fumbled with, then finally lost half the stuff she was juggling in her hands. Two female family members quickly came to her rescue, and Jack looked away in an effort not to embarrass her further.

Then he thought back to the mud slide incident on that first day they met, and how beautiful she had looked, even all covered with mud. Then Jack remembered the day in the garage when she fell off the ladder, and also the time she told him she stepped on the skateboard and fell down the stairs. Then how embarrassed she'd been after being slightly injured in two accidents on her bicycle, when he thought somebody was beating her up.

As Jack slipped outside for a cigarette, he remembered yet another black eye Carmelita received, which was the end result of stepping on a rake while engaged in her gardening activities.

Despite the numerous minor injuries, Carmelita usually managed to cover these mishaps with a certain amount of dignity and poise, and a total reticence to discuss her klutziness. Sensing this, Jack never broached the subject.

While standing in the front yard having a smoke, Jack noticed a low riding vintage Chevy sedan full of cholos cruise by the house a couple of times.

A carload of gangbangers in this neighborhood was not an odd occurrence, but it was something that caused Jack some concern, considering Angela's recent brush with that side of life.

After the cholos third pass by the house, it also crossed his mind that in some circles, shooting a white guy, is an acceptable form of Saturday night entertainment. Jack decided to crush out his cigarette and return to the interior of the house.

Later that night, Jack and Carmelita found a dark corner in the backyard behind some bushes. They shared a long tender kiss, but they both kept their eyes wide open, mindful that they were only partially hidden from view.

"Tonight, I must stay here, but tomorrow night, I sleep at your place. You pick me up at five. I tell my family I have to go back to work at Mr. Dan's house one day early," Carmelita whispered conspiratorially.

Jack was amazed at how well Carmelita was now speaking English. He felt his Spanish somewhat lagged in comparison to her progress.

"Si bienes mañana a las cinco," Jack said, then added, "I love you."

"Te quiero, Jack," Carmelita replied, then she glanced around cautiously, before she kissed him again.

Si. Te quiero siempre. Yes, I'll love you always, Jack thought, as he savored Carmelita's sweet kiss.

XXXIX

Jack picked up Dan at five in the morning and drove him to a hotel near LAX. Jack always wondered what Dan was really doing with all these clandestine meetings at odd hours. He often met people near the L.A. Airport. They would only be in town a few hours, and Dan's meetings always seemed to leave him tense and frustrated.

Dan had promised Jack that he would be finished sometime in the early afternoon. This time Dan was true to his word, and Jack was finished and back at his motel just a little after noon.

Again, Jack was pretty well spent due to lack of sleep. He was supposed to pick up Carmelita at five, and he had some important errands to run that afternoon, before he saw her again.

He decided to lay down on the bed, and rest for an hour or so, before he set out to take care of his chores. He really didn't want to go to sleep, so he flipped on the television.

First, the TV exposed Jack to George Bush the both, with some sort of retrospective on the lives of the father son Presidental office holders. It had not yet been a year since Bush the lesser had won the highly contested election. Not much had happened so far in his administration, and it struck Jack as a little bit too early for any kind of intelligent analysis.

Next, he switched to the History Channel and got a show on Ike. Well, he won World War II, and ran the country for eight years, so at least there was something to discuss in terms of his career.

Then he bounced to the E Channel where Howard Stern was busy Playing a game of Striper Jeopardy. Three almost naked stripers were serving as contestants. Jack really found the answers challenging. Not the questions, just the answers.

Next, he landed on a local news program, and low and behold, Brad and the other dot-com boys were the subject of a news story.

A couple of incidents had occurred recently at the office, that involved Brad Rodriguez.

First, about a week ago, while Jack was having a smoke on the parkway, he saw Brad pull Dan aside for a little chat just outside the front door of their office.

Was this little private conversation held to relate some recent awesome sports accomplishment, or had one of Jack's icy glares hit the mark?

Was it tattletail time? During Brad and Dan's discussion, Jack just stood there on the parkway smoking, ready to strike like a coiled rattlesnake. He'd totally had it with Brad's haughty asshole attitude. Jack realized it was immature, but he was also just itching to kick that butt sucking arrogant yuppie's ass.

Thank God, I'm in love with Carmelita, he thought. Hopefully that will keep me from slapping that piece of shit in the mouth if there's some kind of confrontation. Brad always reminded him of the jock types he'd hated since high school. They always had their tongue at least ten inches up the administration's ass.

In an effort to not tap into his pernicious side, Jack often felt that his whole life lately around the office, was nothing less then a cruel exercise in anger management.

Fortunately, his boss and Brad's little pow wow ended without creating a confrontation with Jack.

The next day Jack found out that Brad and company, being on the cutting edge of the new dot-com technology, were among the first to tank in the Thousand Oaks area. Was the tony community of Westlake Village on the verge of economic implosion, with the threatened loss of the Brad type brain trust? Only the future would tell, Jack thought.

Long faces abounded around the office that day, as the three or four dot-com guys who worked with Brad, brooded in mass.

Scuttlebutt also had it that Brad was about to lose his new house, and talk of an indictment was in the air.

Later that day, Jack saw a couple of Brad's cronies corner his friend, Lance the lawyer, in the parking lot. Jack couldn't hear their conversation, but by all appearances, Lance didn't look the least bit interested in offering counsel.

Well, the local news show Jack was watching confirmed it, the SEC was charging Brad and company with a litany of offenses.

Strange, only thoughts of love now filled Jack's mind, and he found little satisfaction, or for that matter, interest in the rest of the story about Brad's apparent well earned demise.

He hit the remote returning to the E Channel and Howard Stern's stripers, who at the moment were stymied by the question; When was the War of 1812?

No answer was forthcoming, so Jack clicked off the TV.

Jack was successful in not falling asleep. When he got up, he had rested for just over an hour. He made some instant coffee, smoked a couple of cigarettes, then set out for a flower shop located in the Thousand Oaks mall, some ten miles north on the 101 Freeway.

He bought a dozen roses, then got an idea as he passed a nice jewelry store on his way out of the Oaks Mall.

Initially, he'd planned to take Carmelita with him when he went to shop for an engagement ring, but suddenly the idea of making it a surprise appealed to Jack's romantic side. He entered the store roses in hand.

At another flower shop in Pacoima, far from the upscale Oaks. Mall, Carmelita selected a dozen red roses, and a card in Spanish that she felt summed up her feelings for Jack.

Carmelita soon left the flower shop carrying a dozen roses. She inhaled their beautiful fragrance, then placed them in the basket mounted on the handlebars of her bicycle.

Before she left her house, she noticed the seat and handlebars had been reset to a different height. She and Angela were the same size, but her sister always changed everything when she borrowed Carmelita's bike. Carmelita was wearing one of Angela's sweaters, so she figured they were probably even. She was also wearing Angela's favorite ball cap.

Very pleased with her purchase, she smiled and peddled away enjoying the warm glow of her romantic thoughts, on what seemed like a perfect sunny Sunday afternoon.

Jack left the jewelry store wearing a big smile, and carrying a small gift wrapped package along with his flowers. His mood couldn't have been higher as he headed back to the motel.

When Jack returned to his room, he placed the dozen roses on the nightstand next to his clock. The time was 3:30. He would leave to pick up Carmelita in an hour.

Next, he toyed with the small gift wrapped package. First he put the little present next to the flowers, then he placed it on his pillow, then back by the roses.

After a few moments, he put it back on the pillow. He just couldn't make up his mind.

Wasn't love wonderful, he thought. The most pressing thing in his life at the moment, was where to place the engagement ring he had purchased for Carmelita. Tonight would be so very special.

Tammy put the last cartridge in the revolver and slammed its cylinder shut. She then stared at the loaded weapon with great resolve.

XL

Arlo Wells, one of the first paramedics on the scene, saw the dozen red roses strewn in the dirty gutter next to the curb. A small crowd had gathered and the police were already on hand.

Carmelita's damaged bicycle was nearby. Within minutes, the ambulance with Arlo behind the wheel, sped away with all its red lights flashing and its siren wailing.

Jack was still fooling around with the placement of the small package as he prepared to leave. He had taken a shower and was now wearing a shirt that Carmelita had complimented in the past.

Just as he started out the door, he noticed the blinking red light on his phone, which was partially hidden by the flowers on the nightstand. Jack guessed the phone must have rung while he was in the shower.

He quickly dialed the code that accessed the motel voice mail, and listened to the frantic message from Angela. A look of total horror crossed Jack's face at the same moment a sharp pain slashed into his heart like a knife.

The following Friday night, the elegantly appointed banquet room was abuzz with a group of well dressed chatty guests, who were just digging into the main course of their tasty gourmet meal.

Tammy, dressed to the nines, was standing just outside the big banquet room, in a narrow hallway that led to the noisy kitchen.

Tonight, Tammy's stylish outfit was accessorized with a modest sized elegant shoulder bag.

After glancing around to make sure no one was watching, she surreptitiously slipped into a small supply room.

Once inside the cramped store room, she removed the revolver from her shoulder bag, and checked its cylinder to make certain that the pistol was loaded properly. Assured that the gun was ready for some action, she set it on a nearby box.

Next, Tammy reached behind a stack of crates and retrieved a blue burka that she had carefully hidden there earlier. She quickly pulled the flowing female Arab garment over her head, and adjusted the consuming outfit.

The burka totally covered her from head to toe. Even her eyes were hidden behind a thin strip of matching mesh cloth.

Tammy's hand emerged through one of the arm slits and grabbed the gun. Concealing the weapon beneath the flowing fabric, she slipped out of the store room and quickly entered the big banquet room.

Among the dinning guests were a smattering of folks who were also dressed in Arab attire.

Tammy quickly approached a table of eight, lifted the weapon, and and fired three times with the gun pointed at the back of a man seated at the table.

Startled people screamed, as the target man fell forward, face down in his linguine. Tammy took another step toward the man, and fired two more times. The man's body jiggled in response to each shot fired.

With one bullet left for her get a way, Tammy took off running toward a side door.

As she ran past the last table, a man in a Saudi robe, dark glasses and headdress, jumped up to grab her.

Tammy fired her last bullet and the Arab went crashing into a nearby flower covered serving table, sending food, plates, and floral displays flying.

Tammy quickly vaninshed out the side door without missing a beat, leaving the banquet room ablaze with confusion, screams, and two dead bodies.

Once outside, she whipped off the burka, threw it in an open trash bin, and immediately reentered the hotel through another emergency exit that Annie Horwitz popped open for her right on cue.

Jack was always amazed at how wrong people could be about things.

He had gone to great lengths to reassure Carmelita that there was no murder plot afoot.

Laying in bed together one night, Carmelita had repeatedly said, "But what if somebody gets killed, and we didn't try to do something to stop it? How are you going to feel then?"

She repeated this in English and Spanish several times, Jack recalled.

"I guess, I'll feel awful," he had answered.

Then passion interceded, and the subject was dropped again. Sex always seemed to sidetrack them, creating absolutely the most pleasant diversion Jack had ever known. He knew Carmelita was never completely convinced, but he was sworn to secrecy.

Again, Jack was always amazed at how wrong people could be about some things.

Several days before Tammy's performance at the banquet room, Jack had met Annie Horwitz at Dan's house.

Amidst piles of papers and armed with two lap tops, Tammy and Annie were arguing passionately.

"He has to die!" Tammy implored.

"But if he dies, who kills her?" Annie retorted.

Jack had entered the den during this heated discussion. He was completely taken aback when Tammy introduced him to Annie Horwitz. He had heard her name bandied about, but he had never actually met her.

Annie Horwitz was the most beautiful African American woman Jack had ever seen. She was absolutely stunning, dressed in tight shorts and a revealing little halter top. Her hair was pulled straight back, and her face looked like it belonged on the cover of Cosmopolitan. Jack had met her husband Allen once, and he had pictured the traveling wife in a totally different way. Like maybe white, and Jewish.

Tammy and Annie loved to write and perform in murder mystery dinner theatre, and they argued passionately about the body count in each new play. Tammy usually won.

"Honey, this is Jack Hardin, my husband's driver." Tammy always called her best girlfriend Annie Horwitz, Honey.

"Hi," Jack said, as he extended his hand.

"Hi, there. It's nice to finally meet you," Annie purred, as she gave Jack a firm and friendly handshake.

Annie's astonishing beauty actually made Jack quite nervous. Like Tammy, Annie was definitely the kind of woman who could get anything she wanted.

"Honey, I know Jack can give you a ride. Right?" Tammy said, as she glanced at Jack.

"Okay," Jack replied.

"Somebody stole her car in front of the Dockside Terrace, and her car insurance company hassled her about getting a comparable replacement. We just talked to 'em, and we won! Can you give her a ride over to Calabasas Mercedes Benz?" Tammy asked.

"Sure," Jack answered. "Dan just gave me the afternoon off."

"I know," Tammy said. "We fixed that, too."

Jack learned from Tammy later, that Annie and Allen were both the offspring of Sixties Berkeley radicals. He also learned that the couple liked to practice their own form of social rebellion, with wild costumed sexual encounters in public.

So Allen Horwitz was Zorro, Jack mused.

So far they hadn't been caught, but Tammy worried that it was probably just a matter of time, especially now that a big reward had been posted.

This prompted Jack to wonder if Westlake Village's most famous criminal attorney, his friend Lance the lawyer, would be retained at any cost, to defend this one? He could picture Lance on Good Morning L.A. adding a modicum of dignity to what would otherwise be a rather randy case of freedom of expression.

Tammy almost had a heart attack that day in the parking lot in front of the Dockside Terrace. She didn't know the cops were responding to Annie's stolen car call. She thought that they had probably been busted for one of their public sex romps.

In the beginning, Jack had also read Tammy wrong. She was the master manipulator. He even got shanghaied into playing the Saudi Arab who got shot and crashed into the serving table.

Also, he was sworn to secrecy. First, the integrity of the plot was sacred to Tammy. Secondly, Dan was stretched thin money wise, and he hated the idea of Tammy hustling Allen Horwitz for dough.

Every play she did lost untold thousands of dollars, due to Tammy's high production values, and lack of business acumen.

During Tammy's first visit with him at the motel, he was very concerned about how to handle the situation if she put the moves on him sexually.

Jack didn't know exactly how he would deal with it, but with his time proven weakness in that area, he knew it would present a very dangerous dilemma.

That night, with Tammy sitting on the edge of his bed looking sexy as hell, she almost immediately set the situation straight, right after taking her first sip of tequila. She had just told him that she and Dan hadn't had sex in over six months, and she thought that Jack could help her out.

Of course, Jack took that to mean that Tammy wanted him to hit the sheets with her. Judging by the look on Jack's face, she instantly picked up on the misinterpretation.

"I don't want to have sex with you, stupid. I want to win Dan back. I love him," Tammy stated, in no uncertain terms.

"Oh,…so that's why you always look so…"

"Hot?" She retorted.

"Yeah, hot," he replied.

"Of course. Why? Did you think I was doing it for you?"

"Ah,…no," Jack said, sort of stammering with his answer.

"I want you to help me win Dan back, and I've got a plan," she said. "You're with him all the time, and I want you to drop some hints. I have something I want you to say tomorrow."

"Okay," Jack agreed, not knowing what else to say.

"Oh, and by the way, I think Carmelita really likes you."

"Oh, really?"

Had Carmelita said something to her, Jack wondered, or was Tammy just intuitive?

"She thinks you're very handsome."

"Oh, yeah?"

"She also told me, she thought you were kind of a fun guy."

"Really?"

"Si, por un Gringo," she added, employing a slightly theatrical Spanish accent.

Jack and Carmelita did have fun together. Like the time he volunteered to help her learn how to drive.

They took Jack's old sedan to the far corner of Albertsons big parking lot one quiet morning. They found an area that was a good distance away from most of the parked cars and traffic.

Carmelita slipped behind the wheel, buckled her seat belt, and prepared to drive with a look of determination on her beautiful face.

"¿Lista para manejar el carro?" Jack said, hoping he had just asked her correctly, if she was ready to drive the car?

"Si," Carmelita replied, with confidence.

Carmelita depressed the gas pedal and instantly took off with a loud squeal burning some rubber in her wake.

First she hit an empty unattended shopping cart, just before she jumped the curb of a small circular island surrounding a tiny tree which she narrowly missed.

Then she came within a couple of inches of colliding with a fast moving car that had entered the lot rather suddenly. She continued to sail across the tarmac as Jack hung on for dear life.

"Carmelita, no gasolina! No gasolina! Las brekas! Las brekas! The brakes! Hit the brakes!!!"

Carmelita heeded his command and slammed her foot on the brake pedal driving it to the floor, which caused the brakes to lock.

The car skidded into a wild slide, then did a. 180 before it screeched to a bumpy halt.

"That was very good," Jack said, calmly. "Muy bien."

"¿Si?"

"Si," Jack said. "Absolutamente perfecto."

"Gracias," Carmelita replied, graciously.

They shared a big laugh, then she cautiously nudged the car forward again, this time exercising a little more control and much less speed.

XLI

This all led up to that day when Jack had that nasty encounter in McDonald's with the angry Gringo.

Jack had just gotten a three day stunt job, and he had darkened his hair to double some actor whose name didn't ring a bell, but the gig sounded like fun. He was scheduled to do some driving sequences, a big chase, and a crash.

While speaking Spanish to his Latina friend Blanca behind the counter at McDonald's, Jack had used the term Gringo during the course of their conversation. He failed to noticed the surly and impatient Gringo standing behind him in line.

Blanca had just complimented Jack on his rapid progress in learning Spanish, and he had just replied, en espanol.

"Muy bien, por un Gringo. ¿No?"

"Si. Muy bien," she replied.

To the unschooled ear, and with his newly dyed dark hair, and his light blue eyes obscured by sunglasses, Jack's crude Spanish had caused the rude white guy to mistake Jack for a Latino.

Then, when the burly white man, who was accompanied by a woman, heard the term Gringo, he immediately confronted Jack in a very nasty aggressive manner.

"Why don't you filthy people learn how to speak English?" The man growled, apparently unable to contain his xenophobia.

This unexpected ugly comment startled Jack. It also mirrored two recent incidents while he was out in public with Carmelita.

On both occasions Carmelita had begged Jack not to fight, and he was still seething from backing away from what he considered a righteous reason to kick some ass. He was sick and tired of these racist Gringos, and today Carmelita wasn't there to stop him.

In light of these recent events, and others that he had dealt with or witnessed over the last few months, he was in no mood to put up with another racist white trash piece of shit.

When Jack turned abruptly and confronted his verbal assailant, he noticed that the man also reeked with the small of alcohol. Jack's anger was instant, and he only barely tried to contain his warrior instincts.

Jack realized he'd been mistaken for a Latino, and he set the record straight in short order.

"You ever hear of the First Amendment, pal? That's the one right up there on top! You know, freedom of speech. I think I'm entitled to say anything I want, in any fucking language I want! Now, if you have a problem with that, you can kiss my ass! Am I comin' in loud and clear?"

The burly antagonist was taken aback by the sudden revelation of Jack's ethnicity and his assertive rapid reply.

"Oh, you're an American? I thought you were a,…"

"You know, I really don't give a shit what you thought," Jack responded in a very terse tone.

"Hey, I heard you call me a Gringo! The surly man said, in a menacing manner.

"I wasn't talking to you, or about you!" Jack replied, his patience running thin.

Outside, two Sheriff's Deputies were just about to walk into the restaurant on their lunch break. Blanca noticed the two cops, Jack did not.

Jack turned his head slightly and again addressed Blanca, but he also continued to speak English.

"You know, I wish some of these dumb ass Gringos would learn to speak Spanish. I think there'd sure as hell be a lot more understanding!"

Outside, the cops were almost at the point of entering the establishment. Blanca tried to say something to Jack, but he cut her off as he switched back to Spanish for the sole benefit of antagonizing his adversary.

For a moment he thought about the woman he loved, and briefly wondered if he should hold back a little, then he noticed the pure hate in the man's blood shot eyes.

"No me gusta la actitud mala de algunos Gringos," Jack said, looking the man straight in the eye. "Yo odio racismo, GRINGO!"

"Okay, that's it!" The burly one spat out the words, along with some other vile phrases, as he quickly drew back a clenched fist and started to take a swing at Jack.

Jack instinctively blocked and grabbed the offending fist and twisted it up the burly man's back as he slammed the man's face into a nearby soda dispensing machine. In an instant, the man who outweighed Jack by sixty pounds, broke out of the hold, and knocked Jack back.

The big man then unleashed another savage round house swing. Jack blocked the punch and violently delivered a hard right hook that connected squarely smashing into the man's jaw. Jack's expertly placed blow resounded with a loud bone breaking crack.

The powerful punch knocked the big man off his feet and caused him to go crashing again into the beverage dispenser, before he fell to the floor with a dead weight thud at the feet of some startled bystanders.

The two cops who had just entered the restaurant, immediately jumped into action.

The cop's nightstick slammed into the side of Jack's head with such force that it instantly send him into oblivion.

While laying on the floor unconscious, Jack's mind relived his last dinner with Carmelita at their favorite restaurant, Le Cafe in Westlake Village.

Le Cafe was a large upscale French Country style restaurant that abutted the local Country Club.

They had dressed up for this romantic dinner, and they ordered Carmelita's favorite French dish, Due L'Orange for two.

Actually, in French it was Canard L'Orange. Jack explained to Carmelita that in English, the word canard meant, cruel joke.

Carmelita laughed, and said, "Well, I guess to the duck it is."

Jack chuckled. At times, Carmelita had such a cute sense of humor.

This romantic repast was followed by more, tengo amor, and Jack's mind remained in this area until he drifted into a deeper state of unconsciousness.

Within minutes after the fight, five more police cars were present outside McDonald's, along with an ambulance and a ever growing curious crowd. As always, the cops tended to over respond in Calabasas.

Jack was now outside, only a few feet from where he had fallen$ sitting on the ground next to the door with his back against the wall of the restaurant.

A County Medic had looked at the big bump on the side of his head moments after he regained some semblance of consciousness, and had promptly pronounced Jack unhurt.

Jack was amused by this quick diagnoses, designed he assumed to concur with the Deputies' incident report. His head hurt like hell. He felt like he'd been hit by a truck, and Jack was sure he had at very least a bad concussion.

After the Deputies heard his side of the story, Jack watched the swarm of cops converge on the now semi-conscious corpulent casuality of the fight, who was securely strapped to a stretcher.

A couple of County Medics were attending to his injuries which included a severely broken jaw, and a gaping laceration where his head hit the coke machine.

The man's female companion was totally hysterical, and had to be restrained by a couple of cops. Like her compadre, she too reeked with the smell of alcohol.

While two male cops wrestled with the hysterical woman, one female Deputy was assigned to stand guard over Jack. His vision was blurred, and the intensity of the pain in his head was growing. He also noticed that time was beginning to move more slowly.

Jack watched as more cops arrived. They were in L.A. County territory, but an LAPD unit pulled into the lot, followed by two cruisers from the California Highway Patrol. Jack's vision was a little hazy, but he still marveled as he sat there and watched all the cops from the various agencies arriving at what was at best a minor incident. The Redcoats are back, Jack thought, but now they're wearing khaki and blue.

Carmelita suddenly swung into the parking lot driving Jack's old sedan. She had quickly recovered from her bicycle accident, and the driver who hit her was charged with drunk driving.

She banged into a trash can, then bumped into a curb, before she finally managed to park the car properly. She jumped out of the sedan and rushed to Jack's side.

"¿Que paso, Jack?" Carmelita asked, with a sense of panic in her voice.

"Nada," Jack replied, calmly.

"¿Nada?" Carmelita responded, glancing at the huge welt on the side of Jack's head, and all the police and confusion around them.

"Es nada," Jack answered, again.

"¿Que paso, Jack?" She said, once again asking what happened?

"Well, some honky heard me speaking Spanish, and thought I was a Latino, and mouthed off about it, so I whacked him."

"Oh," Carmelita replied, seemingly satisfied with his answer, then she asked, "You okay?"

"Si. Bien, bien. I'm fine," Jack said. He hoped this wouldn't count as another lie, but he didn't want to worry her.

On the day of the McDonald's incident, Carmelita and Jack had planned to go looking for an apartment. She had moved into his room at the motel, but it was now time to find a larger abode.

The two lovers had gotten married almost immediately after she was released from the hospital.

It was a beautiful ceremony that was attended by all of her family, Tammy, Dan, the kids, and some of Jack's stunt buddies.

Angela, who was now engaged to Johnny Lopez, served as the maid of honor.

The lavish reception was held at Dan's house, orchestrated by Tammy, the consummate party giver. Every detail was planned to perfection, and the whole spread was probably very expensive, Jack thought. Dan picked up the tab.

Jack had learned that Dan had pulled off the business deal of the new Century, and a somewhat altruistic one to boot. He had made a ton of money on a complex venture that involved transporting food and medical supplies to Third World Countries.

Dan had brokered the entire deal for hundreds of airplanes, making the massive logistic effort possible. He took only a modest commission on the sales, but still walked away with over twenty-five million due to the immensity of the project.

Boy, these business guys, Jack thought. A modest commission, and he scores 25 mil. Thank God, he wasn't greedy.

Also, Dan's business feat, would no doubt insure the life of Mystery Dinner Theatre in the Conejo Valley for decades to come.

Dan's drinking buddy Al, practicing attorney, had negotiated with Dan's recent girlfriend the night the two paid her a visit.

Al had offered her a generous on the spot settlement. Dan's squeeze for half a year, took the sixty grand, and figuratively kissed Dan a fond good bye.

Also, there was another new development. Al would soon need a driver. He had recently received his third DUI, while he and Dan were leaving the Country Club, following a long afternoon of very heavy drinking.

"You sure you're okay?" Carmelita asked, again.

"Yeah, I'm fine. Don't worry. Estey bien," Jack reassured her.

His head hurt bad, and he felt dizzy as hell. Jack had had concussions before, and from what he could recall, if his skull wasn't fractured, he'd be okay in a couple of hours, but he would probably have a head ache for at least a week.

Carmelita looked up at the female cop guarding Jack. She just didn't trust the police.

"I worry for you Jack," she said, a look of true concern now emanating from her beautiful dark eyes.

"Por favor, no te preocupes, Carmelita," he said telling her not to worry.

When Jack spoke to Carmelita in Spanish, the stern female cop standing guard glared at them. Carmelita noticed this, Jack did not.

"Otro subjecto," Jack said, asking Carmelita to change the subject.

"Okay," she said. "Did you pick up the dry cleaning?"

"No, sorry. I didn't get quite that far," Jack answered, with a slight laugh. Carmelita did have a great sense of humor.

"Oh," she said, feigning disappointment.

"Aveces, tu eres muy graciosa," Jack said, telling her that sometimes she was very funny. As he was saying this, he uneasily struggled to his feet.

"Be careful, Jack," Carmelita said, as she assisted him.

"Esta bien," he said, reiterating that he was okay.

"You think I'm funny?" She said.

"Si. Aveces."

"Yes? You say you like girl with humor," she said, somewhat over pronouncing the word humor with a strong Spanish accent.

"Si, verdad."

"I want you to speak English," she said, as she helped him steady his balance. "I need practice."

"Okay. You're not only funny, sometimes, you're absolutely beautiful, and I love you more than I can say in any language."

"Yes?" She said, as she cracked a cute coy smile.

"Te quiero, te quiero, te quiero," he said, saying I love you, three times.

"Me too," Carmelita replied.

"¿Mucho?" He asked.

"Yes, very much," then she added. And for always."

"Si, siempre," Jack said, as he took her in his arms.

They shared a long loving kiss, as the watchful female Deputy considered intervening, but didn't.

This is heaven, Jack thought, as he continued to hug and kiss his beautiful new Señora.

Carmelita wasn't pregnant yet, but they were working on it night and day. They both truly wanted a baby, and the fun filled necessary prerequisite for this endeavor continued to be their favorite pastime.

Holding Carmelita in his arms, Jack recalled with fondness the rich melodious sound of the Mariachi band Tammy had hired for the reception. They were a great group, with a strong brass section, and sixteen violins on the string side. Tammy certainly knew how to spend Dan's money, Jack thought.

The big band preformed a wide mixture of Mexican selections, as well as some lively contempory Anglo fare. They had also been asked to learn one song in particular for the occasion.

Several times, at Carmelita's request, the forty piece band had played her favorite Irving Berlin song, 'ALWAYS,' as the two happy newlyweds danced under the stars.

In his head, Jack could still hear the words, 'I'll be loving you, always. With a love that's true, always.' He recalled the Mariachi's brass trumpets and violins, and thought of the word, siempre, which in Spanish means, always.

Jack hugged his beautiful wife, as he said to himself, si, siempre. Yes, always.

As he held Carmelita tight and kissed her again, he felt his knees start to get weak. He was about to tell her once more, that he knew he would love her till the moment he died, but her soft sexy voice interrupted him before he had a chance to speak.

"Jack, I'll love you, always," she said.

He opened his eyes and looked at Carmelita's beautiful face.

Her hair was hanging around her shoulders, with the top part held back away from her forehead with a pretty Spanish style tiara.

Suddenly, he noticed her features were beginning to blur, and an excruciating pain shot through Jack's brain as his legs gave out, and his body fell.

At that moment, Jack Hardin died in the arms of the woman he loved, at 11:47 that morning.

The official cause of death was listed as exacerbated brain hemorrhage, caused by the violent blow to his head inflicted by an L.A. County Sheriff's Deputy, during his lunch break.

Word of Jack's death never made the news. The next day was 9/11/01, and what happened at the Twin Towers World Trade Center, in New York City, dominated the media that day, and for months to come. An event that became so deeply etched into the modern annals of American history, that it changed the course of this country forever.

As a result of her wrongful death law suit, Carmelita Hardin received six hundred thousand dollars from the County of Los Angeles.

Soon after receiving her settlement, Carmelita left California and went back to Mexico, vowing to never ever return to the United States of America.

THE END

About the Author

Want to know more about the author? Read *STILL ALIVE IN LITTLE SAIGON*.

CPSIA information can be obtained
at www.ICGtesting.com
Printed in the USA
BVHW031025100721
611640BV00005B/39